Wicked Words 4
An erotic short story collection

Look out for the nine other *Wicked Words* collections.

Wicked Words 4

An erotic short story collection

Edited by Kerri Sharp

BLACK LACE

Black Lace books contain sexual fantasies.
In real life, always practise safe sex.

This edition published in 2004 by
Black Lace
Thames Wharf Studios
Rainville Road
London W6 9HA

First published in 2000

Marilyn's Frock	© Julie Savage
Still Life with Fruit	© Alison Tyler
Screen Dream	© Portia Da Costa
Room Service	© Maria Eppie
Scratch	© Astrid Fox
Up To No Good	© Tabitha Flyte
The Mayfair	© A. J. Ivanov
Permanent Waves	© Tina Glynn
Isobel's Brass Bed	© Kate Dominic
Something to Remember You By	© Tracey Allyson
Melinda	© Mitzi Szereto
Hands Up	© Maria Lyonesse
Girls Are No Good . . .	© Ms. Steak
Thatching	© Roxy Rhinestone
Nita	© Kathryn Anne Dubois
The Trouble with Guys	© Verena Yexley
A Great Job	© Juliet Lloyd Williams

Typeset by SetSystems Limited, Saffron Walden, Essex
Printed and bound by Mackays of Chatham PLC

ISBN 0 352 33603 X

Contents

Introduction

I am delighted these wonderful Black Lace erotic short story collections are getting a new lease of life, and in such fabulous eye-catching new pop-art covers, too! The series has been hugely successful, and sales of *Wicked Words* anthologies have proven how popular the short story format is in this genre.

Fruity frolics abound in this fourth anthology of sizzling stories and, as ever, there is a wonderful outpouring of the joyful, the horny and the downright filthy. What a wonderful thing the liberated female sexual imagination is! How many men will write erotically about having their hair done (*Permanent Waves*), or getting their roof thatched (*Thatching*)? Or explore all the exquisite shameful emotions of a young monk being seduced by a Viking priestess (*Scratch*)? There has always been creativity by the kilo in *Wicked Words* stories. Black Lace girls find eroticism in the most unexpected quarter. They aren't limited to the physical appearance of their characters for the turn-on. It really isn't about size – it's about attitude and imagination, of which there is ample in *Wicked Words 4*. And the fun doesn't stop with these reprints. There is much more to come from the series next year.

As from February 2005, we will be publishing themed collections – which will be a fun way of diversifying the list. The first books will be *Sex in the Office* and *Sex on Holiday*, and after that we will be having *Sex on the Sportsfield* and *Sex in Uniform*. I can't wait! In the meantime, *Wicked Words 3* is also published as of this month – September 2004 – to be followed by *Wicked Words 5–8* through October and November. If you never got the chance to buy all the books when they were first published, you can now complete your collection and be the envy of your friends! Look out for the colourful covers – guaranteed to stand out from everything else on the erotica shelves in bookshops.

Do you want to submit a short story to Wicked Words?

By the time these reprints hit the shelves, it will be too late to contribute stories to the first two themed collections, but the guidelines for future anthologies will be available on our website at www.blacklace-books.co.uk. Keep checking for news. Please note we can only accept stories that are of publishable standard in terms of grammar, punctuation, narrative structure and presentation. We do not want to receive stories that are about 'some people having sex' and little else. The buzzwords are surprises, great characterisation and an awareness of the erotic literary canon. We cannot reply to all short story submissions as we receive too many to make this possible. Competition-style rules apply: you will hear back from us only if your story has been successful. And please remember to read the guidelines. If you cannot find them online, send a large SAE to:

Black Lace Guidelines
Virgin Books
Thames Wharf Studios
Rainville Road
London W6 9HA

One first-class stamp is sufficient. If you are sending a request from the US, please note that only UK postage stamps 'work' when mailing from the UK.

Marilyn's Frock

Julie Savage

You know the Marilyn Monroe frock, *that* one, the *Seven-Year Itch* white one with the cross-over bodice that outlined her breasts and the pleated skirt that blew up and showed her pants? Well . . .

Once upon a time, I . . . er . . . in it.

Once upon a time, before you and I knew each other, I was a curator in a movie museum. One particular year, we were doing an exhibition of key clothes from the movies, particularly Hollywood classics. We had Bogart's cool white jacket from *Casablanca*, Celia Johnson's I'm-just-an-ordinary-housewife coat from *Brief Encounter*, a Busby Berkeley feathery headdress two foot high: you know the score. The exhibition was a big-budget number, as you can imagine: megabucks to borrow the costumes from the film studios, US costume and private collectors; big dosh to courier it all across the Atlantic; a fortune and a half for the insurance and additional security.

The pièce de résistance, the thing that would draw all the crowds and Sunday supplement photographers, was Marilyn's White Frock. And it was my baby. I'd wanted it. I'd fought for it. I'd got it.

1

The day it was to arrive, off an American Airlines jet from LA, with a courier from the Hollywood Museum of Historic Costume, I could hardly breathe. I dressed up to meet the plane at Terminal One, as reverently as if I'd been going to meet Marilyn herself. It felt like an honour much greater than being blessed by the Pope or touched up by the President or knighted by the Queen. My best toffee-coloured leather jeans, a golden brown chenille cut-off sweater, Versace tortoiseshell shades, even though it was only April. It worked well with my sleek blonde hair, sweet complexion and fuck-you walk.

And I stood at Heathrow arrivals waiting for the courier to come through, feeling as if I should be surrounded by a posse of guards with machine-guns, maybe even armoured cars, in case anyone hijacked The Dress. I'd barely given the courier a thought: just scrawled

Tim Morgenstern
Hollywood MHC

on a placard for him. Art couriers are usually anal fusspots, and nonentities. As this guy was in dress history, he was bound to be gay. My job would just be to allay his anxieties, take possession of It and get him on the next plane back, pronto. Out of my hair.

I couldn't wait to get the frock in my clutches, to handle it, put it on the model, pose it. You'd be the same, wouldn't you? The loaners had of course issued the strictest of instructions about where it should be displayed: air temperature, humidity, distance from the public, proximity to light. But I wanted just an hour – well, six – alone with this wonderful frock.

But then this tall, lean, more-saturnine-than-James-Dean-type comes pacing in from Customs. He's sexy, he's all in black, he'd got more style than most movie stars, he's

2

distinctly masculine and he's heading towards me. With a big flat box being wheeled on the trolley next to him, all straps and buckles and reinforced corners.

'Dr Crammond?' You know what Californian accents do to my belly.

'*Alexia* Crammond ... Tim.' I find myself smiling so widely that the grin pushes my shades up a little. 'I hope you had a ... non-tedious flight?'

'I would have done if you'd been sat next to me.'

His smile goes straight to my pussy, just nipping over my nipples on the way down. With such a sock-it-to-me start how audacious is the end of our contact going to be? I can't wait – as usual.

'Perhaps some post-flight compensation, then?' I murmur. 'Let me ...' I'm going to say, 'buy you a drink before you go back', and am wondering if I am being precipitate in trying to work out if we could possibly shag in my Frontera in the grey concrete gloom of the car-park, bay J8, when he announces, 'I'm staying for a few days actually ... I have a couple of buddies in Holland Park.'

'Are they meeting you?' I try not to show my disappointment and anxiety. Surely he won't be snatched out of my hands so soon.

'Actually not.'

'Then may I drive you to ...?'

'Your place!'

I swallow. The nerve of him. Never before has someone who attracts me been so keen on me in return. They usually take months of fishing for, don't they. Yet here is a man who I fancy more than anyone in years – and he is going for me. I know I look good, despite pre-exhibition panic. But I wonder what I have done to deserve what is surely going to be nine inches of the most stunning cock to cross the Atlantic that day.

'Unless you're anxious to get the dress settled in?' he taunts.

'What dress?' All I can think of is 'but I'm not wearing a dress, and how quickly could I get a dress off if I was . . .' and what's this 'settled?' . . . Then . . . 'Oh, *that* dress, well . . .'

I gulp. He's used the excuse of crowds of new arrivals pressing through to edge closer to me. Somehow his hand is at the small of my back, pressing those tiny indentations in the sacrum that vibrate like piano keys, sending different pitches of reverberation through my entire body. Jeez – this is surely going to be a winner. The kind of guy you want to spend at least a week in bed with.

'Your car?' he prompts me, smilingly aware that my brain, as well as my legs, have just turned to jelly.

'Er, over here,' I motion.

You can imagine how crap my driving is, on that journey back home to Islington. It isn't just his presence, and the thought of what might be. It isn't just that Marilyn Monroe, by proxy, is in the back of my motor. It is his hand on my thigh. And worse, it is the teasing bastard's determination to not let those adept fingers go any higher than halfway up, no matter how much I hopefully slide my leg around to edge his hand higher, nearer my cunt.

'I'm gonna make you beg, baby,' he says maliciously, bending to take a bite of my left nipple as we stop at a Shepherd's Bush roundabout jam. I pull his hair, hard, and want to get violent-ish with him, now. Instead we both seethe, lasciviously. It's delightful.

Throughout the journey home, which takes an infuriating two hours, I only occasionally give a thought to 'Is the bed linen clean-ish, when did I last Hoover, have the cats pooed anywhere horrible?'

Everything is focused on the effect on my whole body that his practised fingers on my leather thigh are having, and the growing bulge in his black jeans that I can see in the corner of my eye, as we head through central London.

By the time I let him in the flat door my whole body is screaming so much with lust that I think I'll have to yell or else go insane. He goes ahead of me, pulls off his shoulder bag and puts the frock box down in the hall.

Marilyn's frock in my hall! For a minute the thought overwhelms me then I turn back to look at him. I expect an embrace, our first kiss, to involve me being yanked towards him forcefully. No, there he is, Mr Cool-as-a-Cucumber man, looking round the flat. Looking at books, my bloody books, for God's sake! You can imagine how irrelevant that seems at this point.

'Tim . . .?'

'Dr Crammond?' he smiles.

'Come and fuck me rotten.'

'Mmm . . . could do.'

'Hey!' I walk up to him and begin easing off his jacket. Should I play lady hostess and be concerned about his jet lag, offer him facilities for a nap, a hot drink? Nah, I want his dick shafting me, fast.

He pulls me down on the couch and starts kissing me. His hair smells of a shampoo brand I don't know and his tongue is long and practised. It matches his fingers, which by now have got the measure of my bra-lessness, the buckle on my trousers, and the towering state of my nipples.

'Oh, let's fuck!' I groan.

'All in good time, lady.'

He stands up and starts to undress. First the soft slightly Angora black sweater. His chest is lean and the dark hair runs down it in a central line, waving out into two thin horizontals under his breasts. It looks like he works out a bit, and his golden skin is certainly a tribute to the California sun. He shimmies his crotch at me and I lean forward to breathe on it, grabbing his buttocks to pull him closer to my face. Then I ease up on the sofa

5

arm, legs apart, and jam one of his legs between mine, up against my fanny.

'Bloody couriers. They should do as they're told,' I growl.

'Damned customers. They should be grateful for small mercies ... Except, I've only got a big mercy to give you.' He cradles his bump at me. I can't wait to find out the exact truth of this, but he breaks away.

'Oh no, what are you doing?' I gasp.

'I've got ... a little ... idea.'

'I thought we'd both got a big one,' I complain.

'The frock.' He walks over to the box with Marilyn's frock in it.

'You want her to watch us?' I ask, as he props the brown official-looking box upright on one of my yellow, much kissed-upon, armchairs.

'Better than that.'

'What then?' I'm mystified.

'You'll see. Get it out.'

'I can't. Not in my grubby little flat. It's Marilyn's, it's God's, it's sacrosanct,' I burble.

'Undo that box.'

'Christ!' But I get up – stiffly, because my clit is so sensitive, and go over to the box.

My clit is pressing so hard against all constraint that I have to take off my trousers. I do it so functionally that I forget that it might turn Tim on. And as I turn to address the box I sense him come up behind me. The heat of his hands is near on my thighs and on each side of my slender hips. As I bend over the box to undo the first of the many leather straps he slides his hands up my jumper and presses his naked chest against my back as his fingers reach round to cup my breasts.

'Oh, those titties,' he sighs. They feel wonderful in his hands, like golden syrup puddings made of compressed hot buttercup petals, each one pulsating with life. I lean back against his chest and arch my spine, the better to stick out my breasts for him. The frock is forgotten even though the impress of the heavy steel buckles is still on my fingers.

'Ooh, baby!' He takes the weight of my breasts fully in his palms. And immediately I come. I come. Not with a shudder but just a gush. It's as sharp as if I've weed myself. And I feel wonderful.

'Oh baby,' he says again, moving a hand down to my wet fanny, cupping my mound through my saturated moss-green lace knickers.

I am helpless for a minute, and shocked at what has just happened. It has never never been like this before. I take in the smell of him, the remnants of a horse chest-nutty kind of shower gel, some deodorant like the sea, aftershave a bit lemony.

He's tender, in the sunshine that comes in through the sitting-room window and lights us up. He understands that for a minute I am defenceless girl, not capable woman. He hums to me and rocks me a little, my back still to his front, as we gaze at the big brown still-trussed box.

'Think what it's going to be like later,' he murmurs, 'if we're like this together now.'

'How long can you stay?'

'As long as it takes, Alexia.'

'That could be a very long time.'

'So be it.'

I need to sit down, I am still so shaken by that unexpected coming. I totter to the sofa and he says, 'Shall I open the frock box?'

'Actually, I'd rather have a cup of tea,' I confess, 'before I cope with anything else.'

He smiles. 'The English. Well, it is tea-time I guess –' he looks at his watch – 'somewhere in the world.'

'Will you make it for me . . . us?'

'Sure.' He goes into the kitchen and finds his way around competently, as I knew he would, while I just tremble on the sofa, in my wet pants and rumpled sweater, gazing at the frock box.

'Ms Monroe, darlin', what have you brought me?' I breathe. If this is what it's like for starters what state am I going to end up in?

The container full of white folds that once encased her sits silently, of course.

I sprawl there, huge gusty sighs coming from me. God, this is likely to be a marathon – it could mean days off work. And I can't wait for it to re-start.

The mobile rings. Stuff it, it will be Evalinda, my secretary, wondering if I'd had any problems with Customs. Well, I am no more prepared to speak to anyone about duty than I am to take a slow boat to Alaska. What I have on hand – or rather, what I am going to have in my hands and in my cunt – is far too important. Let them wait.

Tim, bouncy with pre-jet lag adrenalin, comes back in with a tray and turns my cup handle towards me.

'Ready for a bit more?' He grins.

'Getting there. Slowly . . .' and then he puts his hand on my right breast. Immediately it surges into his palm. 'Well, maybe faster than I thought,' I groan. 'Clear off, for a minute. I need my tea or I'm going to die.'

Smiling he takes his tea over to the window seat and begins crooning, 'The way she . . . sips her tea . . . can't take . . . away from me.'

'It's a great frock, you know.'

'I know.' I sip my tea and think that 'gratefully' is actually a good way to describe the way I am drinking it. If sex with him is like this already then surely I am going to need gallons of brandy to help me recover from all Tim is going to do to me later.

'I guess we could say it's probably the greatest dress of all time,' he muses.

'I don't know. Maybe it wouldn't have been without the air blowing it up, and her holding it down. It was her in it, and the gush from the air vent, as well. The three factors make it great.'

'You know, it was her idea to stand over the air vent. She posed it herself. The photographer had been shooting for a while and not getting it quite right, when she started larking about and tried that pose.'

'Brilliant.'

'Did you fancy her, in it?' he asks.

I hadn't thought. Maybe I'd wanted to *be* her, in that frock. But to *fuck* her ... no, it is more that I want to just join in that fun, of playing with our dresses blowing up.

'Maybe I'd have liked to be there with her, giggling, fighting the draught,' I reply.

'Don't you just want to put your hand inside those white panties?'

'Yes, a bit. But more to slide it inside the folds of that bodice and find her breasts all tight inside a white lace bra, and pinch her nipples and make her squeal ... And I suppose, yes, then I'd like to ease my hand into her knickers and see if it had made her wet.'

He begins unbuckling his trousers as he sprawls in the chair, rubbing the mound from left to right. 'I want you.'

I smile. 'You want me and Marilyn, both going down on you?' I smirk.

'Yeah, all right.'

'You want her to climb astride you, in that dress, only this time without any drawers on. To climb astride you, and pull that bodice down and stick those glorious tits in your face for you to suck and then ease down on your big long prick and say ...

'"Fuck me baby, only me, fuck me like you'll never let me go."'

'You like clingy women?' I am shocked.

'It'd be an honour to be clung to by her.'

Talking him through it has made me horny. *I* long to climb on top of him, thrust *my* breasts into his mouth, have him groan as *I* ease *my* wet fanny down onto what I hope will be a long, thick, dark and eager dick.

He is watching me, and knows it.

'Can you take all I've got, baby?' he drawls.

'Come here and prove you've got it,' I tease. 'Unbundle that kit and let me take a look-see.' I lick my lips. I don't just want to look, I want to touch, and taste and bite and absorb every single bit of it.

He slouches over to me, unbuttoning his jeans slowly, the belt falling away. He draws his cock out of his jet black underpants and I can't help but groan with pleasure. It *is* big. It is dark. And it looks every bit as juicy as I had hoped. And I love the way his curly hair clusters round his balls, thinly enough so that I can see the skin on his groin. I reach out to touch.

'No, I'm going to do it in that frock.'

'What? Tim! You're mad. That's thousands of dollars' worth of frock. It's practically a holy relic!'

'You heard. I'm going to fuck you like there's no tomorrow, but in that frock.'

'You'll . . . we'll . . . ruin it.'

'No, we won't. Anyway, Marilyn would like it. It's a good use. Better than having it lie mouldering in some upgraded Beverley Hills thrift shop.'

I look at him. He's right. And so adoring that I can hardly believe it.

'Can you get into it, Tim?'

'Yes, just about. I just don't have the right bits to fill it out.' He gestures towards his breasts and begins putting it on. I sniff and wonder if there is any scent of Marilyn still left on it. If walls retain memories of what's happened within them, then do clothes too? Suppose she fucked the President in this? Am I going to feel like JFK or Marilyn screwing JFK? Will I now start to sort-of know what it felt like to be Monica Lewinsky?

'Do you have an electric fan?' Tim asks.

'As a matter of fact I do.' My eyes gleam. Jeez, this is going to be so saucy.

First I help him on with the frock, as carefully and thoroughly as if I was Marilyn's devoted theatre dresser, or a cardinal helping the Pope on with his most sacred vestments. Tim smoothes it over himself, turning and admiring his flat chest within that bodice, his hard buttocks beneath those skirts. While he is looking in the mirror I go and get the fan heater, hoping its airflow will be powerful enough.

'Put it on the floor, here,' he commands.

Switching the controls to 'warm' I lay it on the carpet near the fireplace, where there is lots of room. On it goes. The air whooshes out. I stand in the electric breeze, letting my hair blow awry, deliberately with my back to Tim to tantalise myself.

Then, on a whim, I lie down next to it. That way I can do what I and half the world have always wanted to do: look up Marilyn's frock.

The skirts billow out well in the air stream, just as in the photo. It's a turn-on, rather than ridiculous, to see that dark erect dick beneath the snowy, girly skirts. I groan as I see that nude powerful shaft that is going to be for me, in a minute, lurking there where Marilyn's clean white pants had been, covering a fanny that had been penetrated by a President.

Tim places his legs astride me. Dancing, crooning a Marilyn number about wanting to be loved by you alone, boo-boopey-doop, he lines his cock up with my eyeview.

I am overwhelmed. Marilyn's frock, in my living room! And in a minute I am going to have it next to my skin. Her dress is going to be crushed against the sexiest man I'd seen in years.

It is almost scary. I reach down to my fanny for consolation, slipping my fingers inside the sodden moss-green knickers. But instead of comforting myself I find that I am turning myself on, and so fast that I can barely see the frock and Tim's dick. It is a blur. Suddenly I feel the frock brushing my face.

'I wish you were wearing her white knickers,' I groan.

'I could wear yours,' he offers.

I yank mine off and hand them up to him. It almost feels like making an offering to a priest, to put on the plate and be offered up to God. My knickers where Marilyn's should have been. My green pants next to that white frock. My drawers over the place where her backside would have been. I just can't believe it.

'Tim, fuck me,' I beg.

'On the chair.'

He gathers up his frock. Then, sitting back in my ordinary chair, just off ordinary seedy-groovy Upper Street, he folds up the skirts of the most-fantasised over dress in the world so that I can sit astride him.

And slowly, as Marilyn might have done, I breathe 'Shaft me like there's no tomorrow,' and lower myself down till my hot wet frills are just touching the tip of his dick.

The famous frock brushes against my legs. He reaches up and strokes my lower back.

'Come to me, baby,' he croons.

And I come to him, and come all over him, many thousands of times, sometimes sliding my hand into Marilyn's bodice so I can feel his nipples, sometimes just stroking that frock, and his legs in it, so sinewy against its soft fabric.

'Oh, Marilyn, oh, Tim.'

'Oh, Alexia, oh, Marilyn,' he murmurs.

And that is the story of why, if you see that frock in the Hollywood Museum of Historic Costume today, you may well see a slight blemish on the left of the skirt. It's my come, where it shot out at some point during those manic hours. Try as we might, afterwards, we two museum professionals, we semi-experts in textile conservation techniques, couldn't get that stain out, in that kitchen in Islington.

Which is why there were insurance problems. And why Tim had to sweet-talk – or sweet-a-bit-more-than-just-talk – Lorna, his director in LA, into accepting that accidents do happen if you do – ah – this. Like – ah – ah – ah Tim – this – this!

And surely, Marilyn would quite understand that this is a frock to orgasm in. This is the most comed-over frock in the world.

Still Life with Fruit

Alison Tyler

*F*ood is my life. As an assistant chef at a hip Los Angeles eatery, I spend most of my waking hours in the kitchen. My thoughts are constantly consumed by recipes, menus and the specials of the day. Still, no matter how fulfilling I find my job, I have always looked at ingredients and envisioned meals, not mayhem. Snacks, not sex. Sure, I've heard of lovers who play with chocolate sauce or zucchinis, but I chalked those ideas up to silly talk by people who simply had too much time on their hands.

That all changed when the café owner hired Jesse Martin as the new head chef. From the moment I saw Jesse, I caught a spark of the rebel in his attitude. He looked tame enough at first glance. Tall, with sandy-blond hair and a short goatee, he arrived at work each day in his black-and-white plaid chef's pants and crisp white hat. You can't get much more subdued than that. But I've always had a thing for bad boys, can smell them out, and Jesse had my alarms blaring. Something about the way he caressed a melon, the manner in which he hand-whipped cream, made me think he was picturing other items entirely.

The *real* bad boys are the ones who don't advertise it on the surface.

When we moved by each other in the kitchen, it was as if we were doing a dance, a sexy little samba. I could envision us naked, pressed against each other, his mouth hot on my skin, his hands roaming over my body. He must have been visualising the same things, because it wasn't long before it happened.

During a slow afternoon, after the lunch crowd had left but before the restaurant re-opened for dinner, Jesse fucked me on the counter top, his pants undone and pulled down. He didn't bother to strip me, simply slid my pants and panties down to my ankles. The tile was cool under my naked skin. The heat of the stove and the smell of food swirled around us. He fucked me hard, the way I like to be fucked, so I can feel it. He kept his eyes on the door while he drove inside me, as if he didn't want us to be disturbed. I thought that it was too late – we were plenty disturbed already.

'Like that, Bridget?' he murmured, his mouth against my neck, then his tongue, licking me, tasting my skin. 'You like that, don't you?'

The way that Jesse was touching me made it nearly impossible to answer his questions. His cock between my legs plunged back and forth so that I could feel sparks of pleasure shooting through my body. Yet Jesse seemed to want to hear me talk. He stopped in mid-thrust, keeping his cock in me, but not moving it. I craved the motion, would have done anything to make him continue.

'You like that?' he said again, his lips now just a sliver of space away from my own. I understood that he wouldn't give me what I wanted until I responded, and I worked to find the answer within myself. All I had to say was 'yes'. One single word, one simple syllable.

'Don't you, Bridget?' he asked, probing, steel-blue eyes glinting with mischief.

'Oh, yes,' I finally managed to sigh, my voice unrecognisable to my ears. I was lost in him, desperate for more, striving forward by squeezing him with my inner muscles. Jesse grinned at me, impishly, then continued. He worked forcefully, his hands climbing up and down my body, stroking me under my shirt, pinching my nipples through my bra. His cock seemed to swell as he fucked me, reaching to tickle all those sensitive places within my body. Every place he touched felt awakened, alive in a new way, and I almost cried at the release when the climax finally flowed over me.

Soups bubbling on the stove sent out their warm, enticing fragrances. Breads, fresh from the oven, cooled on nearby metal racks. Jesse, inside me, dipping inside me, made the sweetest cream ever, stirring me with his cock, turning me inside out and upside down with the steady, sinful motions. And when we finished, just a quickie, just a blink, I was undone.

After closing the restaurant that evening, we retired to his apartment. It was obvious that what we'd done together earlier in the day was only the appetiser. Now, we were both ravenous, ready for the main course, and Jesse had it all planned out. He led me into the kitchen and then turned to look me over. For a moment I thought that he would kiss me, hold me, say something sweet. Instead, he stripped me. Quickly. Effortlessly. My pants discarded into a pile of soft material. My blouse up and off, bra tossed along with it. My panties down and kicked aside. He took off his own clothes while I observed and admired his handsome body. Then, standing there naked, I watched as he set a bowl of cream on the white tiled floor.

At first, I didn't know what to do. I've worked with cream in many different ways. I've beat it until it turned into pillow-like mountains. I've added it to soups and poured it into sauces. None of these activities were what Jesse had in mind.

'Lick it,' he said softly. 'Like a kitten.'

This was brand new, but amazingly the action seemed like the most natural thing in the world. As I lapped from the bowl, Jesse entered me from behind, pushing my face forward, getting my lips, tongue and chin wet with the cream. A fist wrapped firmly in my dark hair pulled back so my head came up and he could lean forward and lick away the wetness. He let me go, let me bend on hands and knees and drink with tiny flicks of my tongue, taking in droplets of the sweet cream.

Coming around to kneel by my side, he moved the blue glass bowl so that he could dip his cock into it, coat the tip with the cream, sit back on his heels and let me lick it clean. 'Be a good little kitty cat and drink it all up,' he said, dipping his cock again and then waiting for my pink tongue to bathe him, to catch every drop. I didn't suck him, I licked the cream away, licked each bit and watched him strain for it, yearning for my warm mouth around it.

Dip and lick. This game could have gone on for ever. The cool cream on his skin followed by the warm wet flick of my tongue. He lowered his cock deeper into the bowl, pushing down on it with his fingertips so that the head and the shaft were coated with the rich white liquid. This time I sucked him, took his hard cock down my throat, swallowing and tasting the cream and then the first liquid that came from inside him.

He grabbed the bowl, moved it between his legs, dipped down so that his balls skimmed the liquid, then stood so that I could raise myself on my knees to lick the dripping cream. I opened my mouth and let him dip his balls again, this time coming to rest against my outstretched tongue. I was so turned on that I couldn't help but reach one hand between my legs, stroking myself as I worked him.

When Jesse saw what I was doing, he brought me up from my knees to standing so he could kiss the wetness from my lips, lick each drop away. Then he spread me out on my back on the tile floor and, not caring about the mess, poured the rest of the bowl of cream between my legs, holding my pussy lips open with his fingers so that the stream of liquid fell in a cool rush over my clit.

He was the cat, now. Not a kitty, but a tom-cat, on hands and knees licking the milky white cream away, making a different kind of cream rise to the surface. The bowl was forgotten. The pool of cream on the floor was slick and cool. My ass was wet, but it didn't matter. All that mattered was his tongue, the flat of his tongue against my cunt, running the length of it, from the opening between my legs to the pubic bone. Wetness formed on my inner lips. He held them wide, licked away the moisture, the feeling of his tongue making me wetter.

With his mouth against my cunt, his lips around my clit, he sighed, pulled back, and said, 'You taste like cream.' He licked again, mouth open, hungry, eating from me. I fed him. This pleased me. From my body, the juices of my body, I fed him.

From then on, we were like wild creatures, especially in the kitchen. Any ingredient seemed destined to join our sex play. Sweet clover honey. The grated chocolate kept in silver shakers to add to desserts. Sinfully rich butterscotch pudding. I was in constant agony at work. Every time Jesse reached for some item, I envisioned how we might put it to use elsewhere. Even kitchen utensils were fair game: the spatula, the wooden spoon, the rolling pin. Grocery shopping became an extended form of foreplay. Bottles of marshmallow fluff found their way into our cart, alongside liquorice whips, tapioca, sundae sauces . . .

I mourned the time I'd lost thinking of only the

functionality of food. I'd been so restricted before, but no longer. Jesse had set me free.

'Do you ever shop at the Santa Monica farmers' market?' he asked after one of our mid-afternoon romps in the restaurant kitchen. Not exactly the kind of after-sex cooing one might expect, but I was starting to understand that Jesse was someone who enjoyed the unexpected.

'On Ocean Boulevard?' I asked, not looking away from my reflection in the polished window of one of the ovens. My gold-streaked chestnut hair was a tangled mess that I worked uselessly to comb with my fingers. There was no denying that I looked as if I'd just been well fucked.

'Meet me there on Sunday morning?' he asked next, grabbing a spoon and starting to stir one of the pots on the stove. Jesse always recovered from our romps a little quicker than I did.

Now, I glanced up at him, locking on his gaze. I couldn't decipher the look on his face, but I sensed excitement, and I readily agreed just as the kitchen help came back in, instinctively knowing that their break was over. They eyed me, the young boys, obviously understanding exactly what we'd been doing. One scrubbed the counter top, *our* counter top, smiling at me the entire time.

Jesse said, 'Go get yourself ready for work, Bridget. I'll start the rémoulade.'

I nodded, wishing I could kiss him, touch him, lose myself in his scent. Instead, I met eyes with one of our smugly smiling assistants and left the kitchen, already daydreaming about what Sunday morning would bring.

In Santa Monica, farmers congregate on the weekends in a parking lot across from the ocean. They begin setting up tables and large fawn-coloured umbrellas long before dawn, preparing to sell their wares. The market has a European feeling to it, with the glittering white sand and silvery waves as a backdrop to the canvas umbrellas and aromatic fruits and vegetables. On Sunday, I was wearing a white linen sundress and my favourite straw hat, black ribbons tied around the brim and falling in a loose bow over the back. The sun warmed my skin, my bare arms and shoulders, but when Jesse brushed against me, he gave me goose bumps.

'What do you recommend?' he asked, scanning the table of polished crimson tomatoes, so fresh they still clung to the vibrant green vine. His large hands palmed the ripe, red fruits and made them seem indecent. I had a vision of him suddenly squeezing his fist closed, of the tomato bursting, slippery seeds sliding through his long fingers. My heart raced, and I lowered my eyes, embarrassed. Jesse acted as if he didn't notice my reaction, yet I could tell that he knew exactly what he was doing.

At the next stall, he ran his fingers through the wicker buckets of perfectly round plums, judged the quality of several fuzzy peaches, skimmed his fingertips over the array of yellow and dark green squash.

'Come on, Bridget,' he urged. 'Do you see anything you like?'

'You tell me what you like,' I said, finding the nerve to challenge him. 'You're the head chef.'

It was a hot day, but the heat seemed as if it radiated from him. He picked up a zucchini, hefted it, grinned at me. 'These look good.'

Dirty, I thought. His fist around the dark green vegetable, an evil glint in his grey-blue eyes. Coming close to me, brushing my long hair aside, lips to my ear, 'We could have fun with this, don't you think?'

His words brought an instant flash of us in bed. I could easily visualise it. Crisp white cotton sheets, a bottle of expensive virgin olive oil on the nightstand. Afternoon sunlight staining the walls gold, puddles of the oil on his mattress, on the floor. Fruits and vegetables all around us. The pale green pulp of a honeydew melon, cold and wet. The long cylinder of a yellow squash. A rainbow of produce ready to be used, inserted, removed and discarded. Whoever said not to play with your food had obviously never met Jesse.

'I know exactly where I'd like to put this,' he said next, as if watching my fantasies with me, from inside my mind. The round little fruit vendor narrowed her hazel eyes at us, correctly guessing that we weren't planning on marinating her precious zucchinis or blending them into a rich bread batter. Something in the bend of Jesse's head to my ear let her know that he wasn't sharing recipes for pasta sauces or fried zucchini flowers. Add flour, a bit of cheese, toss in oil and watch them bloom.

'You'd like to be filled, wouldn't you? Me in your pussy, this in your ass. That would be exactly your speed, wouldn't it, naughty girl?'

I pawed at a purple cabbage, not answering, pretending that I was a normal, sane shopper. Pretending that I wasn't imagining him spreading my asscheeks wide, spitting to lubricate my hole, plunging the larger of the vegetables there, where I would be able to feel it when he fucked my cunt with his cock, the two rods creating a delicious friction between them. How did he know the way to talk to me? How could he have guessed that his words were stirring a riot of feelings inside me? That my panties were drenched, my body responding instantly to his suggestions.

'Filled,' he repeated. 'We could arrange that, Bridget. We could make all of that happen. All you have to say is "yes".'

Yes, I thought. *Yes.*

He lifted another zucchini. 'Which is more your size?' he asked, all business now. 'This one or this?' he wondered, hefting the two. He watched me carefully, and as

21

my eyes widened, he nodded to the woman that he'd like to pay for them, then telling her that no, he didn't need a bag.

'Maybe you'd like both at once,' he said, grabbing onto my elbow, dragging me away from the throngs of people, off in a corner against a fence. A healthy vine crawled through the metal openings, poking in and out of the chain link. Honeysuckle bloomed around us, perfuming the air so sweetly with the heady fragrance, but it was Jesse's conversation that made me dizzy.

'One for your ass and one for your pussy. You can keep your mouth busy around my cock. That would take care of all your holes, wouldn't it?'

Yes, I thought again, but for some reason, the word didn't come out.

Cars whizzed past us on Ocean Boulevard. We were exposed to the world, on display to anyone who wanted to look. At the same time, we were cloaked and protected by a false sense of seclusion. How many lovers had felt like this before?

'Wouldn't it, Bridget?'

Finally, I nodded, my heart racing.

'This afternoon,' he said, his voice growing lower. 'I need you at my place. In my bed.'

Say 'yes', a voice inside my head urged me. *Yes. Yes. Yes.*

His fist around the zucchini. I could see it in my mind, my eyes half-shut, my mouth half-open. Jesse behind me, parting the cheeks of my ass, pouring olive oil down that sinful split of my body. Not simply lubing me up with it, a dab of the oil on his pointer and middle finger, but *pouring* it on liberally, overturning the bottle and running a river of the thick golden liquid down that valley, between my thighs, the scent of it hanging thickly in the air.

I could see it, taste it, smell it. Jesse's fist around the zucchini, pushing the first inch of it into my hole.

Talking to me the entire time, making it easier to take because he was keeping up a running monologue. 'Naughty girl. You like this. It's dirty and you like it. Or you like it because it's dirty. Doesn't really matter does it?'

Eyes half-shut. Mouth half-open.

I leaned against him, seeing his hard cock, throbbing, ready to enter me, but not yet. He had his toys out, his brand new shiny slick toys, fresh from the garden. He was going to play, first, and I was going to let him because this was going to make me come. Ripe melons cut and dripping their sweet nectar down the hollow of my throat. His mouth following the line of sticky syrup, drinking each drop. Slices of honeydew cupped over my breasts. Strawberries squeezed to paint with, red circles around my nipples, crimson designs over my flat belly. Blueberries staining my skin and his sheets in dark violet patterns.

Jesse described it for me further, telling me about holding a squash, one in each hand. Being filled with something that was malleable. When I squeezed with my muscles, the vegetables would give inside me.

'I'll push them in deeper,' he whispered, 'they'll slip in my hand, slide into you, the oil and the sweat combining for easier access.'

Mentally, I dove further into the world of fantasies as he spoke. Cucumbers, shaved of their skins and watery nude, slippery. What other phallic foods were there? What other items could he put inside me? Japanese eggplants, dark purple and smooth with the subtlest of curves at the narrow tips. Nubby carrots, short and fat, their skins still holding onto dirt in the knuckle-like cracks . . .

'When can we meet?' he asked, and suddenly I was pulled back to the corner of Ocean Boulevard. I could see the shimmering silver waves between the two condominiums across the street. I could see the hot sand

and people spreading out blankets in the shade of colourful umbrellas. Sun shining through the thin nylon painted the sand a kaleidoscope of colours, echoing the multi-hued baskets of produce in the market.

'Four o'clock,' I told him. 'Your place.' And then, the blush on my cheeks as ripe as those plums we'd seen for sale, I hurried back to the market to lose myself in the crowd.

That evening, before we made love, he drew a bath for me. He adjusted the temperature carefully, then lit candles and placed them around the rim of the tub. As he generously added milk to the bath water, he explained, 'Milk is supposed to be good for your skin.' But I knew that he just liked to watch me bathe in water that looked like cream. As usual, he enjoyed every indulgence.

Once I was in the bath, he took photos of me, my body caressed by the liquid, so different from ordinary water.

'What will you do with the pictures?' I asked.

'Blackmail,' he said, winking. I waited. 'Stare at them when you're not here,' he amended. 'Think of other things to dunk you in.'

'You make me sound like a cookie.'

'Something sweet,' he said, 'definitely.'

The candlelight flickered over the walls of the bathroom, shooting shadows up to the ceiling as Jesse slid out of his faded jeans. He joined me in the porcelain bath, submerging us both in the milky water as the level rose around our bodies. We washed each other slowly. It was dirty, what we had, kinky and wicked, but somehow everything seemed pure when he rinsed off my skin, towel-dried me, took a picture as I sprawled out on his bed amidst all of the produce we'd purchased earlier in the day. Purchased to fulfill our deviant fantasies.

I could easily visualise the photo, see it on display

with all those other X-rated pictures I had stored in the gallery of my mind. Mental snapshots of us fucking on the marble counter top at work, making love on the tiled floor in his kitchen, fondling each other in the aisle at the grocery store. This one was different. It represented how far my attitude had changed. Food equalled life, and sex equalled life. Didn't the two have a perfect place together?

In our world they did.

Screen Dream

Portia Da Costa

*T*he first thing he saw when he entered the room was the Coromandel screen.

It wasn't the best one he'd ever seen, but he could have sold it at a nice profit, no problem. It was the sort of thing the Goths liked and they were always prepared to splash out on something black and symbolic-looking.

But he wasn't here to think about flogging cheap antiques, was he? He wiped his hand across his brow and found he was already sweating. When he looked back at the screen, he seemed to see something else entirely.

There was a woman sitting behind that lacquer-covered surface, and in his mind's eye she was also black and shiny and desirable. She was wearing a vinyl catsuit that gleamed like varnish, and clung to every curve and indentation. She was like the screen in another way too: not young, but well preserved. She had large breasts, a narrow waist, and her thighs looked like ebony in their vinyl carapace – hard enough to crush a man's skull if he put his face between them.

'Take off your clothes.'

Oh God! Oh yes! That voice . . .

It was low, rich and earthy, yet somehow also quite posh. The cut-glass diction seemed to dance along the length of his cock and make his balls vibrate. He felt as if he knew her somehow. Really. He'd heard that incredible voice somewhere else and now he wanted to hear it say the filthiest of things to him. He'd do anything to hear it purring obscenities. Inside his trousers, he was rigid with thwarted longing.

He felt as if he were a boy again. On the day he'd got his first car; the night he'd fucked his first willing girl; at his first big auction and scoring a bargain worth ten times what he'd paid for it. As he slid off his coat, his heart thumped and his cock got harder.

Weirdly enough, she always enjoyed this much more when she couldn't see the man. Concealed behind her beloved black screen, she could make the punter into a much hotter property than he really was. In her mind's eye, he was a gorgeous movie star, a wild, hard rocker, or even somebody she fancied from an advert. Anonymity gave her total control over him. Not seeing his face or his probably deeply inadequate body, she could just remodel him into any man she wanted.

So the little CCTV monitor stayed blank as she listened to the sounds of him taking his clothes off.

'Are you done yet?' She kept her voice light, but with backbone. She knew he hadn't had time to be anywhere near ready yet, but this way he'd have to speed up, get in a panic, and be anxious. She was turning the screw, but that was the whole point of the exercise, wasn't it? She imagined him fighting with his zipper – sweating and shaking – and she immediately wanted to touch herself.

'N-no!' he stammered, 'not yet.' She heard the jingle of a belt, then a bump and a muffled curse. He'd probably stumbled and knocked himself on the heavy mahogany side table where the props lay. She put her hand over her mouth to stop herself laughing, and pictured him rubbing a bruised hip or thigh, bronzed muscles flexing in his shoulder as he did so. That made her less inclined to giggle, and more inclined to do other things. It was a delicious image, and she fixed it in her mind.

'You may call me "mistress",' she said after another long pause. In her experience the cool, measured approach was far more undermining than snarling and shouting at them. He would be thrown even more off balance now, not knowing quite what to expect, and certainly not getting precisely what he'd specified.

Strict dominatrix demands you follow her orders.

It was corny, but always a winner. The punters loved it. It was amazing how much power a cliché had, and how much money desperate men would shell out in pursuit of it. But even so, she couldn't find it in herself to despise them. The tried and true kinks paid for nice things like antique screens and Georgian side tables. Her other employment paid for the basics, not the frills, as celebrity faces earned much more than unknown voices . . .

'I'm ready, mistress.' His quiet voice surprised her. It wasn't usual for 'slaves' to speak up. They were supposed to be tongue-tied and to wait for instructions. This man sounded respectful, yet stoic – which appealed to her.

'Indeed?' She kept the smile out of her voice. 'Well, I'm not. So just keep quiet and stand still until I'm ready.'

Did he sigh? She wasn't sure. If he had sighed, he'd have to pay for it. Unseen by him, she grinned and ran through a few particularly fiendish humiliations. She fancied something out of the usual run. Something a bit 'extra' – which he'd enjoy, if he'd got the bottle for it, just as much as she would. The beauty of it all was that she didn't have to do a thing herself, not really. All she had to do was talk, use her vocal training and her imagination, and let the man do things to himself. There was no surer way to demean a punter than that!

Was he already erect? Unable to resist prising open her own clothes, she reached in to touch her quim. Tonight was just getting better and better. She couldn't work out why it was so much more fun than usual . . . but it was.

'What's your name?' She looked down at her own body as she pictured his again.

Would he be as aroused as she was? Would the tip of his cock be as wet and sticky as her slit was? She imagined a pearl of juice hanging suspended from the end of his penis, and saw it slowly descending towards the polished floorboards beneath his feet.

Should she order him to touch himself yet? Or even taste his own juice? Ooh, that was cruel! Perhaps he was already masturbating? If he was, he was keeping it quiet.

'My name's John.' The words were tight and staccato with controlled tension. He *was* nervous, but he still had some control over himself, and she liked that. She'd been right; things were really getting better.

'Well, John, I shall call you "slave",' she said, touching her fingertip to her clitoris. The tiny little bead felt moist and polished, and the jolt of pleasure was astonishing. She couldn't believe how much this feeling always managed to surprise her, no matter how much and how often she played with herself.

Circling, she rolled her clit like a ball bearing, and bit her lip to stop herself moaning and panting. It was as hard to master her own urges as it was those of the man she was supposed to be mastering.

'Not very imaginative, I know,' she went on when the surge had crested and retreated, 'but it'll have to do.'

'Yes, mistress,' replied John from beyond the black lacquer that divided them.

'Don't speak yet, slave,' she admonished gently, reaching into her clothing again, with her other hand, and adjusting her bottom cheeks so they were spread against the upholstered surface of the chaise longue. There were two layers of fabric between her anus and the moquette, but even so, it felt grubby and perversely voluptuous as she wriggled. 'Not until I tell you to,' she added, pressing her bottom downwards.

'Caress your body, slave,' she said after a moment or two. It was amazing how just a few heartbeats could ramp up the tension. 'Rub your palms and your fingers over your naked skin ... but whatever you do, don't touch your cock yet. Do you understand me?'

'Yes, mistress,' he said, and near silence followed. Straining her ears, she could just about hear the faint swish of skin against skin.

The picture in her mind was irresistible now. She saw him squatting slightly, long bronzed thighs flexed as he ran loving hands over his chest, his belly and his bottom. His hips swayed, and his erection – huge and angry pink with hyper-stimulation – bobbed and jiggled to the rhythm. His eyes were closed and his strong, handsome face was taut with the effort of *not* touching himself, and the stress of *not* coming.

She breathed heavily but silently. Part of her wanted to say 'sod it!' and then crawl out from behind her shield to kneel before him and take that juicy shaft into her mouth and suck on it hungrily. Either that, or lie on the panelled floor, legs akimbo, inviting him to push his swollen rod inside her ...

But that wasn't what he wanted of her, was it? And if she broke the spell by revealing herself, and seeing him in turn, it would be cheating them both.

So instead, she swivelled her wrist and thrust two fingers slowly into her vagina. This was a better way, she thought, beginning to thumb her clitoris.

* * *

Touching himself was a test of his self-control. Rarely in his life had John felt as aroused as he did now, staring at the black screen and focusing hard so he wouldn't come.

With his hands on his thighs, fingers itching to stray to his cock, he took a silent step closer and peered at the four lacquered panels. The even number meant that it was of oriental origin. European repros tended to have an odd number. He'd had lacquered screens like this in the shop many a time – and some a lot better than this – but never one with this strange, almost living quality. It was like a third person in the room with them, and now he was closer, he could see more wear and tear . . .

'Are you still stroking yourself?' Her diction was still exquisite, but also huskier now.

Was she as affected by all this as he was? John licked his dry lips and prepared to reply. Behind her screen was she turned on too, her body hot and horny inside its slinky suit of clinging black plastic?

'Yes! Yes, I am,' he managed to murmur at last, stroking the pads of his fingertips up over the hollows of his groin, brushing his wiry pubic hair. Going close, so very close to his rigid penis.

'But not touching your dick, I hope.' Her voice was as clear and golden as honey, yet dark as blasphemy. 'Not fondling your stiff, red, aching dick . . . Your hard-on. Your rod. Your erection.' She seemed to roll the words around on her tongue as if she were swirling the tip of it around the very organ she named. He looked down, saw the head of his cock jerk and weep thick silver goo. His rod looked as hard as a bar of mahogany and it ached as if she had it in a vice. He clenched his hands against his hips so he couldn't grab himself and wank to oblivion.

'Aren't you going to answer me?' she asked, and across the crazed black lacquer, a vivid picture grew sharper.

She was lying on a Victorian, scroll-ended chaise longue, her sleek body upholstered in firm flesh and gleaming black vinyl. Her slim legs were splayed, and between them an ingenious zip lay open. Her gorgeous slit was open too, the pink folds swollen ripe like segments of red fruit.

'No! No, I'm not touching myself, mistress,' he said, as in his mind's eye she did the thing he wasn't allowed to.

A single long slender finger, the nail painted with a polish as black as her suit, slid into the peachy channel and sought out the very heart of her desire. There was no sound, because it was a silent movie, and any noise from within might make him miss any real sounds, but his mistress's mouth formed a rosy, perfect 'O'. The finger flexed, and the 'O' grew rounder than ever.

'Do you want to?' The fantasy fractured and John saw himself reflected in the screen's blackness again.

The surface of the lacquer had seen better days, and the image was fuzzed, but he saw the faint outline of a white-skinned man, of medium height, with lightish, curly hair. At his groin, there was a shadowy smudge – his dark brown pubic tuft – but no clear detail of his pointing, rampant penis.

When he looked downwards, it was a different story.

He was huge. Bigger than he'd ever been. Bigger than it was possible for him to be. His flesh was red, the skin stretched and shiny with an angry inflamed sheen. His swollen glans seemed to yearn towards the screen and for a moment he had the mad thought that if he struck it against the nearest panel it might shatter the ageing lacquer.

Without thinking, he laughed.

'What's so funny?' There was humour in her voice too, but the fact that she didn't shout frightened him more than anger.

'Me, mistress,' he said quietly. 'My hard-on ... It's sticking up. It's ridiculous.'

'So ridiculous that you don't want to touch it ... to caress it?'

There was a smile in the beautiful tones. She was toying with him, playing with him subtly, lightly, almost with kindness.

'No, mistress ... I mean, yes, mistress.' He felt confused, angry with himself for getting confused; yet more and more excited because of it. 'I do want to touch myself ... I'm aching. It's driving me mad. I've never felt this hard before.'

'Oh, surely you're exaggerating,' she said. 'That's what all men say ... They're always the hardest or the biggest. The soonest ready, the longest lasting ... You men are always the best and most of everything.'

She was mocking him. Putting him down. She didn't care about him at all, and why should she? He was just a client to her, a source of revenue.

And yet ...

He couldn't hear anything. She'd given nothing away. No rustle of clothing, no uneven breathing, nothing. Yet still he sensed she was enjoying herself. And that made his own pleasure greater. His cock felt as if it had grown another inch, and he didn't care what she said; it *was* the hardest ever!

'But it's true, mistress,' he said boldly. 'I've never been harder. Honestly!'

It was her turn to laugh now.

'All right. I believe you. Now describe it to me.' She chuckled softly. 'Tell me all about your prick and why you think it's so wonderful.'

Oh, he'd been good, she thought afterwards, rubbing her brown hair dry as she sat on the chaise longue wearing men's pyjamas and dressing gown. She'd just had to shower again and that didn't usually happen.

But there had been something about this John, and the way he'd described his cock and what she'd made him do to it, that had got her going. Unknown to him she'd masturbated furiously throughout the whole diatribe!

As he'd wanked, she'd rubbed and worried at her clitoris; as he'd described pushing a butt plug into his own anus, she'd reached around and fondled and played with her own bottom.

As he'd climaxed, gasping and gulping, she'd come too. It'd been bloody hard to keep her own moans in check, but she'd managed it. And she'd also resisted the temptation to call him back, afterwards, so she could take a look at him.

She felt a pang of regret that the only memento she had of John was the nice pile of banknotes he'd left on the Georgian side table, but there was always a chance he might become one of her regulars. Sometimes that happened; sometimes she never 'saw' a customer more than once.

'C'est la vie,' she muttered to herself, abandoning her towel and counting the payment again.

Generous John had left a tidy bit extra, and what with that, and her latest cheque for a series of television voice-overs . . .

Well, it was time, she thought with a smile, to hit the antique shops!

It's a top screen, really it is, thought John, as he arranged his latest acquisition to its best advantage. Technically it was far better than the one that had concealed 'mistress' and yet because it hid no mystery, he didn't like it nearly as much.

Three weeks had passed now, and a dozen times a day he'd considered ringing her number again, but something had happened that made him even more in awe of her.

He'd seen her in an advert on the box. Several times.

She was beautiful, blonde and sleek, but somehow not quite how he'd pictured her. The voice had been the same though, and he'd almost come on the spot when he'd suddenly heard it one evening while he wasn't really paying any attention to the telly at all. Deep, dark and complex, it had made a banal advertisement into a siren's song that had stiffened him instantaneously. It even worked now, just from hearing her in his mind.

Embarrassed because there were people in the shop, John moved away to his work area, and opened a sale catalogue. A moment later, though, his concentration drifted. A woman was studying the black, lacquered screen.

Not his mistress, alas. This woman was no television blonde, just an average-looking and slightly dumpy brunette. She looked even less remarkable when she put on a pair of glasses to lean up close and inspect the screen's inlaid design.

But when the woman smiled – presumably in appreciation of the screen – the erection that had just subsided twitched into life again. And it jumped even more when the woman looked across and smiled at *him*.

'A very fine Coromandel screen,' he said when he reached her, and then found himself launching into a rushed and rather jumbled sales pitch. She wasn't looking at his crotch, but he had a feeling she was aware that his penis was hard. The woman said nothing, but nodded knowledgeably now and again as he spoke.

'So, are you interested? I think I can make you a very fair price,' he said in an attempt to stop babbling. The woman was looking him in the eye now – and down at his groin from time to time – in a way that made his head light and his cock as heavy as lead.

Then the woman spoke. In those rich, measured, perfectly modulated tones he'd heard in every dream he'd had since he'd visited her apartment.

'No, thank you. I have a screen already.' She licked

her lips and gave him a slight, yet powerful smile that transformed her ordinary face into a beautiful icon. Until a few moments ago, he'd never seen that face before yet it was totally familiar. 'Have you anything else that you'd like to show me?'

In the space it took to draw a breath, questions were posed, then answered in John's mind, and he realised that the face you saw on a TV screen and the voice you heard didn't necessarily have to belong to the same person. And what you *thought* you wanted to see wasn't always what you actually wanted.

'John?' she prompted, her voice so resonant and glorious it seemed to make his cock sing.

His own voice was thin and light, yet it also had strength. 'Whatever you want, mistress. I'll show you anything . . .'

She smiled and nodded, and then – his shop and his customers forgotten – John fell to his knees before her and started tugging at his zip.

Room Service

Maria Eppie

M y fucking boyfriend! Just because he's famous and successful, he thinks he can behave how he wants; he thinks he can treat me like dirt, with no comebacks.

See, Will, my fucking boyfriend, is in a band. You might have heard of him. If you're into indie gee-tar bands, that is. He's been on MTV and everything. No shit. You would know who he was if I hadn't changed his name (to protect the guilty). Now wouldn't you like to know who he is; a juicy bit of gossip? Well, tough tits, 'cos I ain't telling. Why not? I mean, you're thinking why not dish the dirt and expose the jerk and enjoy seeing him with egg all over his face? Well, for one I like going out with someone famous and, for two, I have my own way of getting back, and that I will tell. It goes like this.

Kathy and me are kinda best friends, and all best friends have their secrets. It started one night when Kathy and me were doing our 'adoring girlfriends' routine while Will and Matt (bassist and Kathy's boyfriend) sang to their adoring public. (Note: a lot of adoration here, very necessary for musos, along with copious coke and pills and sex. But only when they feel like it, of course.) Anyway, it's hard having a boyfriend who's famous, because you've got the ego problem. You have to sit there and listen while they perform, and they do that all the time. Their life's a fucking performance. So, if you're the girlfriend, you're practically on duty all the time. Even the groupies get more fun than us, and they are every fucking where: male, female and in between. Believe. We're not supposed to get wild and raucous. We're not supposed to talk to anything with a dick. We're not supposed to do anything but sit and look beautiful and totally wrapped up with what the boys are doing. Like I said, adoring.

We get to look good, mind you. No, make that we *have* to look good, as befits a rock chick and tonight, as usual, we do. I'm wearing a skin-tight cropped T-shirt that shows my skinny belly to it's full advantage. The material's so thin you can see my nipples (which I'm particularly proud of) like they're painted on the outside, and I'm wearing my new hotpants that cut into my fanny a bit but they make my arse look great so who gives a shit. Kathy's gone for a kinder-whore schoolie look. All tousled blonde hair in bunches and smudged eye liner and a pelmet of a skirt that just covers the cheeks of her fine big arse.

Anyway, we were good girls right through the gig so we were looking forward to letting rip a bit at the aftershow party. There's always an aftershow party when you're touring. Even if it just means everyone piling back to the hotel and doing a few lines. And that's what happened 'cept the boys decided to carry on playing, which is the worst case scenario 'cos you can't do anything; you can't even talk. Like I said, you sit and listen and look adoring.

So, me and Kathy were sat in a corner bitching. We'd been drinking steadily all night and were getting towards loud and raucous. I could see Will glancing over at us. Kathy started shouting out requests for karaoke tunes. Some liggers who didn't know who we were came over and started bullshitting about how they were music biz execs and asked if we had an act. I said, 'Oh yeah, we have an act,' took a swig of my Bolli and pulled Kathy's face towards me and kissed her. I let the champagne run from my mouth into hers, and then licked her neck where it had dribbled. This guy was practically creaming by the time I'd finished. That was when Will came over and told me that I was acting like some pissed old slapper and that I was an embarrassment to myself as well as him. This from the guy who had Groupie Number One practically joined to him at the belly. I said, 'Yeah, and you'd know all about pissed old slappers, wouldn't you?'

He just smirked and said, 'Right now she's more of a lady than you'll ever be,' and told me to fuck off and went back to strumming his gee-tar with her draped between his legs.

'Bastard!' I shouted and hurled my glass, and then the bottle and then my chair after him. Everyone had stopped what they were doing now and were just watching. Matt shouted over, 'There's room in our bed if he's kicked you out, babe', and then Will had a pop at Matt and everyone started snarling at each other until David the tour manager said, 'Are you happy now, you selfish bitch?' To me!

So Kathy told him to fuck off and said, 'C'mon. We're going.'

When we got into the hotel corridor, I started crying. Kathy just hugged me and held me. I thought it was nice the way she was so concerned about me. We had a good friendship, all things considered. We weren't competitive for a start. Boy, that's a plus in musos' girlfriends. I wasn't sure of her at first, mostly because she was blonde with long legs and a cleavage to kill for, i.e. totally one hundred per cent babe. Me, I've got really dark hair, my skin is really white Irish (the sort that never tans) and I'm skinny with tiny little tits – but I'm wild. I thought, who needs this babe? I mean, I wouldn't have minded Courtney Love as a mate but not some sunbed bimbo. I needn't have worried, though, 'cos Kathy turned out to be wild at heart as well, and a girl's girl through and through. Not the sort who's always sucking up to the lads and telling tales behind your back. She's more the kind who winds up other girls by being more outrageous than them. When I said she wasn't competitive, I didn't include this. Being honest, I sometimes have trouble keeping up with her. She's dangerous. But she never scores points in front of the boys, which I like.

Anyway, our rooms were on a different floor and we started wandering round and round a maze of corridors trying to find the lift. We'd been walking for what seemed like miles on this endless burgundy carpet and Kathy said, 'I'm getting bored of this,' and started trying all the doors. One of them opened and she dragged me in, closing the door behind. I was like, 'Kathy, what are we doing here?' She just shrugged and whispered back 'Trespassing'. The room was occupied but empty, if you see what I mean. Kathy went straight for the minibar and emptied it. 'We get the booze, they get the tab!' Kathy started rooting through drawers. I was nervous. 'C'mon, Kath. What if someone comes?'

'So? We're rock chicks. We're off our heads, we got lost.' It was a man's room, a middle-aged suit by the style of the clothes in the closet. Kathy took out an earring and slipped it into a shirt breast pocket. 'Let him explain that to wifey!'

I started sniggering, 'Oi, I want to leave something too,' and rifled through his clothes. Rows of neatly ironed boxer shorts. I took out a lippie and smeared just enough round the edge of one of them's fly. 'Fuck,' said Kathy, 'I need a pee.'

We were in the bathroom when he came back into the

room. He was not alone. He had a woman about ten years younger than him in tow. She did not look like a wifey. She was wearing a little black dress and fuck-me pumps and she was pissed. He was all over her as soon as he got the door closed and pretty soon, the pair of them had collapsed onto the bed, moaning and groping. Kath and myself were spying on events through the crack of the bathroom door. We just looked at each other, open-mouthed, and then she started sniggering. I tried to shush her without making a sound myself but, truth was, I was having problems keeping it bottled as well.

Before we knew it, the woman was pulling his shirt out of his pants and he was unbuckling his belt and then, next thing, his suit pants and his underwear were round his ankles. He didn't have a bad body for an old bloke. He looked like he went to the gym and stuff, but he must have been forty odd and his belly was acting its age, even if he wasn't. At first he was trying to suck that big old belly in, but he must have lost concentration when she ripped her knickers off. He just let it all hang out while his hand was working away, massaging his cock, while the woman was saying, 'Give it to me, baby,' or some such shit.

And, all the time, he was going 'Oh yeah, baby, I'm gonna give it to you, I'm gonna shove it right up you,' or some other nonsense that people who iron their boxer shorts think would turn a woman on. So she kept saying 'Give it to me, baby,' and he kept fiddling with himself and it was obvious that these two were just *not* gonna get it together.

Then the woman said, 'Hey, let me have a go,' and he said, 'No, no, I'll be OK. Just take your clothes off.' So she pulled her dress off and I tell you, she was actually wearing sussies. Then she unhooked her bra and she didn't have a bad set of tits, if they were a bit droopy, but none of this seemed to help our man out there. Then

Sussie Woman pulled off his trousers and shirt and got Company Man to lie back on the bed while she made all soothing noises and went to work on his flaccid dick. She pumped it, she nibbled it, she sucked it, but it didn't show much in the way of a response.

I glanced at Kath and she was watching intently. She noticed me and looked up with a smile and raised eyebrows and crooked her little finger. Neither of us were giggling now, we were fascinated by the floor show. Sussie Woman seemed to know her stuff (a talented amateur, I suspect), because she was working two handed on matey's member. The fingers of her left hand were squeezing his balls as she stroked the stem with her right while her head bobbed up and down, nibbling and swallowing and blowing like a demented horn player. Eventually, his cock was just about demi-erect – a bit swollen at the base but still pretty wrinkled at the top. Not much you can do with that, girl, I thought.

Then, Sussie Woman had a bright idea. She got his necktie and wound it a couple of times round the base. 'Hey, what're you doing?' asked the man, but she had her mouth too full to answer him. Anyway, it worked. Soon, the old ostrich neck was craning ever upwards till it was plump and shiny and glowing. The Angry Purple, as Kathy calls it. In fact, it was a king dick by now, very respectable and solid with it.

Sussie Woman had stopped sucking now (she probably couldn't fit it in her gob) and bravely got astride and pushed and shoved and worked away until she had forced most of the huge pile of flesh into her cunt. Then she started a rocking motion till, gradually, they had built up a nice little rhythm together, accompanied by the regular quota of 'I'm-gonna-give-it-to-you-baby's from him and a fair sprinkling of 'Oh-you're-so-BIG's from her. Soon, they were really slammin' and Sussie Woman was being bounced further and further up in the air.

Well, that was their mistake. As soon as she lifted her hips more than the critical distance off the spreadeagled punter, Company Man popped out with a desperate groan. There was a lot of hurried clutching and shoving again and Sussie Woman was saying, 'I can't, it won't . . .' and then the man yelled 'Oww, OWWW!'

It was at this point that Kathy let out her big guffaw. Not a titter, not a snigger – a huge great belly laugh. Both the parties on the bed froze. The man sat bolt upright and looked towards the bathroom. Then he roughly pushed Sussie Woman out the way, swung his legs off the bed and stomped towards the bathroom with a meaningful look in his eye and seven inches of livid flesh leading the way.

As you are probably aware, there are rarely second exits from hotel bathrooms. So we were trapped. The man flung open the door and confronted us, cowering together on the toilet seat. Neither of us could look him in the face. After a brief standoff, he said, 'Who the fuck are you?' and Kath sniggered and said, 'Chambermaids'. It struck me that this was not the cleverest of responses as neither of us were what you'd call demurely dressed and I guess he'd noticed this too. The colour of his face was starting to match that of his dick and I could see an explosion coming. But somehow, neither of us could tear our eyes away from the monster that was waving at us from six inches below his belly button. The best bit was that his rather fetching, navy-with-tiny-red-polka-dots patterned tie was still neatly knotted around its base. It was nice to see that a middle-aged man could still maintain some decorum in such a situation.

Then he took a step towards us and I completely lost it and started screaming. Kathy kept her cool and snatched up a rather large loofah and whacked the member with it. It swung about like a demented noddy dog. By now, my screams were mixed with laughter. Kathy whacked it again and again till she was crouching there, practically fencing the thing. Then she just yelled, 'Run for it!' and hurtled out the bathroom, barging the man against the wall. After a couple of seconds, I regained the wit to follow her but, by then, the man had hurled himself at Kathy as she tried to open the catch on the door to the corridor. I rushed out, grabbed the tie that was dangling from between the cheeks of his arse and yanked. He collapsed in a heap and we were free.

We hurtled down the corridors till we found the stairwell, charged on up to floor six and crashed straight into Kath and Matt's suite, totally hysterical and breathless. After a couple of minutes' recovery time, punctuated with lots of 'My God, did you *see* the look on her face?' and 'Did the dick have red polka dots as well or was that my imagination?' and similar hilarities, Kathy piled the miniatures we'd nicked from Suit's room onto the glass top of the coffee table with a smirk. Then she clicked her teeth in annoyance, 'Nulle champagne!'

'No problemo!' I replied and picked up the phone. 'Bolli, now! Room 603.' Kath started chopping lines on the table. 'Ooh, I so love it when you're masterful, babe!' We both had a snort and by the time there was a knock at the door, we were buzzing.

Kath opened it and in walked Room Service. Young. About seventeen and cute in a barely legal way. Kath winked at me and purred 'Hey, babe, got a tip for a nice young man?'

I emptied the contents of my purse onto the floor and rummaged round through the make-up and keys and tissues and whatever. 'Uh huh! Oh dear, looks like we'll have to pay some other way.'

'Oh no!' shrieked Kathy with mock-shock-horror. 'Not payment in kind!'

The boy started making apologetic noises but it was too late for that. Kathy and me were now both too well inclined to screw *some* fun out of the evening and anyway, from my position on the floor I could see that

the idea titillated him. I circled round him on my hands
and knees, growling, till I'd backed him into Kathy who
wrapped her arms around him and then collapsed backwards, pulling him down onto the couch. This was
perhaps more than he'd bargained for. The poor boy
was starting to sweat. I knelt in front of him and ran my
nails over his crotch and growled some more for proper
effect: 'Rrr-our!' He blanched. 'This doesn't look very
comfortable! All cramped up in there, how about we let
him out for a bit of exercise?' The boy was still protest-
ing, but weakly. I undid the button, unzipped his fly
and immediately slipped my hand inside and rummaged. 'Ohh, all tangled up, we gotta do something
here, Kathy!'

'Get him out and let him get some air before he's
suffocated!' said Kathy and bucked his weight upwards
with a practised toss of her groin while I yanked his
waistband down. His dick sprang out like a jack-in-the-
box, long and taut and veiny. And definitely somewhat
stringy. 'Ah, man,' I said. 'Just our luck, it's a pepperoni.'

'I gotta see,' said Kath, pushing the boy from off her
lap and peering into his groin very closely. 'Fuck. A boy
dick. Not like Big Daddy we saw before! But, hey, we
know what to do here, don't we, babe?'

'We certainly do,' I replied.

I loosened his regulation Room Service black tie and
Kathy wound it round the base of his dick, knotting it
neatly just above his balls. Room Service must've been
having second thoughts by now, 'cos he had a definitely
wilted look about him. Kathy whipped one of the two
scrunchies she was using to keep her hair up from off
her head and slipped it round the boy's dick for good
measure. Room Service sat there, backed up in the corner
of the settee, with a fetching little pink-and-green patterned frill round his now shrinking member. Kathy
asked him, 'You like, babe?' and flicked his dick with
her nails. The poor creature retreated even deeper into

its little burrow while its owner desperately tried to find words to extricate himself from his predicament. 'Tcha, Room Service!' I tutted. 'You just can't get the staff these days.'

'And he's not wearing his tie properly. It needs to be tighter!' said Kathy and pushed the knot firmly up till it pinched into the skin. Room Service made a throttled sound. By now, he had a nearly terrified look on his face. He clearly thought he was trapped in a room with two crazies who were seriously considering doing something unspeakable to his genitals. He forced himself up off the couch and shuffled like a penguin on a mission to the door, trousers still wrapped round his ankles. And when he reached the door, he didn't stop, just hurtled straight out into the corridor and freedom. Kath leaped to her feet and rushed after him, screaming, 'Hey, you! Bring my scrunchie back now or there'll be complaints, I warn you!'

When she finally closed the door, we just fell about. I chopped some more lines and demanded music. Kath found a Steps CD. Genius. The famous Will and Matt hate all Pop, so Kathy keeps a selection specifically to wind them up when they really get on her nerves. Always works, every time. Then she sat down next to me, indulged in a couple of lines and passed the CD cover back to me. After I'd done my bit, I was lounging back on the couch, sniffing when Kathy said, 'I like these,' and ran her hand up my leg to let it rest high up on the inside of my thighs. I'd had a snake design done right there in sequins and glitter and Kathy started tracing the line of the snake. I felt a bit shy but I was stoned and giggly drunk and it was Kathy and it felt unfriendly to tell her to stop. So she didn't stop and she started to trace the crack where my shorts were starting to dig in. They'd ridden right up and my pubes were poking out as well. I giggled and said, 'You do realise this is Will's big fantasy, don't you?'

Kathy smirked and said, 'What?'

I opened my legs wider and said, 'Y'know!'

Kathy pushed her little finger into the leg of my shorts and said, 'This? Yeah, Matt's too. With him watching of course!'

Then 'Tragedy' came on and the pair of us went, 'Aaaagh!' and jumped to our feet. Will and Matt hate this song and most of all, they hate it when we do this, dance to it. Well, fuck him, I thought. Only that little tart groupie probably already is. Kathy must have read my mind 'cos she said, 'Yeah, they don't know what they're missing. Maybe they'd like it better, if we did it like this!' and pulled my T-shirt out of my shorts and started to run her hands up my back. 'Oi!' I objected. 'Steps don't do that,' and I sort of wriggled, but Kathy just wriggled along with me and we squirmed together to the beat. But thinking of Will and what he'd said in the party just riled me more, so when Kath kept tugging at my T-shirt, I raised my arms and let her yank it right off over my head. Fuck it, I thought, and just let rip, dancing topless and wild, arms flailing in the air and hips gyrating madly. Kathy was laughing and giggling at me and crashing around into the furniture. She was wearing a shirt knotted under her boobs so, to equalise the situation, I pulled on the shirt tails where they'd been tied till her breasts swung out, big and brown and braless.

We stood dancing opposite each other, then Kathy stepped forward so that her nipples brushed against mine and I felt them stiffen. My breasts might be small but my nipples are massive and incredibly sensitive. Kathy pinched one and said, 'Shit, babe, your nipples are bigger than your tits,' and laughed. I was embarrassed and wondering what to do next so I said 'What do we do now, fence with them?' After we'd finished laughing, Kathy looked at me kinda funny, then took my hand and led me through to the bedroom. It struck me this was going a bit further than winding the boys up but I trotted along behind her just the same.

Once we were in Kathy's bedroom, I felt overcome by shyness. I wasn't sure what was going to happen next, what should happen next, if I wanted anything to happen next but Kathy just let go of my hand, unzipped her skirt and stepped out of it. She was standing there in her thong, plump and brown and I started to giggle again. 'What?' she asked. I laughed some more and said, 'Give it to me, baby!'

'Oh yeah?' said Kathy and started advancing on me, talking in this he-man voice, 'I'll give it to you, baby.' I started running my hands over my body going, 'Oh, baby, you're so big!' and then I got the giggles again. Kathy lunged at me. I squealed as Kathy's fingers pinched and tickled me and tried to wriggle out of her grasp, but her reach was longer than mine and her grip was strong. I just ended up losing my balance and the pair of us toppled over onto the bed with a crash.

We wrestled a bit more, though I was nearly choking with laughter. Kath forced her knee between my thighs and pinned me down, squashing me into the mattress. My laughter subsided into the occasional chuckle and I looked up at her. She gave me that funny look again and said, 'Babe, you know, you're sweet. Too sweet for that prick Will.'

'Yeah,' I said, 'true.' And then I said, to keep the compliments even, 'And you're too sweet for that prick Matt.' Kathy rolled her weight off me and lay next to me, our legs still entangled. 'We don't need those pricks, do we?'

'Absolutely not,' I said and Kathy said, 'We don't, do we?'

I glanced at her. She was smiling up at the ceiling while the back of her hand trailed absentmindedly up and down the front of my chest. We both lay there for a few minutes. As her nails scratched lightly backwards and forwards across my nipples, I felt little tingles zoom all the way down to my stomach. Next thing, her fingers were stroking my tummy and, without really thinking much about it, I gave a pleased little grunt of appreciation.

Then she rolled over and kissed me. She kissed me in a soft, sensitive, sexy way; better than any guy had ever done. She smooched me. The bottom just fell right out of my stomach and I yielded to those sexy smooches and smooched her right back. And all the time her hands were fluttering up and down my body. Then she started kissing my neck and round my breasts till, finally, she took a nipple in her mouth and started flicking her tongue gently over it. This time the tingle went straight to my pussy and I think my body must have wriggled slightly, 'cos she ran her hand down over my tummy and dived it right into my panties, just like I'd done with that room service boy. I was lying on her bed with my legs open and her hand over my mound. She parted my hairs very carefully and slipped a finger into the gorge between my lips. As she ran her fingertip round the edge of my cunt, I realised how incredibly moist I was. I thought, I shouldn't be enjoying this, she's a girl. It was like Kath had read my mind 'cos she said, 'You like?' and the truth was, I did, and she knew it.

My mouth was dry and I couldn't swallow properly. I looked at her and thought, she's Kathy, my friend. So I just rasped, 'More kisses now, please,' and Kathy returned to smooching me while she removed my panties and I lay there completely naked with my legs as wide apart as I could get them while Kathy gently slipped two fingers in and out of my hole. I think I felt about as dirty as I ever had in my entire life, and that includes the times I played Hospitals with Caroline Quinn in the garden shed when I was seven.

We lay like this for a long while, Kathy fingering and teasing and stretching me with juicy friction. I could take any amount of what she was giving me and, all the time, she was murmuring things in my ear, telling me what a sweet girl I was and asking me if I liked it and I kept saying 'Yes, please,' very softly and urgently. Then, Kathy suddenly switched position and her head was between my thighs and she had clamped on real tight. Before I knew it, she had the tip of her finger up my arsehole and I was pushing myself into her face and bucking my hips and coming, very loudly. It just happened in seconds. Kathy came up for air. I lay on the bed looking up at her and she was grinning like a Cheshire Cat. 'Told you we don't need any pricks,' she said and laughed. 'How was that for room service, babe?'

I managed an exhausted but appreciative groan which made her giggle even more.

Kathy wriggled out of her silky thong (which by now had a distinctly damp patch in the gusset) and lay next to me. 'My fanny's really wet,' she said and took my hand in hers and laid it on her own crotch. Then she took my index finger and started slowly circling it round her clit, which was all plumped up. She looked at me and said, 'Would you do me?' and I said, 'I'm not sure how,' and she said 'You're a girl, aren't you?' and smiled. Then she said 'Please?' very earnestly, like she needed it. 'I can show you.'

So I let Kathy wank herself off with my hand, which she did very vigorously and I enjoyed watching her lie there and take her pleasure, even though my wrist got tired and battered in the process. She built herself up to a real rocking rhythm, gripping my hand with both of hers and then suddenly she rolled over and grasped my thigh between hers and rubbed and pushed her pubic bone into me. Kathy's powerful arse was soon pumping vigorously and she was panting like an animal. I was shocked and excited to see a girl so hungry for it. She made Will's shagging look pathetic. Then she gasped,

'Kiss my breasts,' and pushed one towards my mouth. I wasn't sure I wanted to do this but she shoved a nipple between my lips then immediately came with a long hiccupping sigh before I even had a chance to object. Then she rolled over, puffing and blowing air and grinning all over her face. 'Thanks, babe. You did me nicely.'

'Any time,' I said and grinned as well.

'So?' she said eventually.

'So?' I replied.

'So, any time? You mean it?'

I cuddled up her and said, 'Could do . . .' and I thought, yeah, why not? She had been very considerate and tender towards me and, truth was, I had rather enjoyed feeling and hearing her come as well. We fell asleep for a couple of hours before I crept back to my room. Even though I didn't particularly want to see Will, or have to put up with his pathetic attempts to maul me, even more than that, I didn't want Matt finding us together. As Kathy said, we didn't need those two pricks – not tonight, at least. But Will never came back till the morning anyway, and then he was full of guilty apologies, so I had the best of all worlds; a great fuck, a good night's sleep and Will feeling like he owed me.

And that's how it started, our little secret. We still hang out with Will and Matt because, well, they are famous and they've got dosh and they do give us a good time, occasionally, and we both still like pricks, real pricks, from time to time. And me and Kathy get to spend time in each other's company, which is cool. But now, if the boys want to play the tortured artiste, we just let them. If they get really out of hand, like they're pissing about with groupies or insulting us, one of us gets all tearful and the other gets a bit angry and we go off together in a well-rehearsed little tantrum and then just soft fuck each other slowly for a nice long while, all the time laughing about them not knowing what they're missing. Those two pricks don't even dream what little delights we get up to. I reckon I know ten times more about Kathy's sexy body than Matt ever will and, *naturellement*, vice versa re Will and me. We have discussed about maybe letting the schmucks get involved but haven't come to any decision. Maybe one day, if they're very good boys. Then again, maybe not. I mean, we're doing fine without them, aren't we?

Scratch

Astrid Fox

*I*magine, if you will, a tree. A tree more enormous than the world itself, a tree which itself holds the earth within its scope. The green sweeps of the tree's branches arch out from its trunk like plumage, and the jade-blushed feathers of the leaves are impenetrable and thick, exposing little of the undergrowth. But among the depths of these same leaves and along these same branches stride various creatures, initially familiar but strangely equal in size: a stag nibbling at leaves; a huge squirrel poised on a hidden limb; a vast glittering hawk whose wingspan takes in the breadth of a thousand villages. Beast and fowl alike might be colossal, but they are also dwarfed in the great green cloud of the mythic tree's foliage. Below its dense greenery the trunk curves down, a huge astral trunk of crumbling bark and layer upon layer of new growth, dead wood, new growth, dead wood ... The tree shifts, changes, retreats: the process is endless; the tree is eternal.

Down goes the trunk, down through the constellations and the firmaments, past the gods' abode, all the way down to the world itself, set high above the roots of this Yggdrasil Tree, roots whose base is still watered by the tears of three crones. Yes, the world itself is set high: a world of ice-bright seas and lands of blood and soil, of stench and sex, and a world bound tight by the coils of a great serpent, whose constricting hold squeezes and shakes the very seas on which the priestess's boat now topples, a hold that jars and shudders the invading Viking ship in a shower of foam and dirty brine. With salt water clogging her throat, the priestess prays to the Red Thor to stop the storm, to ease his hammer between the snake's tight spirals, spirals held fast by daggers of its own teeth. With her knife, she scratches a rune into the oak of the ship. At last, there is success. Her words and her carved invocation coax the worm's great fangs to loosen, and all is calm again.

The men are grateful, but no one speaks to the priestess for the next few days of the journey.

They sail for another three and a half days and when they reach the coast the stink from the vessel is terrible. But clear skies hasten the last leg of the journey into the island, and spirits are high. Adrenalin is in the air, too, as the sailors morph into warriors ready to pillage, rape and burn.

The men have avoided the priestess, as much as they have been able to in a cramped ship where a person can scarcely take a breath without inhaling someone's beard. Still, she has kept to herself down by the far end of the prow, and apart from making the usual enquiries as to weather and luck of the battle, the men too have tried their best to keep their distance.

She is a strange woman, and there is no denying that. She admits it herself. The priestess Veleda enjoys her reputation.

In this Year of Our Lord 793, the young monk Cuthbert guards over the incorrupt body of the Sainted Cuthbert, after whom he has been named. His hands riddle over a rosary made of the small white rocks the sea spews up.

Each of these stones looks like a bone-hard tiny sea-creature. Each resembles the Holy Rood itself, each is a little crucifix bead spat out from the sea that surrounds the Holy Island. Already pilgrims take the stones away after they have visited the incorrupted body which young Cuthbert tends, already the stones are known as Cuthbert's Beads, after the saint whose name this seventeen-year-old has the privilege of using.

In this summer month of June, there have been flashes across the heavens of Lindisfarne, great streaming lights across the sky, portents of fire and dragons and trauma. The other monks on the Holy Island are uneasy in the evenings as they whisper to each other after vespers, but throughout the early summer while the other brothers worry, young Cuthbert sneaks off to his cell and strokes himself with pleasure, the comets roaring outside the groove of his window while his fist is on his cock, and he strokes and pulls and gasps and thinks of evil flesh, of men and women, of the smell of his own juice in his hand. He licks his lips, eases his hand along his cock and dreams of soft bodies and hard sinews. Then the pulse comes, and he shudders with a terrible enjoyment; he grunts in satisfaction then cries out as his sin shoots out of his cock, into his fist, liquid and sexual. The comets still tear through the twilight heavens, and Cuthbert hopes then that the other monks have not overheard his efforts.

He knows these self-ministrations are wrong. He knows these thoughts and actions both are evil.

The fighting has quieted, and Cuthbert still waits in his hiding place in the cellar where he has been sobbing silently since darkness fell. He has heard the slaughter above, and he has caught just a glimpse of the yellow-bearded warriors who had landed their boats on the shore and then attacked with such force. The smell of smoke indicates that they might have set fire to the living quarters and they have taken all the holy icons and gold in the church where he is now hiding, but by some miracle have left the holiest item of the monastery untouched: the incorrupt body of the saint.

In his cellar, young Cuthbert spits. These pagans cannot see the true value of sanctity; they see only the glitter of silver and gold; they do not see God's worth. But then Cuthbert censure himself: of course, it is a blessing that the pagans did not take the abbey's most valuable treasure. There is Our Lord's hand in this, somehow.

Though not young Cuthbert's, because his hand had been elsewhere; he had done nothing to prevent the ransacking of the chapel. Instead he had watched through a crack in the cellar beneath the shrine as the filthy warriors had laughed at the saint's body, when they had seen it was only a corpse, and one of them had even reached up and shoved it. Most had seemed hesitant to touch it further, however, and Cuthbert had seen through the crack how the blasphemers had busied themselves with the gathering of silver chalices and golden plates and pewter candlesticks instead, and his heart had boiled in wrath. And then, worst of all, Cuthbert had watched as he saw a female heathen come forth from amongst all the filthy savages, a sorceress of some sort, and saw how she marked the wooden base of the holy shrine itself with a knife, making some sort of devil's symbol, which Cuthbert, because of the angle of his hiding place, could not make out. A female, a most evil Eve, in God's own house, defiling the shrine of a saint!

And now Cuthbert shivers in the cellar in which he has hidden since the attack, for he had been attending to his own dirty lusts in his cell when he heard the first shouts, and had just spent himself in a profane orgasm when, in a surge of deep guilt, he had left his living chamber and had run to the chapel which held the saint's body over which he was supposed to be keeping watch; he had run like a coward, and then, as he had sneaked by the butchery, seeing how the other monks had been slain or raped and bound as slaves, he had crept below the church by an old tunnel he had once discovered, and there it was that he had witnessed the great plunder of God's own riches. Now Cuthbert closes his eyes and shudders. That someone could steal from God Himself! What particular penalties of Gehenna await these murderers, he cannot imagine. Surely a worse hell than the normal one, for the theft of God's possessions is far worse than the theft of those of mere mortals!

Still, Cuthbert can not at the moment fathom a hell worse than the situation in which he now finds himself. Brother Abelard was slain as well as Brother Joseph, and young Brother Jonas, whom Cuthbert had always secretly admired, had been bound up by rope with twenty or so of the other monks, heading towards some evil heathen slavery . . .

But now Cuthbert's breath catches, because he sees the sorceress entering the chapel once more. Anger swills up in him as he watches her light the candles of the church, candles which have been discarded on the ground after their holders were stolen. The sorceress pays no attention to protocol, so she does not care that the wax will now drip and tarnish the holy floor; she rights the pale-blue candles and anoints them with fire anyway, so that soon the whole church is glowing with flame. But it is wrong, so wrong, Cuthbert thinks, because what wicked heathen ritual will now be performed?

Because there is some terrible devil's magic at work here, because though Cuthbert should hate the very sight of the Jezebel, instead he discovers that he does not – worse, the sight of her inflames him with the very passion that is his secret guilt every evening in his cell.

Her flaxen hair seems air-light and sensuous, her lips seem to moisten even as he stares at them, and there is the evil flush of sorcery to her cheeks and her bosom, a flush that makes his chest grow tight. Beneath his robes, he is stiffening at the sight of her. And now, as she bends over to light another candle, a slim tapered candle blue as the sky itself, he can see the sway and jiggle of her unbound breasts, promising a Satan's lushness of silky skin, promising the satiny feel of carnal satisfaction with another human that Cuthbert himself has never yet experienced. Cuthbert's mouth has gone dry, and his heart is pounding.

With a stick dipped in God knows what substance, the sorceress marks a symbol on the floor of the chapel, and this time Cuthbert can make out the stick-like figure. It is no symbol with which he is familiar. He begins to shake. She has lit what seems like a hundred candles, and there is a hellish glow in the chapel now. Cuthbert has never been more frightened in his life.

Yet also, his blood is rushing through his veins, making his cock rigid and urgent with need. He runs his fingers over the white beads of his rosary strung round his neck, but his hands are shaking – he wants to touch himself, but to touch himself in this profane way, under these profane circumstances, under the very shrine of St Cuthbert, is surely a mortal sin. Perhaps it would be justified if in some way he could match the profanity of the spell the northern whore now was weaving. He could desecrate her religion, and by his action then redeem his own.

Candlelight floods in through the crack in the floor of the chapel and quietly, quietly, Cuthbert scratches out a replication of the sorceress's symbol in the dirt with his index finger, upturning the rich dark loam of the cellar so that the rune stands out in relief like a brand. He moves feverishly, his hand cramping, desperate now to fulfil the invocation, to tarnish the sorceress's own spell.

But now he is too full of his own need; he grips his hand round his cock and pushes his fist up and down on himself, as desperate to come as he is desperate to finish this spell of desecration. It is the Jezebel's fault; it is this sun-haired Jezebel who has tempted him like a succubus, tempted him in her whorish manner with her heathen magic.

He feels dirty and unclean, as dirty as a woman, as a shameful daughter of Eve, and it makes him masturbate harder, poison and lust swilling up to the tip of his cock. He has to rid himself of sin. He has to force it out. He looks through the crack at her wet, sly lips and her long white throat and he screws his eyes shut. He wants to come all over that throat, spew over it in a rain of sinful, hot seed. He can feel lust rushing through him now, tight and urgent, like an itch. The whore. The – sluttish – vixen. How – dare – she – tempt – him – like – that. In his mind, he sees her neck and chest covered with his emissions and this makes him even harder, and he jerks more forcefully at his cock.

'Deliver me, O my Lord,' he prays, as the evidence of his temptation bursts out onto the ground in a cool white spurt, over the devil's rune that he had torn into the ground with his own fingernails. And what did it matter? Let sin lie with sin. He feels better now. Clean. Purified. Deep in the cellar, under the altar, young Cuthbert sighs and kicks dirt over the rune, as if he'd never drawn it at all.

The warriors have done their work, and now it is up to Veleda the priestess to ensure the continued success of the raid, for these warriors have never come across such easy pickings before. Not only was the settlement rich beyond dreams, with treasures to be melted down in a molten sea of silver and gold that would shame a dwarf but, amazingly, the defenders of the settlement, though all male, had put up no resistance at all – had not even been trained, apparently, in the simplest art of self-defence. Really, they had only themselves to blame. And now, while her countrymen drink their toasts to a future of many similar raids, it is Veleda's task to purify this stinking church of stone and twigs where the islanders conduct their primitive religious ceremonies, for her countrymen have insisted that the exposed body is in itself a *draugr*, the most unholy of all undead spirits in the form of a living corpse, and it is up to the resident priestess to render the curse of a *draugr* unable to affect the luck of the invaders.

So Veleda puts on her robes, tries to block out the events of the evening – the killing, violence and enslavement were necessary, of course, but not to her own taste – and begins to light the candles that are littered round the dank chapel.

It is good that she does this, because as soon as the chapel is illuminated it becomes a far less fearful place, and Veleda is able to see quite clearly that the body that lies on the shrine is not that of a *draugr* at all, but only a dead man, albeit a well-preserved dead man. She wonders for a moment why he has been attended to with such ceremony, but then dismisses her musings: who knows how the minds of such people work – with their odd little all-male cult on an island off the coast of this foreign land. They no doubt worship death itself, not life, if she is to judge by the decorated walls of the building in which she finds herself – for many of these illustrations depict a pale man hoisted up by his wrists on some type of a frame, with his feet nailed fast, and if he is not meant to be dead, then he is certainly meant to be seriously ill. To Veleda, this is distasteful: she worships life itself, however short or long it might be, and she knows she is only capable of understanding a cosmology such as her own people's – a sacredness of living things like the Great Tree itself. Anything else seems pointless – even abhorrent. Perhaps the men of this settlement all deserve to be killed, after all, so that they do not spread their death-worship even further. As she lights the last of the candles, Veleda thinks of the White Christ missionaries who had visited her country so unsuccessfully, and a frown crosses her brow. The men of this island are of the same type, she thinks.

But now she stands, holy in the middle of the building, and feels herself surrounded by light, by fire itself, and it clears her thoughts. She feels calm for the first time since the long sea journey – she often wishes it were not necessary for there to be a priestess aboard each raiding party, but the raiding sailors insist on it, for luck – and she closes her eyes and lets the candlelight flicker behind the shutters of her eyelids. Her body too relaxes, and her heart slows, and she knows that even if it is not a *draugr* that sleeps there on that platform of wood that she had marked earlier, well, it will soothe her mind and flesh to let herself go once more into the peace of meditation.

So she stands there for a while, eyes closed, and feels the whole power of the Tree flow through her, feels life itself pour out into the church through the channel that is her body, feels the excitement of life-force flicker through veins, out through her fingertips, out through the soles of her bare feet, and then she knows it is now time for the final step of the ritual: it is time to mark the environment with a rune.

Her heart is beating quickly once again as she brings forth the charcoaled stick from her robes; she feels strangely light, excited, aroused. The marking of the rune is always a moment of anticipation, and her body reacts accordingly. She slides her fingers beneath her robe and over her breasts, pinching at her nipples, then removes her hands so that she can write the rune.

She still has no idea which rune shall be revealed to her.

She stands there in the middle of the foreign cult-place, candles flickering around her like many stars, and feels something like a wind rush through her: again she feels full of the life-force; she is driven to write down the rune the Tree has given her. She scratches it out on the stone floor of the church with the charcoaled tip of the stick.

It is a surprise to her: the lines she has drawn spell out the N-rune – *naudr*, need. But I have no present needs, thinks Veleda, I am at the moment quite content, except perhaps for the pleasurable ache in my groin, but that is the usual result of the ceremony.

She stares at the symbol *naudr*, her breath coming quickly.

Then she hears what sounds like a sigh from where the corpse is lying, and at first her blood chills, but then there is another sound underneath it – a scurrying, like that of mice or rats. She knows she is hearing another human, and for some inexplicable reason she now feels *naudr* throughout her body – she needs to fuck, and she will fuck whoever is there, be it a spying countryman – who should know better than to peer in on one of her rites – or a withered male inhabitant of this defenceless but rich settlement.

'Come out!' she commands, but there is silence. The need of the rune courses through her, its magic and its desires, and she repeats herself. Then she takes out her knife and catches the candlelight on it, so that any spy might see that she is indeed a threat and would do well to obey. She has no fear of her countryman warriors, strong though they are, for they are too frightened of her power and they need her services and advice for the sea-voyage home.

But again there is no response.

Veleda walks closer to the altar. There, she sees a crack in the raised floor, and a pale eye staring up at her. She puts her knife down to the crack and shows the eye its blade. 'Come up now,' she says, 'come out from your hiding place.' She knows that even if her tongue is not understood, her meaning is implicit.

Now there is a stirring, and it sounds like a movement below the very stone floor she stands on, and then out from behind one of the pillars there creeps a young man.

In fact he is a very young man, a boy of sixteen or seventeen, perhaps. He has rust-coloured hair and a freckled complexion, though his hair is shaved round his skull. He wears a long brown robe of simple woven material, and around his neck is a string of white beads, which he is clutching in both hands. Compared to her countrymen, he looks effeminate and weak, as if the blood he spilled would be as pale as milk. He looks pious.

And amazingly, he smells of sex. And Veleda, who is well versed at reading faces, can discern that, through the terror evidenced upon his visage, there is also a trace of guilt. She glances down, and sees a dampness evident groin-high on his robes. And she realises that he might have been hiding in terror, but his hands have not been idle, not at all. And as she stares at his crotch, she watches as the swelling there once again begins to emerge.

Ah, the resilience of the young.

Immediately, she wants to bed him. Veleda wants to train those adolescent hands of his to stroke her body; she wants his lips pressed to her anus hot and tight, licking her until she squirms. Already she can see how his breath quickens when he looks at her; how his gaze falters, but then how he tries to sneak a look at her breasts under half-closed lids, for her robe had fallen open earlier when she herself stroked at her cherry-red nipples. Veleda wonders whether this young man has ever seen a naked woman.

Yes, her own land had had the missionaries of this man's ineffectual White Christ before, and Veleda had heard tell of the White Christ's hatred of flesh and pleasure, but this young man seemed to be no stranger to self-pleasuring, even in the midst of a raid.

Veleda feels *naudr* run through her body and she grabs the necklace of the young man and with it pulls him towards her, though in doing so the string breaks, and the beads fall to the floor. The boy doesn't flinch, however, though it is plain that he is aroused, and he stares Veleda in the eye with something like hate. This irritates Veleda. She is a priestess of life, after all, not a stripling of some order that worships death. She stares him back in the eye, perhaps only a hand's breadth between their two faces, and says, 'I am Veleda. I am a priestess – you are merely an acolyte, of some effeminate cult that can't even bring itself to bear arms. I am Veleda,' she repeats, pointing to herself.

The boy glares back at her, and then he mutters something that sounds like 'Cuthbert', a hideously harsh sound of a name, and he points to himself, before glancing quickly up at the corpse above them with something that looks like shame. But Veleda doesn't care about the boy's motives – he has disturbed her ritual, and now he is going to help her complete it.

She points to the charcoal rune. '*Naudr*,' she says.

The boy – Cuthbert? – looks at the rune and spits on it.

Veleda strides up to him and grabs his jaw. He is still glaring at her, but he has also positioned himself so that he is surreptitiously running his fingers against the side of her bosom, as if he thinks she will not notice. She slaps his hand away, and then pushes him down to the floor. He leers at her – has he no shame? – and then, worse, strokes the bulge of his erection through the cloth. He mutters something at her and, for Veleda, this is the final insult.

She tears off her robe, and watches the boy's eyes grow wide at the sight of her breasts, her tapered waist and the fine, full blonde bush of her sex. She motions for him to remove his clothing and, to her surprise, he does so, with no mutterings and with more respect than he has exhibited only moments before. Veleda shoves her hand in her pussy until it is wet with fluid and then holds her hand a finger away from the boy's nose. His anger seems to have dissipated, as is surely typical with men of his weak stock. He sighs, and closes his eyes. Veleda takes the occasion to pause and run her gaze over his body, and she finds it entirely to her liking. Then he sticks out his tongue and licks her juices away from her proffered hand, inhaling her scent with obvious relish, and Veleda understands from his eagerness and clumsiness that he is, indeed, a virgin and that somehow this was why the Tree had offered forth the N-rune of Need, for it is her need too that fills her with desire and makes her thighs sticky with want, even now. For most of her countrypeople are too frightened of her power to approach her with sexual intention.

The young man who calls himself Cuthbert lies back on the floor, passive in his inexperience but still eager as a puppy, lapping and kissing her hand and wrist like a true sensualist, not like a flesh-hater at all. Veleda first resolves to be gentler, but then she kisses him hard, and soon his tongue and mouth are as ardent and even as violent as hers, biting and nipping and probing her lips, like a man dying for water, such is the young man's thirst for erotic sensation. Veleda indulges herself in the sensation, and her nails scratch his back in pleasure. Then she raises herself and steps back for a moment to observe him. He is an avid student, despite his initial anger for her, which she supposes was understandable under the terms of the raid.

The candlelight laps around the two of them on the stone floor, the sticks of blue wax shining across the entire church. Then Veleda sees the white beads, spilled onto the floor from the force of her initial tug on the string round Cuthbert's neck. She gathers up several in her palm, six or seven of them.

Cuthbert is leaning back on his palms, watching with interest. He also looks fearful, as if she were doing something quite forbidden.

Veleda does not break his gaze and she pushes one after another of the beads up inside her pussy, beads which have no particular importance to her but beads which no doubt are filled with some terribly important meaning for young Cuthbert. Her fingers grow sticky with the task, and once more she allows Cuthbert to lick at her hand, a favour for which he seems very grateful.

Then she stretches her naked body down on the cold stone beside him, and guides his mouth to her sex, so that he can continue his licking there, and she feels soft tremors start to flow, and she swivels so that her own bright lips are fastened tight on his cock, which is so urgent that already a drop of moistness appears at its tip. She sucks that moistness away, and is rewarded with a soft whimper from Cuthbert himself.

Veleda can feel him licking out each of the little beads she has pushed up inside herself, and she thinks of the blasphemy he must feel as his tongue curls into her heady juice. With his mouth, he strokes out each little marked bauble. Veleda's mouth goes dry, then she feels herself relax into the slow eroticism of the act, and finds herself enjoying the thought of his young pink tongue moving slowly over the slippery lips of her sex, drinking her. His prick in her mouth becomes harder and more urgent as he licks and licks at her, slurping and swallowing and she slides into pleasure even as she sucks even more violently on his stiff cock. Then young Cuthbert draws his cock away from her lips, his cock with its musky animal scent that inflames her, the scent and flavour that makes her just want to suck and suck and suck.

Cuthbert's fingers enter her cunt, and seek out the last of the little beads. He speaks now, pointing to each X-mark on each bead, beads which he seems to consider sacred, but the words he says – 'crucifix', 'rood', 'cross' – are words which Veleda has never heard before. He draws back so that Veleda can watch him put each into his mouth, her juices mixing with his saliva, her juices corrupting his flesh-hating religion, and this thought makes her burn with even more desire. Her nipples are tight as rocks themselves, her thighs are quivering, her powerful, sticky come is in his mouth.

She stretches her arms out towards him, wants to feel those tender ribs of his, his delicate, cloud-pale buttocks, his ribs beneath his skin, the hot yet tender flesh of his prick. Cuthbert sighs, and puts his hands on her waist, and pulls her on top of him with the confidence of movement from a more experienced man than he is, so that Veleda straddles him and he groans with pleasure. And Veleda, well, Veleda feels the thickness of his cock impale her, as she slides down on him, her cunt tight and moist, for she is dripping liquid, she is so wet she feels as if she were melting into a lake, but here in the lake's middle is a source, his cock, that plunges up inside her and fills her with an itching lust, a need to push down further and further on him.

He moans with her movements.

It fills Veleda with a thrill that she is fucking this boy for the first time, that he is moaning from the pure pleasure of sensation, not the removed fantasies of sex that fill the heads of those more experienced. He wants her, not an idea of her. And he wants the gritty satisfaction she is giving him, as she grinds her hips down. She can see it on his face when she looks down through half-drawn lids, can see the wonder in his eyes and his slack, open mouth. Now she shoves herself down on him with force, and he gives a soft groan and a whimper and stiffens even more inside her. Veleda falls down on him, whilst still moving her hips, so that the pressure on them both is not alleviated. She feels wanton as she nips at his tiny nipples, pale as his lips, bites the taut young skin on his upper arms. She smells his underarms and sticks her tongue into these crevices and licks at his downy fur that she finds, and this sends a pulse down all the way to her cunt, a long string of desire from her wet mouth to the pounding drumbeat of the bead of her sex. As she inhales the scent of his excitement and sweat, he begins a long drawn-out moan and starts to thrust his hips upwards rhythmically, pulsing with a climax he can't long restrain.

Veleda is so aroused by his lack of control, his unconscious moaning, his inability to do anything else but rock his hips towards his own pleasure that she too begins to moan and flush and rock back and forth, so conscious of his stiffness rock-hard inside her, and her hand rubs out a complementary rhythm, sticky and frantic over her own small stiffness. His cock. Her fingers. His innocent face. His tongue snaking out to lick at his lips still smeared with her own juices.

After their pleasure, they lie there for a while on the stone on the warm June night, Cuthbert's fingers playing idly with Veleda's pussy, and she lets him insert and remove his fingers in her wetness until she grows a bit bored with the game. When their breath has returned to them, Veleda gets up and walks to the entrance of the church. She looks outside and sees that her countrymen have congregated down on the beach, where they are drinking. From where the church stands, Veleda can see all the way down to the other side of the island as well, where there are several abandoned boats, and so she beckons Cuthbert towards her and motions to him that he might at this moment make a clean escape while the backs of the Viking men are turned.

As Veleda quickly helps him don his robes again, she smiles. For there, scratched in red relief onto Cuthbert's back in the course of their passion, is a large invocation

of the *naudr* rune. May he never forget or dismiss the
pleasures of the need of flesh again, despite the teachings
of his faith. She hopes it will be a lesson he remembers.
It is the least she could do for the sake of his life-force,
for the sake of the eternal green sap of the Tree that runs
through us all.

Cuthbert is full of wonderment and fear as he rows his
way swiftly to the mainland. And once there, he will
seek out those who will help him recover the Saint's
body. It has been a night of both delight and trauma.
When he looks up across the lap of the waters, he sees
his own abbey, full of flickering light, and he mourns for
those slain and for the future of the souls of those
brothers of his who have been spared, at the heathen
hands of such strange monsters as these invaders. And
yet there is still a resonance in his groin when he thinks
of the pleasure the sorceress has just shown him. Surely
these must be the delights of Eve against which he has
been warned, and rightly so, it seems, for surely the
taste of the sorceress's sex is like the fruit of Eden itself,
the one forbidden fruit. His arms ache and yet it is his
whole body that is flooded with the memory of her flesh.
Though perhaps there is hope for her? She was not
unkind to him; perhaps Our Lord will see fit to save her
soul. Was not Magdalene herself spared? Cuthbert sighs
and feels himself hardening again, even as his arms pull
the last stretch towards the mainland. He has himself
made a small attempt, in any case – he left one of the
crucifix-marked rosary beads behind in the wicked
flower of her sex, so that the message of Christ might
flourish even there, even there in the very source of
tempting sin itself. He thinks of the small white bead
lavished with her juices, and his groin tightens. Though
he concentrates on his rowing, instead. He tells himself
it was a selfless act. It was the least he could do for the
good of her soul.

69

Up To No Good

Tabitha Flyte

I was sixteen the night it happened. Karen had just turned seventeen – it was the week after her birthday. Her parents had gone out for the evening and we were 'house-sitting'. We were under strict instructions not to invite anyone else over but, of course, the first thing Karen did when they left was get on the phone to Robbie.

'Come over, and bring a friend for Susie.'

'Don't be silly, Karen,' I yelled, prowling around the kitchen. Karen's mum had left us loads of food. She was such a worrier, always afraid that we would be up to no good.

I didn't think much of Robbie. Karen had only been dating him a few weeks, and I was hoping she would dump him soon. He was an arrogant pig. Poor Karen, she was so docile and eager to please – she deserved better than a stupid waster like him. If her mum found out about about him, she would be furious!

Despite my protests, I was a bit disappointed when Robbie came alone. It looked like it was going to be a boring night – I knew they would probably leave me in the living room while they went off to use her parents'

70

vast double bed. Karen had told me that they had only slept together twice but Robbie was much better than other boys were. When I asked how, she turned red and stammered, 'I think he really cares about me,' she insisted. 'You know, whether I'm enjoying it or not.'

At the door, Robbie handed me some beers and a bottle of vodka. He gave Karen a big sloppy kiss and a smack on the arse as he walked in. Idiot.

We went into the living room and watched TV, drinking fast all the while. I watched Robbie as he poured the beer down his throat. He wiped his mouth with the back of his hand and then with the same hand, he rubbed Karen's leg, but not with any real interest; it looked more like ownership. Really, he was a slob. His Adam's apple flickered up and down as he drank. He teased her too and she giggled and whimpered. Kar-en, I thought resentfully. She wasn't normally so coy. I suppose I was waiting for him to say they should go upstairs and then really, I thought, I might as well go home, only Karen would beg me to stay – she needed an alibi, you see. I hated being the gooseberry. Instead though, Robbie looked over at me smiling, his overconfident smile.

'Didn't you two want to be actresses?' he drawled.

'Yes,' I said cautiously. 'We still do, at least I still do.'

Karen nodded eagerly. Robbie looked at me intently. And for a split second, I thought suspiciously: he's planning something, and I couldn't wait to see what it was.

'Why don't you copy whoever's on the screen? It's good training, so I've heard.'

Karen had told me that Robbie's uncle had been in a few films. As though that was some big deal!

'OK,' I agreed.

The first thing that was on was an advert for vacuum cleaners. I made them both laugh with my imitation of a bored housewife suddenly awakened by the power of her machine. I jumped around the room like a lunatic.

OK, so I too am a bit of an exhibitionist. Maybe that's why Robbie and I don't get on so well – we're not used to having to share the limelight.

Then there was a commercial for shampoo.

'My turn.' Robbie jumped up. He was so serious as he pretended to be a teenage girl fighting with her mum over a bottle. Karen was nearly doubled over with laughter.

'More drink,' demanded Robbie. I thought he was doing an advert; my confusion made us laugh even more.

There was a cookery show next and it was Karen's turn. She's too self-conscious for games like this. She made a half-hearted attempt at emulating the woman scrambling the eggs, then Robbie took over, extravagantly shaking his arse and saying in a high-pitched voice, 'Do it like this, like this.'

I flopped on the sofa, giggling. My sides hurt from laughing too much.

'You're rubbish,' I yelled and Karen gave me a look that seemed to say, don't irritate him. Still it shut him up for a minute although I felt uneasy. Robbie liked to rule the party. I felt like I might be dismissed at any minute, and I didn't want to be.

'Let's try something else,' he said abruptly and went out into the hall where he rummaged in his bag. He came back with a video.

'Now, this is much better than a tossing cookery show,' he said as he slid the tape in the machine.

He pressed the remote control and this terrible seventies pop music blasted out at us. I started laughing, but no one else did. On the screen, a man and woman were kissing in what looked like a hotel bedroom. The man had one of those big fuck-off moustaches that they used to be fond of twenty years ago, and the woman had a blonde flick and blusher like no one's business. I glanced at the others and saw that they were transfixed.

'Whose turn is it?'

'It's Susie's,' Karen said, and her voice was kind of breathy. Her cheeks were flushed and her mouth was kind of hung-open. The couple on the screen were kissing on the bed and the man's hands were crawling all over the woman's back. Then he pawed off her shirt and her skirt. She didn't seem to mind. She was squirming around in just a black G-string and a lacy bra that made her tits seem awfully big. Then she unbuttoned his shirt greedily. He lay on top of her, filling her neck with kisses. Her legs moved to wrap around him.

'Come on then, Susie,' Robbie said, and he looked at me questioningly.

I felt excited but scared. This was a weird game. I had played postman's knock a few times, and even strip poker, but never this. I wondered what to do. I looked uncertainly at Karen but she continued gazing at the screen.

'We'll keep our clothes on, of course,' I said.

'Of course!' His voice was muffled. He pulled me onto the floor under him, like the couple. Then he started going up and down, bobbing between my legs. I giggled, but he was burying his face in my hair.

'Your legs are in the wrong place,' Karen pointed out helpfully. 'Look, you have to lock them around his back.'

'OK.' I laughed. 'Whatever.'

I spread my legs wide and lifted them over Robbie's back. Then I saw that the girl on the screen had her hands on the guy's arse. I dug my hands into Robbie's jeans pockets. I could feel something nice and warm digging against me. Robbie's face was all funny; he kept wriggling his mouth around. I liked feeling opened up like that. I struggled a little to part my thighs a bit further.

When the man on the screen started rubbing his face in the girl's tits, Robbie started to raise my jumper.

'Oy,' I said. My face was scarlet. 'We're only copying. We don't have to do everything the same.'

Robbie contented himself with drooling all over my sweater. It did feel sexy, and I was embarrassed that my nipples had grown missile hard. I wanted him to lick them, and I would have liked for him to try to touch them again, but he didn't. I especially liked the constant thud, thud, at the crotch of my jeans. I craned my legs further apart and tighter around him. I wondered what it would feel like with no clothes on, with no material blocking us. Karen was alternately watching the actors on the TV and us.

I gazed back at the screen. Yes, we seemed to be copying them perfectly. Robbie was making a sort of diving movement into me, but my jeans stopped him from getting too far. And I had to wriggle more, which I did willingly. Mmm, we created a good friction together.

'You have to make more noise.' Robbie nuzzled into my tits. He was right. The woman was groaning and moaning, crying out for more while the man was silent, busying himself only with the woman's tits. I didn't know what to say. It sounded so funny. Then the man put his hand between the woman's legs, and opened her out, parting her pubic hair so we could see a close-up of what was going on there. She was all pinky red and wet. I felt myself mirror her, soft and inviting.

Robbie put his fingers to my jeans zipper.

'I think we had better stop,' I said. I pulled myself up from under him and stroked down my hair. 'This is silly.'

But the couple on the screen were nowhere near stopping. As the man fucked and fucked her, he massaged her clit with his fingers, and she howled, pressing against him again and again. He moved faster, and I saw that she gripped him so tight that he had tiny indentations in his buttocks from her nails.

I felt confused. We all watched in silence, as the man accelerated. His fingers were playing her cunt, strumming her like an instrument, and she screwed him hard back until they were really going at each other like hammer and tongs. He was grunting and moaning, and then he withdrew and spurted his come all over her tits.

I went to the kitchen and poured myself another much-needed vodka. Robbie was Karen's boyfriend yet I had felt his thingy trying to poke me. There was no doubt that he had wanted to fuck me. And Karen didn't seem to mind. I looked at my reflection in the metallic toaster, and saw that my skin was flushed and my eyes were sparkling.

When I came back to the room, I said, 'What shall we do now?' and Karen said abruptly, 'I'll do the next one.'

'Why don't you take off your clothes?' Robbie said, the dirty bastard. He was grinning like a clown. Karen shrugged but soon started unbuttoning her cardigan. Underneath she was wearing a T-shirt, which she pulled off, and a black bra. Robbie started undressing too. He pulled his sweater over his head. I was surprised that he had such a defined torso. Each muscle stood out, glistening. He unzipped his trousers and stepped out of them. Then he bent over to press the play button, and I saw the sharp contours of his arse beneath his tight cotton boxers.

I was impressed.

On the screen, there was a woman, a different woman, this one had black hair and long nails, and she was straddling a man – the same man as before. I had never seen people like them before, not doing that. She was riding him fiercely like you would ride a horse; literally she was bouncing up and down in his saddle.

I wondered what Karen would do. She was much shyer than I was and, although she was a whole year older, it was me who had told her everything about boys and sex and stuff, and it was me who had lost my virginity first. As far as I knew, she had only ever done the missionary.

Robbie lay down. He had slipped off his pants and all he was wearing was a super stiff cock. Karen hadn't told me how big he was. I couldn't take my eyes off it. It was pointing hard to the ceiling, better than the specimen on screen. And the smooth part of his lower tummy, where there were a few dark hairs, looked absolutely delicious. Karen hovered over him, like she was squatting, and he said, 'Come on, baby, you can do it.'

I watched as Karen lowered herself awkwardly over Robbie's cock.

I looked back to the screen. The dark-haired woman was having a whale of a time, thrusting and writhing. He kept lifting himself up and rubbing his face all over her titties. She was shouting, 'Fuck me, baby, fuck me.' And he was making these guttural groans and sighs. 'Oh yes, you want it, you slag, you want me to fuck you hard.'

'Yes, I want it.'

'You're so wet,' he growled, and she was screaming, 'Harder, harder, more, fuck me.'

It was odd watching my friend as she balanced over her man. I saw her face contort as he slid into her. Then her eyes narrowed and she breathed out, maybe three times quickly in succession. Her breasts quivered, and then she was swinging her head around, squirming. Robbie put his hands up to her breasts, and I watched in amazement as she threw back her head, arching her back. She was almost as turned on as the woman on the screen. Then Karen started saying that stuff too. 'Do it to me, now, fuck me, deeper, oh baby.'

At first, the words sounded really funny coming from her, but after the second or third time, I couldn't really tell which was her voice, and which belonged to the woman on the screen.

Robbie was just lying there letting her bounce around.

His fingers were flicking at her nipples, his face composed. And as the tension built up on the TV, so Karen worked harder, bounding up and down, and he let up on her breasts, and gripped her tight on her flanks, pulling her on and off him. Really hard, he was pulling her too, but she seemed to love it. Her breasts looked beautiful thumping up and down. She had her eyes closed, she looked like she was floating, and her cheeks were scarlet, and still she was begging for more,

'Oh yes, now, oh yes.'

She smashed against him, harder and harder, until he jerked up and she made these whimpering cries. I watched as my friend's body shook with orgasm, and then a smile spread over her face. She bent forward and kissed him very gently on his lips.

I went to the kitchen and poured another drink. Seconds later, Karen followed me in. She had put on Robbie's shirt, but I could still see the tufts of her pubic hair sticking out underneath and the curve of her bosoms. I swallowed back the vodka quickly. She said, 'That was so amazing. I've never felt like that before.'

I said, 'Do you want me to go?' because I was really uncertain what was going on.

'No way,' she said. I can tell when Karen lies, and she wasn't lying then. She put her arms around my shoulder and squeezed me. 'I'm so glad you are here,' she said, pressing her cheek next to mine, like we used to do when someone was taking our photographs. 'That was my first ever orgasm. I'm so happy you saw. Friends for ever?' she asked.

'Friends for ever,' I replied, but I didn't know if I was as happy as she was. I felt really confused. I saw Robbie's come sliding down her thigh, and I had a weird urge to lick it off.

'Come on girls,' shouted Robbie, 'next bit,' and Karen retorted as she returned to the living room, 'Again?' but

I could tell she wasn't annoyed, she was really quite pleased.

'I think it's your turn, Susie,' Robbie said. He looked really self-satisfied, the smug bastard. Why are we doing this for you? I wondered, but I knew I didn't want to stop. The girl now on the screen was a tall, busty, blonde in red knickers and bra. She was dancing in front of a mirror, enjoying herself.

'Copy her?' I asked dubiously.

'Why not?' he said. It sounded like a challenge.

I got up and wriggled around a little, very self-consciously; even the alcohol wasn't helping much. I was too concerned with what was coming next. I faced the curtains at first, away from them.

Karen said comfortingly, 'You're doing fine, Susie,' and I thought, now Karen's telling me *I'm* doing fine! It was a reversal of roles.

The woman on the screen unfastened her bra and then shook her boobs. I boldly pulled off my T-shirt and jeans and was rewarded by seeing Robbie's dark eyes widen at the sight of me. I turned around to face them. There, I wasn't too bad, after all. I knew he wanted me. What he hadn't got before, he wanted now. I swayed around the room a lot, like the woman I was copying. I felt my tits and thought, yeah, they feel good. And then like her, I went to lie down. This was a bit of a dull one, I thought. I guessed that she was going to start masturbating. I decided that I would pretend to do so as well, but I would fake my orgasm. There was no way that those two were going to see me do that. Like her I trailed my fingers between my legs. I might as well take off my knickers, I thought, and I took them down. Robbie and Karen didn't say a word, they were looking at me intently. I was very wet there, that place.

We waited. Then a second person entered the room, only this time it wasn't the man with the moustache, it was the dark-haired woman. She kneeled down and took hold of the blonde's breasts, fondling them and caressing them. The blonde-haired woman, who I was copying, moaned with pleasure. She was biting her lips hard. Then the dark woman leaned right over and not only did she feel her tits, but she put her mouth there. She slurped down the nipple, washing it in her mouth.

'I don't want to copy any more,' I said weakly.

'You have to,' said Robbie. Karen didn't say anything. Instead, she slowly kneeled down next to me. I waited to see what was going to happen next. The woman who Karen was copying raised her arms and then started kissing the other woman. It was a shock when Karen started kissing me. I felt her tongue prod at my mouth, peep through and then we were French kissing like you do with boys and she was stroking my breasts. I kept my arms down at first, but then I really wanted to touch her too. I checked the screen and saw it was OK. I pulled Karen's shirt up and felt her tits. They felt strange, familiar, yet strange. Somehow I knew automatically what to do. We mirrored each other's hands as we reflected the action on the screen. Karen gave out this little whimper, so I knew she was enjoying it. I managed to stay silent, even as she worked my nipples, even as my nipples hardened and reddened and sent little showers of pleasure throughout my body but especially to my cunt.

Then the dark one pushed the blonde down again and parted her legs. She made her spread her legs so wide that you could see everything: the thick bush, the red inner lips, the slipperiness of it all. Karen hesitantly did the same to me. I struggled but only a little. Then Karen opened my vagina up and, like the woman on the screen did, she licked a finger and then coolly, tenderly, put it inside me. I felt her slide up me, and my pussy contracted lovingly around her. I started to sigh.

I heard Robbie say, 'Go for it, girls,' and realised that he was right up close, getting a good look at us both, and that his ever-ready cock was hard again. Then the woman Karen was copying dipped down and plunged her face between the other woman's legs. I didn't think Karen would do that, but she did. She edged down the length of my torso and arrived at the top of my legs. Karen didn't let go of my nipples, she was still pampering me between her thumb and index finger, but then she was up between my thighs. I felt her tongue make contact with my cunt. Hot, sticky and wet. She was moving her tongue up and down my crack, she was doing me like she had been doing this all her life. I pushed my pelvis against her. She took one hand from my breast, but before I could be disappointed she had caught hold of my clitoris and was flicking me there, just as she was licking me all over my hole.

I started groaning. Loud. I wasn't copying the woman on the screen any more; what I was saying was all my own. 'Oh yes, please, I like it, more.' And then the woman who Karen was imitating, swivelled round and perched over her partner. Surely, I thought vaguely, Karen wouldn't, but by then, I knew she would. Karen changed positions and soon she was dangling her moist pussy over me. I closed my eyes, to shut it out, but soon I felt her pubic mound above my mouth getting lower and lower. I didn't want it, but the way my cunt was feeling was kind of chewing up any thoughts of resistance.

'This is fantastic,' Robbie was meowing in the background.

She landed on me, and I felt the shock of the creamy smell of her, and the heat. I wanted to put my tongue up her, to give her the sensations she was giving me. I gingerly slid my mouth along her crack, and heard her give a yelp of pleasure. I buckled under her and I was moving against her, feeling her skin press on mine. Her tongue licked my clit, her saliva was mixing with my juices, and I echoed her, learning from her. Her fingers were working me, rubbing me, taking me higher, taking me away, so that I was only distantly aware of Robbie masturbating beside me. We were going too far, we couldn't stop. Robbie's hard cock was near me, and I reached out to touch him. The screen had turned black, the movie was over, but I gripped his cock in my hands as she buried her face up me, and I wanked him until he spurted out a perfect arch of come. But Karen and I didn't stop, we didn't stop until the convulsions of excitement ran through us; first, I admit, through me, and then through her, and I thought I was going to die or be suffocated or something like that, when she came like a steam engine on my face, but I didn't. I survived.

'Did you plan all that?' I asked Robbie later, as I sucked him off, and Karen fingered me just the way I liked it.

He said, 'No, of course not. Fantasised about it maybe, but I would never have dreamed that you would agree to it.'

When Karen's parents came home the next day, her mum asked us nervously how we had spent the evening. When we told her that we had just watched videos all night, she said that she was relieved that we hadn't got up to no good.

The Mayfair

A. J. Ivanov

*I*f my mother only knew what her sister Sylvia was up
to she would just shit, at the very least. But then, who
would suspect that Sylvia was ever up to anything at
all? In contrast to my mother – doyenne of the Reform
Synagogue Women's Auxiliary, Symphony Board member, top fund-raiser for the Women's Reproductive
Health Association annual book drive, Tennis League
organiser – Sylvia makes sloth into an art form.

I swear, it's like this minor miracle every time Sylvia
rousts herself out of bed at one in the afternoon. The
only reason is that after a while she finds it even more
boring to stay in bed watching the electronic ticker on
CNBC than to wander around their home flicking hairs
off the throw pillows. Sylvia works hard at boredom,
practises it with every gesture, with every suck on her
cigarette, with every slow dip of her eyelids as she
makes a point about some parochial scandal occurring
at the bridge club, where she does manage to crawl off
to every Wednesday afternoon.

Or so we thought that's where she goes.

I am just graduating this spring from University of
Pittsburgh, majoring in Classics. This degree pretty

much guarantees that I have two career choices: either or both work equally well for me – marriage or graduate school. Aunt Sylvia's fuck-off genes clearly permeate my DNA, which peeves my mother to no end, although I have done my best to keep her off my back with A's and B's. With Daddy, who knows what he thinks? He reserves his emotions for his law practice, and as much as I adore him, his attempts at bonding embarrassed both of us to the point that sometime after I turned twelve or so, we somehow concluded to let sleeping dogs lie with respect to quality time.

It's been a rough time for me lately. Howard Lobkowitz, my intended, whom I met my first day at college, backed out of my exquisitely planned country-club wedding just three weeks before the big day, alleging 'lack of readiness for commitment'. Why it took him three years to decide this eludes me, although, in looking back, I should have noticed that there were just too many weekends where his mother needed him in New Jersey, when he couldn't take me to an old friend's wedding, where he just couldn't miss his first stag party, and so on, and where our love-making degenerated into a cuddle and a nap, as he was too tired from his job at his uncle's venture capital firm. Later, I saw his face too close to that of a fat-assed cow-uddered blonde across a table at Pittsburgh's most trendy Vietnamese pho restaurant, as she picked a bit of noodle from Howie's cheek. And I foresaw with devastating certainty that this Howie would be only the first of many inappropriate men I would cloud my happiness with until menopause or death saved me.

After that, life contracted into a little ball. I redoubled my efforts to distract myself with mother's prescription – busyness. I've launched into Hadassah activities, Oprah Book Club sessions, the gym, anything at all to just keep moving. It's had the effect of hardening the agony into a manageable tumour. If I don't touch it, it doesn't bother me too much.

Aunt Sylvia keeps tabs on me as usual without making an issue of it, occasionally having me over for tea served to her in bed by the maid. Last week, to my considerable surprise, she rang to say she was picking me up to attend a benefit fashion show. It was Wednesday, her sacred bridge time. I still didn't get it. However, it was near my birthday and graduation; it would be typical of Aunt Sylvia to be too lazy to shop for me. This way, I could pick out something I wanted at the fashion show.

So, she shows up in her black Jaguar, dressed in a simple mauve silk shantung dress that tells the world she's a size 0. She is close to fifty, although $30,000 of plastic surgery keeps people guessing, at least. She's always aped Lauren Bacall's hair and tone of voice and does a fair imitation of her accent as well. We've been on her back for years to quit smoking, but she's terrified she'll lose her Bacall voice and start sounding like Pee Wee Herman or something, so finally we left off.

We head down Forbes Avenue and, to my astonishment, make a right turn into the parking lot of The Mayfair.

I have to tell you about The Mayfair, or at least about its legend among the Pitt U. girls, because who really knew the reality? This dress shop has been there on the corner for as long as anyone can remember. It's a two-storey free standing white-painted brick building which we figure could have been built anytime from the twenties until after World War II. It's separated from the apartment complex next door by a small vacant lot used, I guess, as a sort of park by the apartments.

Anyway, even from my perspective as a classics major, The Mayfair seems to have no visible business purpose. It is not located near any shopping area; there's no parking lot in front that suggests you'd be a fool to drive by and miss the shopping action. The only sign is the gold script name embossed above the door. You have to really make a point of going there. I never saw a sale sign of any kind or any ads in the paper or the local magazines for it.

However, it does look like a shop. It's well maintained, and there are some tall display windows on the front and side that are always decorated with one elegant outfit each on gilded dressmaker's dummies. There's also a scarf here and there, a little clutch bag, a choker necklace that would help obscure that crepey chin and those age spots. Everything is changed weekly, although nothing ever really stands out. You never say, 'Like, have you checked out The Mayfair windows this week? There's the most incredible Mizrahi gown there! I'll just die if Daddy/Howie/Mother/Jerry (or whoever) doesn't get it for me.'

What I also found interesting, once someone made a point of it, is that each display window is completely closed off from the interior of the store by three high panelled walls that make it into a big box. You just can't see in, which seems dumb to all of us. After all, what's the point of window shopping if you can't get a taste of the rest of the selection inside?

And then there's the second floor, which is not seemingly used by another business. What is it for, fitting rooms? There are, I don't know, at least four to six windows on each wall, as the building is so long and narrow. Every one has identical white-tasslled fabric blinds, each exactly three-quarters pulled down at all times. There's no movement there, except that at night there is often low light coming from some of the rooms. Still, it doesn't feel like an apartment or office, which one would think would have more casual window treatments and at least some activity.

There's no telling about the parking lot. The driveway

runs along the inside wall of the store next to the park and ends behind an impenetrable wall of very high hedges, making it impossible to tell how many people are there and what they drive.

From time to time, we contemplated having a stake-out to see what really went on at The Mayfair, but then of course there was too much real living to do, so we abandoned the idea. Somebody suggested that there was money laundering going on there; I didn't have the nerve to ask what that was, but we all dismissed the thought of drug selling. That would have attracted some pretty obvious types, and the problem was more that there didn't seem to be anyone at all there ever.

So here we are, pulling into the narrow driveway of The Mayfair on a Wednesday afternoon, when Aunt Sylvia was supposed to be at bridge.

'I thought you went to bridge on Wednesdays,' I say.

'You could call it that,' she replies and pulls into one of the last spaces, next to a yellow BMW convertible.

What had been the original delivery entrance had been converted into the main entrance, with a jonquil yellow door and heavy brass fittings under a yellow canopy. Sylvia is ringing the bell and allows herself to be regarded by the eye on the other side.

The door opens and a petite woman with this helmet of hair welcomes us, dressed in a red wool knit trimmed in black, very St John's.

'Mrs Taubman, what a pleasure to see you again. And you've brought a guest, I see! How nice; we have a super little party planned for today.'

She swings back the door and motions for us to come in to the foyer, where this outrageously campy fake French Regency desk squats on legs like a boxer dog. Immediately, a butler steps up with a tray of champagne flutes. We each take one.

'Marge, this is my niece, Rachele Berntsen. Her birthday's next week, and she needs a little perking up, so I thought this would be just the thing.'

Marge beams at me, every tooth veneered to Vogue quality standards. 'How right you are, Mrs Taubman. We've got some darling new young models you're just going to love, honey.' She swept her hand towards the main room. Classical music is playing, and I can hear men's and women's voices punctuated by occasional laughter and glass clinking.

You could have knocked me over; The Mayfair's no clothing shop, to be sure. Instead, it seems to be some kind of weird dating club. There are all these 'women of a certain age' as someone told me the French called them, standing around talking to men. The guys are of pretty much all types – flowing-haired European Adonises in black skin-tight leather pants and sweaters, California beach boys, marines, a couple of Latinos packing penises that looked like they'd split open their pants at any moment, a massive African with a shaved head in a gorgeous orange kaftan, even a Wall Street investment banker impersonator with ostentatious cufflinks. There was a kind of flow to all this socialising, sort of like a Discovery Channel documentary on bees mating, as women weave from one man to the next, checking them out, occasionally touching, taking in a little secret message in the ear, exchanging a toast.

'See anyone you like?' Aunt Sylvia asks as I poured down another champagne.

'I don't get it,' I say.

'This is my gym,' she says. 'Bridge escapes me, frankly,' she noted as if this explains everything.

I look at her totally confused.

'It's not advanced Plato, dear. You just pick who you want, and he handles the rest. Now, what about Paul over there? He's very good. I can *personally* recommend him.' She nods to a collegiate swimmer type in khakis, who looks a lot like a guy who hung around the Pitt Student Union on Saturday nights.

'No, not my type. Too much like everybody I know.'

'Well, you can't leave until you have a go at one. How about the African? He's so big he nearly killed me one time. Best cock action you can get. And he's a former diplomat. He'll teach you everything worth knowing about the effects of European colonialism in Central Africa.'

'Uh, maybe next time.'

'OK, I'm going to book my usual. You look around. Tell Marge what you want and she'll put him on my bill. I promise you, this is going to change your entire outlook on life.'

'But Aunt Sylvia, what about Uncle Mort?'

'What about him?' she says drifting off with a big smile toward the investment banker, who grins back and parts the ladies so that they could head towards the rooms upstairs. 'See you in a couple of hours.'

I just stand there in shock, watching the mating games. Marge joins me and takes my hand. 'She didn't prepare you, did she?'

'If she had I probably wouldn't have come. I'm not ready for this,' I say, alarmed at how much the sadness of losing That Bastard has permeated my voice.

'Ah, a failed love interest, is it?' She squeezes my hand. 'In my experience the best cure is to get as far away as possible from what you've lost. What would be really new for you here?'

I shrug and wish she'd go away, staring out into the clutch of eager bodies. Suddenly, a man descends the staircase, and I am riveted. Then I look around and notice that he has in fact not stopped traffic at all. I am amazed to find that I seem to be the only one who has the wind knocked out by him.

He is actually quite old, maybe in his sixties. Absolutely white hair, longish European cut, tucked behind his ears. He's whip fit, black tuxedoed, with his jacket thrown over his shoulders and his starched pleated shirt like origami. There is a sprig of white lily of the valley in his lapel. I am taken by the elegance of his patent bowed pumps as he descends, his impossibly long fingers, like those of a violinist or pianist, balancing him on the railing.

'That's Count Kalman Burian,' she murmurs. 'Such a tragic life, but such style. He's a wonderful man, so caring. We're all crazy about him.'

Suddenly, he looks down from his halfway perch on the stairs at us. His eyes are as black as his hair is silver. There is something quietly stricken about him; his eyes reflect mine – the equal inability to live or to die. We are caught forever in the moment of deciding what to do and, in not making a move, doomed to a kind of living purgatory. I understand him completely, and know from those eyes that we can heal with each other, or at least create the illusion of this.

'Now, are you sure he's not a little old for you my dear? We've got a lovely young Brit, Nigel, who's also quite refined.'

'Get me the Count,' I say.

I turn away for another glass of champagne, not at all sexually excited, but heart beating nonetheless at the thought of his hands touching my heart.

'Miss Berntsen, allow me to introduce myself. I am Count Burian,' he says in his stunning Central European accent, cupping my right hand in both hands. He bows, bends my fingers down, and kisses the long bones of the top of my hand. He looks up; I cannot breathe or move. His eyes nail me and reach out, as if he is imprisoned in his own body and is begging for release.

'How do you do?' I finally manage, feeling that I look the same way, a small animal just captured and begging to be spared. I think of Howie and my eyes fill up with tears, to my great embarrassment.

'My darling, what has happened to you? So young, and so crushed.' He suddenly pushes a few stray hairs behind my ear and grasps the back of my neck, resting his palm on it firmly but without pulling. 'What shall I be? Your father, your rabbi, your teacher, or just your lover, a real man?'

'Just my lover; show me what it should be, Count.' I am in some kind of trance, feeling like I'm looking at myself looking at myself talking.

'As you like. Shall we waste time here for a while?'

'I hate it here,' I say, amazed at the raw honesty of what I'm telling a total stranger.

'As do I; let us go to my room.'

He leads me by the hand up the stairs. Now, people are looking. I sense their distaste at my inappropriate choice and for the first time, my deep uniqueness, which liberates me. Perhaps I am fully adequate, perhaps better than that. I think maybe I'm like some great wine that ordinary people think is vinegar, but which a few connoisseurs know is superb.

We get to the room, paved with very old red oriental rugs, a Hungarian painted wardrobe that looks to be at least a hundred years old, and a great huge bed with massive oak posts and silken hangings around. I know he has selected these things himself; that this is his lair. I notice that the walls are covered in gold print silk, padded underneath. As he closes the door behind us, I note its extra thickness and the heavy buttoned padding that will make it virtually soundproof.

'It is seldom that I have the honour of savouring such a young and lovely girl,' he says. 'I am delighted beyond imagining that you have chosen me.'

He pulls back the duvet and I slip off my shoes before going under it, fully clothed in my little black basic sleeveless dress I wear for practically everything. He carefully hangs his jacket on the clothes tree and arranges his shoes, just so, underneath it. I sense that these are some of the few clothes he owns, maintained like priceless antiques. I see a tiny hole rewoven at the edge of his pants pocket as he sits beside me on the bed. He acts with gallant concern about my delicacy, as though he were back forty years ago in Budapest entertaining a child bride, and I too am pleased that he has covered me with the feather tick instead of leering at my nakedness.

He leans down and kisses my forehead, smoothing my hair back. 'Miss Berntsen, such a lovely name.' He moves to my eyes, down my nose, laughing as I rub away the tickling of his downy kisses. I lie like a rag doll, while he picks me up and cradles my head and upper back in his arms and delivers the first kiss, delicate as a bit of fluff but full of promise. He reaches behind him, where there is a glass of a clear liquid in which something gnarled and brown is floating anchored by a toothpick.

'Allow me to introduce you to a famous Hungarian spirit, distilled from plums. I think you will like it very much.' He takes a gulp, then shoots it hot into my mouth, smashing my lips. It's like a jolt of burning kerosene and he holds me hard to him, forcing me to take it down, polishing off what comes out the sides of my mouth with his pointed tongue. My whole body starts to burn.

'Do you like it, my pet?'

I nod and lick off what little excess there is.

'Here, I will give you the best part, the prune that is soaked in the spirits. It will revitalise you for what will come.'

He hands it to me on the little toothpick and I nip it off eagerly, spitting the seed into his waiting hand. It is sweet and concentrated with the heavy liquor, and I feel it starting to hit me immediately.

'Yes, yes, my darling, that's right. Now, let us begin

in earnest if you are ready. I want to spend every moment possible in pleasing you.'

I look at him helplessly. It is wonderful to be weak in the arms of a real man, I realise, and thank God I have been given this opportunity to experience the joy of being laid out and fucked like a real lady.

He unbuttons his starched shirt and unties his evening tie. The cummerbund and tie are laid carefully on the shoulder of the jacket and he removes his European ribbed sleeveless undershirt. He still keeps fit, despite the grey rug of his chest hair. There are only occasional tiny areas where a little sag escapes being spread over a taut muscle. I am pleased to see that the muscles of his shoulders, arms, chest and back are still deeply defined. He removes his socks, then his pants and climbs into bed, wearing spotless white silk shorts. His lightly tanned thighs and rear are impressive for a man of any age. I make a note to marry this guy as soon as possible, I am so in love/lust.

I am also glad I wore the little black dress with the buttons down the front. He nuzzles and coos in my hair and ears as he works down the row and slips me out of the dress under the duvet. I am down to my good underwear (which I wore thinking I might have to have a fitting – little did I know what I was going to fit into or over), when he asks, 'May I look at you, dear? Your skin is affecting me so, I must see how lovely it is.'

He picks up the edge of the cover, whisks off my bra, and immediately takes my breasts in his hands. He looks at me with a soft smile and suddenly seems almost a boy again. 'It is so strange the memories one has,' he says with his rich accent, cuddling my breasts in his hands, rolling them about a bit. 'I recall that one year, our prize female rabbit had a litter of little bunnies. They were so wonderful, my brothers and sister and I could hardly bear to be away from them even for an instant. They were tiny, so white and pink and soft. Your breasts

92

are so like them, it is like holding those baby rabbits in my hands again. But it was so strange, once we began to play with them, the mother rabbit – what was her name, Hedi, I think, would not feed them. Every time they went for her nipples, even though she was full of milk, she kicked them away and tried to run. We would have to hold her down and find a nipple for each of them to get them fed. We could see the whites of her eyes, she was so angry at us for saving her babies and forcing her to stay put. Why did she do that? Not even my father knew, and we thought he knew everything. Eventually, most of them survived, but we never bred her again. He finally killed her for stew, and we didn't mind eating it, I can tell you that!'

I look at him and see the pain again for an instant, but he returns to his task and carefully kisses each breast with such sweetness that I can almost believe it is love. His long fingers and palms enclose me as he kisses my sternum and presses my breasts to his cheeks to caress them with his clean shaven face. He takes the hairpins out of my French knot and loosens my hair with his fingers, whiffing deeply not only my hair but the cologne I have sprayed behind my ears and in the hollow of my neck.

The spice of his cologne rises to my nose and I take in his smell hungrily as if it is apple strudel. He cradles my sides in his hands as he licks and kisses the score down the centre of my belly that separates my stomach muscles. I am beside myself with adoration. I take his beautiful mane in my fingers and pull back his head so I can lean down and kiss him. He takes the cue and covers me with himself, as we begin adoring each other's mouths in every way possible. I take his lower lip in my mouth and suck on it, thrusting my tongue along his gums, while he penetrates and tickles the roof of my mouth with his tongue, moving to the corners and over my lips, into my ears and down my neck. His dick begins to press on my groin, hard enough to bruise, but we pay it no mind as we continue kissing anything we can reach. His hair is in my mouth, then I am breathing hot in his ear. He is saying something in Hungarian, something urgent and passionate. His language is ugly to me, but it seems like the right sound for sex talk, all rolling and exotic.

I momentarily think of Howie, who considered kissing as a thing dogs and homosexuals did, and thank God again for my liberation. Kalman has pinned my arms over my head with his own and has begun kissing my armpits, of all places. This strikes me as fiercely erotic for some reason. His hot breath there is driving me to madness. I spread my legs like a female dog and bend my knees, no longer being able to help myself.

Then he does what we have come to do. He expertly loosens my garters, trying his best to keep them from snapping my legs. I let him know that I don't care about taking off my stockings but help him unhook the garter belt and toss it away. He now removes the coverlet and kneels between my legs, giving himself the first complete look of me. His hand goes up to his mouth for an instant, and I am shocked to see tears in his eyes. Everything stops as he regards me, his hand, fingers spread, now tracing down the length of my body. 'Viveka', he says softly. A tear drops neatly into my navel.

I reach up to take his face in my hands, 'My darling,' I say. 'Take me, I love you. Do it now.'

He wipes his eyes and nods affirmatively, resignedly. I notice that his erection is still holding, staining his pants with drops of juice. In slow motion with both hands, he takes the elastic at the top of my panties and pulls them down. I lift each leg to let him remove them. Then, without warning, he brings them to his face, smells them deeply and begins to weep hard. I come up and put my arms around him. He is again speaking in his incomprehensible tongue and I despair for his despair as I rock him in my arms.

We stay this way for a long time, he crying into my panties as I encircle his lap with my legs and hold him to me. Finally, I cannot wait longer, and so tentatively because I want him to continue to think of me as a lady, I lower my right hand to slip just inside the elastic of his very brief shorts. I bury my face in his chest and breathe in his beautiful animal smell, undimmed from age and tragedy. It awakens both of us.

'Will you make me beg, your excellency?' I ask as I pull him down with me to the bed.

'Never, my precious. I am all yours, believe me. I am just a silly old man with too many memories. I beg you to forgive me. Can you do that?' He is over me now, my legs still wrapped around his back. A lock of his hair sweeps his face.

'Touch me, I am begging you, *mon amour*,' I choke out, grabbing one of his wrists and trying to move it from supporting him to my aching pussy.

'Let me work, my child, let me work,' he says and pulls my legs off his back, arching backwards until his bottom is balanced on his feet. He again attends to my pussy, but this time it is to study its structure and function. I watch as he examines every aspect of my pussy as if he has never seen such a unique thing. He pulls apart my labia, peels back the foreskin of my clit to reveal the deep rose organ of my real sex, palpates it lightly a few times, pulls on the dark smaller labia and runs his finger meditatively around the surfaces, sometimes in circles, but mostly up and down from the top of my sex, where it merges with my belly, to the perineum below my hole.

I am breathing as if I'm hitting the Wall in a marathon, scrunching the silk duvet and presenting my privates to him, pushing my package near his face, planting my feet on the bed and thrusting my pelvis up to within a few inches.

'Would you like me to kiss it, my sweet? Would you like daddy to love your little pussy the way it deserves? Do you need your daddy to take care of you?' he looks at me and smiles.

'Oh, yes, father. Nobody can please me like you can. Give your little girl a special treat, today, please? I've been so good,' I coo, stretching and pulling up my long dark hair beneath my fingers so that it spreads across the pillow.

'Very well,' he says gravely, with a last trail of his finger down my clit.

He leans across me and takes another draught of the clear liquor, which he swallows with deep attention and respect for its flavour. Another swallow is deposited in my waiting mouth. He grabs my hair and pulls back my head to kiss my throat and breasts again. They sting a little from the remains of the liquor on his tongue. I close my eyes and await the blessed moment I have never ever experienced myself and have begged for from those few boys I have been with.

There is an instant where his only contact is his fingers moving down my body and grabbing the insides of my thighs to hold me still. I cry out just from the impact of his breath on my clit. And then he is There, grabbing it lightly with his teeth and beginning to suck on it. He deposits a little of the plum liquor directly on my quim. I burn, itch, and swell with the alcohol.

I cannot help myself; I begin to scream from the perfect complement of pain and pleasure that I now know to be a woman's ultimate thrill. He pulls, he twirls it in circles, he runs his tongue up and down its length, he uses his tongue to separate the layers until he exposes the exquisitely refined sensitivity of the inner thread of nerves under the foreskin. He continues this for seconds or minutes, I don't know, until I am wrenched with pleasure and about one suck from coming.

Then, just as he knows I'm going to go off, I feel his tongue pierce my entrance and dance inside my deep reaches. He enhances me with his fingers, which I eagerly fuck until he finds my G-spot and begins to rub me in earnest. His fingers scrape the top of my quim in a come-hither movement, rolling off and on my G-spot, and I find myself raising up even farther. At the same time, he returns his mouth to my clit and begins the final sucking crescendo to my orgasm, matching the rhythm inside with his long fingers. It feels as if his entire hand is within me, plucking at the bundle of nerves on the other side of my clitoris.

I am wailing now, shuddering fast with my body as I take his rhythm for my own. And then I come massively, feeling the come shoot out of my pussy as I raise my pelvis one last time to meet his lips and to savour him sucking my life energy out of my clit.

My body is devastated. I lie there panting as if I'd been tackled by twenty football players. Then, I am amazed to experience over and over something that can only be described as aftershocks as if from an earthquake. It's like a series of little orgasms that wash across my body and through my vagina every few seconds. I watch my stomach muscles ripple like little waves and am pleased to see his huge hand soothe my stomach, leaving a trail of juice behind. I cannot speak.

He lays down beside me, stroking my body with the tips of his fingers. I almost cannot bear the stimulation, but I turn toward him and put a kiss where I can reach, which is on the elbow he is leaning on. He seems suddenly radiant, youthful and proud of himself. He smoothes my hair, being careful to work out the little kinks before they pull. Then he leans over me and begins long slow kissing, in infinite variety over my mouth and lips. He traces my lips with his fingers and tells me I am better than candy, a delight to every one of his senses. And the strangest thing is that I know I can believe him.

I kiss back, with every bit of ingenuity I can muster. I want him to love me, to be impressed with my experience, limited as it is; in short, to want to be with me for ever.

'What are your plans?' I ask him.

He smiles sadly, shrugs, kisses my shoulder.

'Why are you here, doing this? Who is Viveka?'

'Don't ask these things; it is a long story. She was my wife and she died, that's all,' he said, but I didn't feel pushed away by his tone of voice.

'When did she die? Recently?'

'No, it was a very long time ago. You remind me of her. I haven't felt this way in a long time.'

'Do you have children at least? Family?'

He laughs, 'Oh no, that's why I'm here, doing this. Would I be an old gigolo in Pittsburgh, Pennsylvania if I had a family who took care for me? How could I dishonour myself in front of them?'

'Kalman, on the contrary, you have honoured yourself and me; you have saved my life, and you know it. This is not sex; this was something profound and important we shared. Your tears prove it, don't you see?'

He shakes his head. 'You are so young, so romantic.'

'I'm not!' I say, sounding extremely young and romantic even to myself. 'Kalman, I'm truly in love with you. I don't have to be old to know it; I don't have to develop love for you over time. It's just there. We need to be together; I need to be with you. I come from a rich family; we can make this work, I promise. Just let me get you out of this!'

He kisses my hand again. 'I'm afraid you must go now, my child. I am ashamed to say that I have another regular client to see.'

'Kalman, listen. I have a car and a bank card. We can

leave right now! Or tonight after you're finished, just tell me when and where.'

'No,' he says firmly. 'My place is here. This is my destiny.'

'It is not your bloody destiny! That's so Old World, I can't believe you're saying it. Our destiny is together, maybe in California or somewhere, just enjoying each other's love. I'll cook; we'll drive along the ocean. You'd like that, wouldn't you?' I say, sounding more desperate and ridiculous by the minute.

'Next week; come back and see me next Wednesday. We'll dream some more together; be here late in the day. We can have supper after. Make an appointment with Marge, yes?' He is assembling my clothes and hustling me into them.

'There's a good girl.' He kisses me on the temple and escorts me down the stairs. Aunt Sylvia is having a Bloody Mary and laughing in that tinkling fake way she does on the arm of her ersatz investment banker. She waves gaily and minces over. 'Time for a nap, eh? Unusual choice, but then you always were Daddy's Girl.'

I look back as she steers me out the door, complaining that Mort will kill her if she isn't home in ten minutes. Kalman has gone.

Permanent Waves

Tina Glynn

I was soaked to the skin and shivering. For the past five minutes I'd been staring miserably through the rain-spattered glass door of the salon, trying desperately to find the courage to go inside.

The temptation to go back to Maureen and ask her for my old job back was almost overwhelming, but I didn't dare. Colin, my fiancé, would've killed me. Taking the stylist's job at Sybarus had almost doubled my salary and what with the wedding, now only two weeks away, to pay for ... Colin was right, I told myself, taking a deep breath and a firm grip on the door handle; fifty-three prawn cocktails, Aberdeen Angus roast beef dinners and strawberry brulées (plus coffee, petits fours and karaoke disc jockey) weren't just going to pay for themselves.

As I pushed open the door, my ears were immediately hit by deafeningly loud electronic music. It echoed around the empty room, reverberating off the walls, its bass turned up so high that the very floor seemed to be vibrating.

I cast my eyes miserably around the uninviting interior: a strange mixture of blinding white walls, mock zebraskin and polished chrome, where the only form of ornamentation was a few gigantic twigs in three-foot-high steel urns. The stark, trendy surroundings were about as far removed as you could possibly get from the cosiness of Maureen's Salon on the corner of Allsop Street, where there were OAP discounts on Wednesdays and plastic rainhats for sale by the till.

To the rear of this airy, minimalist room, behind the row of shining metal washbasins, was a door marked 'STAFF'. With a heavy sigh, I dragged my reluctant feet towards it; my heart sinking even lower into my comfortable leather sandals as I passed a poster advertising their 'Piercing and Body Art Parlour'.

What kind of place was this? I'll give it a day, I told myself, it was only fair, but, as I opened the staffroom door and caught my first sight of my fellow stylists, 'just a day' suddenly seemed like an eternity.

Two young girls sat smoking on either side of a low, rectangular table, their animated conversation tailing off the moment I crept noiselessly into the room. Keeping my gaze firmly fixed onto the floor I whispered an apologetic 'hello'.

The blonde with the nose ring glanced up and clawed back her curtain of hair with her witchy, amazingly long nails.

'You're Hilary. Right?' she asked indifferently. 'I'm Stacey and . . .' she flicked her head towards the other, stunning, raven-haired girl with a straight bob that shone like an oil-slick, 'this is Jaimie.'

Jaimie regarded me coldly through narrowed, supernaturally green eyes and blew a smoke ring in my direction. I forced a weak smile, trying hard not to stare at the naked, tanned flesh of their thighs, clearly on display beneath breathtakingly tiny PVC skirts. These girls had a body language consisting solely of four-letter words and, with their outrageous platform sandals and metallic-blue painted toenails, oozed the sort of self-confidence I could only dream of.

They watched in amused silence as I hung up my wet mac on a vacant hanger, their crimson lips pressed tight together to suppress their laughter. I felt so ridiculous I wanted to cry. There had been a uniform of sorts at Maureen's; all right, it was only a mauve nylon zip-front overall, but at least I never had to worry about what I wore every day. Now, in my newest Laura Ashley floral skirt and neatly ironed white blouse (both birthday presents from Colin), I felt like a circus freak.

Slags. That's what my Colin would have called them. Just like the girls in the magazines he kept on top of our wardrobe, tucked beneath his *AA Book of the Car*. Magazines with some pages mysteriously stuck together. Magazines he had forbidden me to look at. But I did. Every Thursday night, when he went to football practice, I'd lie back on the duvet and drink in the images of perfect-breasted girls with lips always open; sometimes just slightly, teasing and tantalising, just a glimpse of their even white teeth showing and sometimes wide open, as they screamed with erotic joy, orgasmic rapture; their pink-brown sexes plump, voluptuous and strangely exciting.

My favourite magazine featured a photo-story of one of these girls being fucked doggie-fashion by an iron-torsoed man sporting a bushy, black handlebar moustache. The couple, according to the red italics in the corner of the glossy page, were called 'Letitia and Luke' and the series of photos followed their progress from 'foreplay' (a word I'd come across in an old *Cosmopolitan* in the dentist's waiting room. It was Maureen who'd explained, laughing raucously, what this meant. Colin had told me it was a rugby term) to full, juicy fuck.

I'd never seen pictures like these before and I viewed them cynically at first. Oh yeah, I thought to myself, of course Letitia keeps on her six-inch spike heels in bed without so much as snagging the satin sheets and, sure, Luke keeps on his studded biking jacket and Harley Davidson helmet, and ... and ... her tits, well, they've got to be implants and his cock ... his cock! My eyes nearly popped out of my head! The glans was the size of my clenched fist. And my Colin had told me that his slim five inches (I knew it was five inches because he liked me to measure it for him) was about as big as you could get.

Anyway, in frame one Letitia is on all fours. The picture is taken from behind. A real close-up; zooming in on the inviting split of her puffy, vivid red cunt lips and the deep, dark, rosy circle of her arsehole. Then the camera turns to his meaty, purple cock head as it prods the flesh between the pucker of her anus and her pussy, like it couldn't decide which to penetrate first.

I can remember putting down the magazine at that point and, suddenly curious as to what my sex looked like from the rear, placing my dressing table mirror behind me on the bedroom carpet. My sex looked almost identical to hers except that my pussy-hair was darker and a bit more unruly. Reaching behind me, I tremulously parted my slit with my index finger ... I shuddered, it felt so good. I decided to continue reading the magazine in this position, imagining myself as the gorgeous, wanton Letitia.

In the next frame Luke has made his decision and has rammed his huge cock into her welcoming pussy. I was light-headed with the delicious thought of that bulk of rigid flesh forcing its way into Letitia's neat, pretty little hole. I was so excited by now that I was able to effortlessly slide three and then four fingers into my own slippery sex. I thrust them in and out rapidly, devouring the sight of Luke cupping the weight of her tits in his hands, imagining him pounding into her deep and hard – his pelvis bouncing brutally off her quivering, soft, white buttocks – her liquid arousal a satiny glaze along the shaft of his cock.

In the last but one frame they've changed position so that he's straddling her chest, eyes shut tight, teeth gritted, jerking furiously on his thick foreskin until he spurts an unreal quantity of grey/white come into her face. Then the final frame shows the pink point of her tongue darting around her lips, searching out the creamy ejaculate.

By the time I'd reached the last picture, I was fingering my clit wildly; bucking back and forth until I felt the fibre of the carpet burning my knees. The force of my orgasm left me flat-faced on the floor, bathed in perspiration, wondering why Colin had never made me come like this . . .

The arrival of Wes, the senior stylist, put paid to my most private of daydreams. I'd met Wes briefly at my interview. He had a sort of sun-bleached blond crew-cut and today he looked amazing in black leather trousers, a black T-shirt that clung to his broad, muscular chest and bulky motorbike boots with gleaming chrome toe pieces. His clothes reminded me of somebody . . . a lightning bolt of excitement shot through me. Of course – Luke! Even if he'd never so much as sat on a motorbike, I'd bet he dressed like this. I felt the colour rush to my face, my heart beating just a little faster.

'All ready for your first day?' Wes asked, the corners of his brown eyes crinkling into a warm smile.

A truthful answer would have been 'No, and I never will be,' but I nodded.

'Have the girls explained the salon rules?' he asked, his smile giving way to a more serious demeanour.

The two stylists looked as puzzled as I did.

'OK,' he continued. 'No customer leaves the shop until you've found out if they've got a boyfriend or girlfriend or been on holiday yet this year.'

'This information goes onto the computer's "customer record system",' added Stacey, catching on fast.

'And it saves us the bother of asking them again on their next visit,' was Jaimie's throaty contribution.

My brow was pleated in confusion.

'Don't worry,' said Wes. 'We don't expect you to take it all in on your first day. In fact,' he added, staring sympathetically at my hair-turned-rat'stails by the rain, 'we've nothing booked in till after ten. What do you say we treat Hilary to a hair-do?'

I looked pleadingly at him. Colin didn't like change of any description. He was the only person I knew who still had a Betamax video, and he stubbornly refused to buy CDs instead of vinyl claiming they just didn't sound the same. He certainly wouldn't take too kindly to my shoulder-length mousey hair becoming a half-inch crop.

'Don't worry,' Wes said, reaching across and removing my tortoiseshell plastic comb slides, 'just a few layers to give it some shape, and . . .' he turned his attention to my badly bitten fingernails, '. . . I think we might even throw in a manicure.'

I couldn't quite explain it, but there was something reassuring about Wes. Something that persuaded me to put my trust in him; made me follow him, disciple-like, through the still pulsating music, to the washbasin and then, willingly, tip back my head for him to do as he pleased.

Usually, for a hairdresser, I make a terrible customer – holding the armrests with a white-knuckled grip – audibly wincing as my neck is bent backwards over the painfully hard edge of the bowl. But today was different. The fluffy white towel which Wes wrapped around my shoulders felt warm and comforting, made me feel pampered, indulged, like a small child. And then, to my surprise, the water he started to spray over my hair was the perfect temperature, though to be honest, if it'd given me third degree burns, I'd have been too polite to say so.

He began to massage my squeakily wet hair in a slow, circular motion, manipulating my scalp with his large, skilful hands. So blissful, so soothing was his touch that before long my eyelids became unbearably heavy, my limp body dissolving into the chair. I could feel myself drifting slowly towards sleep, now only fuzzily aware of the languorous probing of his fingers beneath the thick halo of coconut-scented foam.

Occasionally, scooping up some errant soap suds, Wes's hand would brush against the skin at the nape of my neck or the back of my ear. Even in my drowsy state I felt a slight stirring, a spasm of arousal deep within that made me tense my buttocks ever so slightly.

Though my eyes were closed, I knew that the girls must be about to begin my manicure. Through the music I could hear their voices, but they were muffled, as if spoken through a thick gauze. I felt their hands, deliciously cool on the clamminess of mine. I expected them to begin filing the jagged edges of my stubby little nails, but instead, they were turning my hands over so the palms faced upwards. Then they were trailing the tips of their fingers slowly, deliberately, along the sensitive insides of my arms, making the flesh there tingle and dance, sending shivers up my spine. What were they doing? Probably some sort of new-fangled relaxation technique. They obviously didn't realise the effect their attentions were having on me: their every touch was sending signals to my sex that I was finding impossible to ignore. I was anything but relaxed!

Then I felt Wes's hands on my shoulders, gently massaging the muscles there, easing away any remaining tension, making my head sway backwards and forwards in time with each gorgeous, lazy, squeeze of my soft flesh.

Maybe I was imagining it – perhaps it was accidental?

But it seemed as if Wes's hands were inching over my shoulders, delving lower and lower. I sighed as his questing fingers stroked the goosebumpy flesh above my breastbone and then stopped, maddeningly, just before the swell of my cleavage. I felt my nipples harden beneath my bra. Wicked, sexual thoughts flooded my mind. Excitement fluttered in my stomach as I imagined how it would feel if, right then, he tore open my blouse and took my tits in his hands, or better still, his mouth. My God, I could feel the crotch of my panties growing wetter and wetter. Maybe I could just pretend I needed the loo? Then I could lock the door and rub my clit like crazy.

But I never got the chance. There was a sudden, soft crunch of cotton and, in one swift movement, my skirt was lifted to my waist. My legs felt cold, exposed. I pressed them tightly together. What the hell were they doing?

Stop!

That was what I knew I *should* say.

In my mind I practised its vocalisation. But . . . oh, the ache, the persistant pulsing in my sex. How would I ever get the word past my lips?

Then there were hands, two pairs of hands on my ankles, encircling them, teasingly tracing a path higher and higher, skilfully drawing out my juices until they reached the tops of my legs and hesitated. I had to stop this . . . had to stop . . . but their fingers were pushing, trying to burrow into the heat of my inner thighs, urging my consent.

They were open! My legs were open . . . splayed . . . waiting . . . my sex yearning beneath the white cotton crotch of my panties. I could clearly visualise this part of my body with the few stray dark hairs spilling out at the sides of my white knickers, my hard bud pouting, bulging impatiently through the tight, straining fabric and the opaque stain that grew bigger by the second.

There was a sudden heat directly above my sex – a moist heat; one of the girls was blowing hot blasts of air onto my pussy and then nuzzling my clit through my damp panties. I gripped her head in my hands, whimpering with pleasure, wildly impatient for whatever she would do next.

But where was Wes? I heard the clank of heavy boots. It got closer and closer, until I sensed he was by my side. His large hand clutched mine and guided it towards the metal buttons of his flies. I tugged frantically, desperately, at them, but my hand shook too much. Wes helped. The buttons tackled, he lifted my hand to the waist of his silk shorts. With one pull, the luxurious fabric slipped over his rigidity. His coarse, prickly hair was cool and crisp in the palm of my hand as I cupped his weighty scrotum and squeezed hard. Then, twisting my body towards him, I took his thick column of hard flesh into my mouth.

Though my eyes were still shut tight, I could imagine his powerful, athletic thighs, the bucking of his pale buttocks and the angle of his cock, as he wildly mouthfucked me. I visualised his face, gripped in concentration, as I, Hilary Needham, soon to be Hilary Pettigrew, sucked dick with the expertise of a Singapore hooker . . .

Whilst I sucked greedily on Wes's prick, a sharp-nailed hand pulled my panties to one side. I caught my breath, thinking I'd die from sheer pleasure as one of the girls parted my pubic curls with her snaking tongue and then closed her hot mouth around my throbbing clit. I was writhing in the chair, pushing my pelvis into her face. Only the fact that my mouth was full of cock stopped me from howling with pleasure as she began to rhythmically lick me.

But a tongue was soft. Right? Soft, supple, like wet velvet . . . This one wasn't. There was something strange about this particular tongue. It was more than just a slithery strip of pink flesh. The middle part of it was sort of hard, unyielding, like metal. That was it! Her tongue was pierced! What felt like a round metal stud dragged repeatedly over my granite clit, making my juices pour from me. She inserted a few fingers into my creamy opening. My cunt had never felt so ready, so desperate to be filled.

The hands of the girl who wasn't eating my pussy began to pull at the the buttons of my blouse. I felt a cool draught, sensuous as silk, on my perspiring flesh as my aching tits were released from the stiff confines of my Playtex bra. Immediately her mouth was upon them, drawing wet circles around the hard peaks, rubbing them softly with the palms of her hands, increasing the need for Wes's cock to put an end to the insistent, painful, pulsing inside.

As if reading my mind, Wes withdrew from my mouth and waited while the girls slid me towards the edge of the seat. Their methodical hands pulled off my lust-soaked panties and raised my violently trembling legs, holding them wide, wide apart. By now I was in a delirium, head thrashing from side to side, unable to think of anything but relief. The electronic music had changed slightly; there was a wailing, a chanting, a strangled voice ... a voice that sounded strangely familiar, coming, as I then realised, from my mouth.

'Fuck me ... please fuck me,' I begged in a near scream. There was a creak of leather as Wes kneeled before me and began rubbing his fat cockhead against the sopping entrance of my quim. Then he lifted me slightly and, with a brutal thrust that made me cry out loud, slid right inside me.

I was so aroused I wanted him to split me in two. As he pounded into me, my cunt muscles squeezed his shaft so tightly that I could feel every thick vein, every delicious inch of slippery prick.

Just when I thought my pleasure couldn't get any

more intense, Wes pushed a hand between my pussy-lips and began to tease my clit, see-sawing the length of one of his fingers over the explosive little bud whilst simultaneously hammering his wet cock in and out of me. The girls, now either side of my chair, continued to stroke my breasts, squeezing my hard nipples between their fingers. Wes's rhythmic pounding was increasing in tempo, faster ... faster ... faster ... until he was pumping so hard that the room seemed to be spinning around me, my clitoris ignited by his relentless fingering, my orgasm building, pushing me to the brink of ecstasy until, finally, he let out a strangled, animalistic grunt and I felt his cock spasm deep within me.

The sensation; his hot, fast finger on my clit; the wetness of his spurting; these all combined to make me lose control. I shook. I screamed. Arching my back and rubbing my breasts wildly together, mouthing obscenities into the sex-soaked air, I came and came and came.

My legs still shook involuntarily minutes after they'd been released from their human shackles. As the sweat cooled on my skin I lay there, head slumped back, breathing laboured, with only the vaguest, uncomfortable notion in some recess of my mind, that I was in the middle of a salon with my crumpled skirt around my waist and tits and pussy clearly on display.

'Coffee, Hilary?'

I opened my eyes with a start, instantly recognising the hoarse voice as Jaimie's.

'Yes ... yes, please,' I replied as my bleary eyes began to slowly focus on my surroundings.

I could feel my head being patted roughly with a towel, the chemical perfume of ammonia filling my nostrils and jarring me back to consciousness.

Looking sharply down I saw to my confusion that my still shaking legs were respectably covered by my skirt.

My hand flew to my neck and, yes, the buttons of my blouse were securely fastened.

I could now see that the salon was a hive of activity. There was the familiar hum of hairdryers. Foil-headed customers chatted loudly. An acne-speckled apprentice with a vacant expression manoeuvred a soft brush between the seats and the perm roller trolley rumbled noisily across the wooden floor.

But it had all felt so real, I protested to myself. I was still breathless in the afterglow of an orgasm that had rocked me to the core. My pussy felt both raw and tender. My cheeks burned . . .

I blinked a few times, but the other customers, the activity, failed to disappear. I must have had a dream, that was the only explanation; a dream brought on by my horny thoughts of Colin's porno mags. Oh God! A terrible thought suddenly struck me: what if I'd really screamed out like that? Colin was always complaining that I talked in my sleep. I bit my lower lip and sank further into the chair, trying my best to be invisible.

'There you go,' said Jaimie, who'd returned with the coffee.

It was when I reached forward to take the cup and saucer that I noticed something; something that made my eyes widen in astonishment and my heart momentarily stop beating. It was my hands. Both of my hands, back and front, right down to my fingertips, were covered in intricate, brown-red patterns . . . dots, dashes, scrolls, hearts, even small birds.

Jaimie smiled. 'Relax, Hilary. It's only Mehndi, henna-tattooing. We do it in the Body Art Parlour. It's an Eastern tradition. They use it to beautify brides, that sort of thing.'

I swallowed hard, unable to take my eyes off the exotic, strangely beautiful skin decoration that made my Argos catalogue diamond solitaire look faintly ridiculous. 'Does it . . .?'

'Come off? Yeah, it should wear off in around four weeks.'

Four weeks! How would I explain it to Colin? He'd go absolutely raving mad. I could picture his thin lips quivering with rage as I explained feebly, 'But Colin ... it's Mehndi ... it's exotic.' I could also predict his outraged reply: 'Hilary, you cannot walk down the aisle of St Francis's Parish Church in a silk dupion crinoline dress with hands straight out of a bloody harem!'

Suddenly, inexplicably, I started to laugh. It started as a giggle, but in a few moments tears of hysterical mirth were rolling down my cheeks.

'Of course,' Jaimie added sulkily, 'if you dislike it *that* much you could get it off more quickly. It just means putting your hands in water more often than usual.'

'Oh no,' I said, wiping my face and then fixing my eyes firmly on hers. 'I love it ... I really, really love it.'

Isobel's Brass Bed

Kate Dominic

'*T*omorrow, Isobel, the decorators will tour the estate. You will waken when we enter this room and our voices rouse you from your dreams.' Adrian kissed away my tears as he again clamped his cruel jewellery on my sore, well-used nipples. 'Our bedroom will be the last stop, beloved. It is here that we will conduct our business.' He tugged mercilessly on the chain, his grey eyes glittering silver as he laughed and leaned over to take my cries into his mouth. I arched towards him, straining against my bonds, drinking in the pleasure of his cruel laughter as the pain again flamed inward, lust-hot, to the core of my pussy.

'So beautiful,' he murmured, his lips touching mine as his fingers slid low over my belly. 'Tomorrow, you will lie naked on our lovely brass bed and you will spread your legs for me. You will close your eyes and stroke your luscious pussy.'

I whimpered, shivering as his long, dark hair trailed soft as whip tresses after his hands. His fingers, thick with my pussy cream, brushed into my slit, exploring, seeking, demanding, and my throat opened to moans at his touch.

'You will be embarrassed, Isobel.' Adrian's voice was thick with passion as he sank his fingers into me. 'I know how you love that, how your honey flows from knowing you are being watched by other men, desperate men who are trying in vain to hide their glances and their hard-ons.' His thumb circled my juice-slicked clit and I cried out, thrusting my hips towards him as his other hand twisted the nipple chain.

'You will orgasm for me, Isobel – in front of those men. Just as you will come for me tonight, every time I tell you to.' He pressed harder, working my pleasure nub as a frisson of fear ran through me. Adrian had never shared me with anyone in our home before. I closed my eyes and turned my head, losing myself in the luscious heat of my humiliation and the hot flush of anticipation spreading across my body. Adrian laughed softly as he pulled my face back to him.

'Don't hide your pleasure from me, precious one. I enjoy watching you blush.' With no warning, he pinched my clit, hard, smiling as I gasped and shook. 'You are so beautiful, my love. You have pleased me so well this evening. Come dawn, your face will heat even more, like a rose opening to the sun. It will be my pleasure to watch you tease these men, as you so love to do.' I twisted beneath him, panting as the pain of his touch blossomed towards orgasm. 'Oh, my Isobel, I will get so hard watching you display yourself, even here in our private domain.'

Then Adrian released the first nipple clamp, and bit. I cried out, writhing as the anguish pierced my breast, willing myself to be quiet as the echoes of Adrian's torture vibrated deep into my belly.

'Very good, my pet.' He laughed softly, his lips curling against my skin as he teethed. 'You obey so beautifully when I am hurting you.'

I whimpered as he tugged on the chain to the other clamp. Tears leaked from the corners of my eyes. I concentrated on the dull throbbing in my second nipple, knowing how my skin would scream when he released the clamp, and again brought his merciless teeth to my pain-washed flesh. I looked up into Adrian's eyes. The silvery lust in them made me shudder.

'You are so precious,' he whispered, his voice suddenly husky. He spread my legs roughly and mounted me. I cried out at the all-consuming heat of his stiff, thick cock sliding into me.

'Adrian,' I begged, arching up against him, unable to control my voice any longer. He ground into me, his hair falling onto my face as I shook helplessly in his arms.

'Hush, love. I give you permission to indulge yourself tomorrow, to display your beautiful, naked body. Your pussy honey flows so sweetly when you flaunt your submission. God, it makes me want to fuck you.' His hoarse laughter rang in my ears as I wrapped my legs fiercely around him. I clenched my cunt muscles around him, milking him, relishing the sudden thrill of power as his eyes glazed.

'Give me,' he demanded harshly, thrusting viciously into me. I opened myself, spreading my pussy impossibly wider, lifting my hips and begging him to take me deeper and harder as he pounded against the pleasure spot deep in the walls of my cunt. As the first waves of my orgasm washed over me, Adrian took his weight on one hand, released the second clamp and leaned down to suck my nipple between his teeth.

I shrieked out my climax, my pussy swallowing his cock like it was drinking strength from his semen. Over and over again, I cried out my submission as my body once more convulsed with the joy of serving him. And through the haze of my climax, I heard his harsh command.

'Keep your eyes closed tomorrow, Isobel, and think only of your service to me as you flaunt yourself for the anonymous men who desire you.' Then Adrian was shaking above me, emptying himself into me, the hot cream of his climax bathing my cunt in the only juices that could ever soothe my hunger for him.

I stretched into the warmth of the morning sun, my breasts and cunt quivering as my flesh remembered both the exquisite pain and the pleasure of my service to Adrian. My body was still lushly sated, my clit and nipples sore and my pussy sticky from loving. Just as Adrian had said, there were male voices in the hallway, low and controlled, moving inexorably closer. The voices of men of authority negotiating. I squirmed against the sheets, circling my palms over my tender nipples, relishing the embarrassed echoes stirring deep in my core – memories of pain and orgasms and the lust for more of both, and awareness of Adrian's unwavering love, and of the way he manipulated, for his own purposes, the sometimes overwhelming curiosity that warred with my submission to him.

When Adrian truly didn't want me to see something, he blindfolded me. I twisted my nipples, telling myself that must mean he was toying with me. He would know that, without a blindfold, my curiosity would make me look. That must be what he wanted. Firm, decisive footsteps entered the bedroom. All conversation stopped abruptly. Instinctively, I closed my eyes and arched high, indulging in a full-body stretch, spreading my legs wide as I offered the visitors their first view of the naked, willing pussy that pleasured my husband. And while they were distracted by my 'sleeping' form, I peeked.

Adrian was the only one not staring at me. Though the front of his white linen trousers was swollen, he was carefully facing a distinguished-looking older man. The gentleman, trim and fit in a grey suit that spoke of the monied power he carried so easily, paused only the briefest moment before clearing his throat and turning back to Adrian. As they spoke, eyes locked together, both men reached down and discreetly adjusted themselves. I knew at once they were the only ones who were truly conducting business this morning. This was the man who would bargain and profit from letting his business – only his business – serve Adrian. They would play ruthlessly, and that part of the game would make Adrian hard with lust for power over money.

But I was greedy to see who Adrian was playing with to amuse himself. My lash-hooded eyes passed quickly over the attentive young assistants who so assiduously shadowed their mentor. The tallest, the one who stood closest to the grey-suited man, was unremarkable save for a beautiful face and the clipboard he suddenly clutched possessively over his crotch. I passed him over quickly. Adrian would have no interest in a lackey, nor in the handsome, slender young man beside him – a decorator I recognised, but one who would have more interest in watching the men around him than in either my service or my body. The last man, though ... I pressed my legs together hard, seeking the touch of skin on skin. I feasted my eyes on a lean, hard body encased in arse-hugging jeans and a tight T-shirt. This was no doubt the site foreman, the person in charge of the physical labour necessary to improve my husband's property.

This strong, sun-tanned man with the short-cropped blond hair had the kind of work-sculpted body I could lick for hours. Adrian on occasion gave me to such men for his pleasure. Blindfolded, I knew them only by the taste of their cocks and the smell of their crotches where their balls hung heavily against their legs, and by the deep racking gasps that filled my ears when their come spewed onto my face.

The foreman made my pussy hot. I snuck one more long peek at him. He was smiling at me. His clear blue eyes burned with desire, and I hesitated, stunned that he was watching me, not just my body. While the others talked among themselves, the foreman reached down, and just once, as though he were also resituating himself, cupped the thick bulge in his groin and squeezed.

I closed my eyes quickly, feeling my face flush hot as I tried to think only of Adrian. He loved giving me to other men, loved watching me climax, calling his name, while my lips and hands and pussy made other men's cocks spurt uncontrollably. But my husband had not given me to this man I suddenly desired so strongly. Adrian had told me to keep my eyes closed. Perhaps, this one time, he had meant it.

I concentrated on my husband's handsome, aristocratic face, on the way his eyes flashed when he was torturing me, on memories of how his firm, red lips kissed me so gently and smiled so lovingly, so sadistically, against my skin as he inflicted his exquisite pain on my quivering body and roused me to screaming heights of ecstasy. I lived to serve him, to pleasure his raw, animal instincts. I stroked my hands down my belly, digging my heels into the sheets and arching my body wide as my hands slid into the burning heat between my legs.

'Adrian,' I whispered.

The conversation stopped abruptly. I froze, stunned at what I had done, trying to not even breathe as I waited for Adrian's reaction. I was supposed to stay silent when he was displaying me. Always, always silent, unless he bade me to speak. My relief was almost palpable when Adrian once again started to speak. His tone mirrored his displeasure – I would be punished later – but I was somehow still playing his game. There was no true anger in his voice as he once again ignored me completely to conduct his business.

'This beautiful brass bed will, of course, remain the

centre of the room. All decorating will enhance it. Your thoughts, gentlemen?'

Amid frequent coughs and throat-clearing, the men discussed the walls, the floor, the curtainless bay windows that overlooked the garden, even the bed itself, but no one mentioned my naked body lying like a centrepiece on the stark white sheets. Hungry for attention, I stroked my hands up over my breasts, cupping and squeezing, wiggling my bottom as I pulled my sore, tender nipples into my fingers and tugged fiercely.

My body was hungry. I stroked lower, petting down over my neatly trimmed pubic thatch, caressing my slippery labia with long, wide strokes. I dipped a finger inside myself, shivering as I drew out my juices and teased a tiny patch of hair to a sticky peak. Each time I spread my pussy lips, the thick, musky scent of last night's sex filled the air. A deep, authoritative voice coughed discreetly as I put my fingers to my lips and licked, my cunt clenching at the tangy smell and taste of fucking.

As I sucked my fingers, I wondered what the blond foreman's cock would taste like. Would he be uncut like Adrian, with an exquisitely sensitive head for me to tease up out of its hiding place? Or would his bared head swell and lengthen uncovered onto the back of my tongue? I whimpered as I slid my fingers back down between my legs. My slit was swollen warm and wet. I slipped one fingertip over my clit, shivering as I stroked my tiny woman prepuce back. If Adrian gave me to the foreman, would he tie me spread-eagled to the bed the way Adrian did? Would the foreman clamp my nipples and whip my naked pussy with a deerskin flogger until I screamed out my climax? Would his kisses taste the way my fingers did – like Adrian's lips when he had seen fit to take his pleasure by eating my pussy?

I rubbed myself and wondered if the foreman's mouth would taste the way Sondra's had earlier the evening before. For the first time, Adrian had given me to a woman. She took me at her house, in her guest room, with Adrian watching. I was so nervous. I shook when she drew me tenderly into her arms. But from her first kiss, she had me trembling beneath her. She tasted me like I was fine wine, licking and sucking, softly, then harder, before she opened her lips and tongued me. My mouth, my clit, my pussy. When I was almost mindless with wanting, she moved lower, her tongue slick with her saliva and my juices, and she licked my secret lower petal. The one Adrian never kisses. The one her tongue slid in so easily as I opened to her like a flower, crying out with pure joy as my newly awakened sphincter lips sought desperately to kiss her back.

'Give to me, precious,' Sondra had whispered, her hot breath tickling shudders from me as she softly licked and sucked. 'I'm going to tongue your pussy juices deep into your hot little bottom hole.'

Adrian had tortured my nipples as Sondra's tongue invaded me. I cried out as she rubbed her thumb mercilessly over my clit, pressing her fingers deep into my cunt. I shook to my bones as my pussy clenched her fingers. Then she pressed harder. I screamed in ecstasy as for the first time I gushed juices when I came. Sondra laughed as my virgin anus orgasmed around her tongue and my pussy nectar trickled down my open crack.

Then Sondra fucked me. She took a huge, nasty, wicked dildo and she slathered it with warm, slippery cunt juice and cold, slick lube, and she fucked my bottom until I cried and cried and cried at the overwhelming pleasure of having someone else control every last part of my body. When Sondra was sated, Adrian drew me in his arms and kissed me, a single sweet, chaste kiss, soft and full on my mouth. Then he took me home to our big brass bed.

'You pleased me greatly tonight, my precious.' Adrian's breath had been warm and sweet on my skin.

He held me closely, licking my tears as he comforted me with his exquisite torments. 'Sondra's dildo looked so full and thick, glistening with lube as it slid in and out of your puffy pink anus. I could see your nether lips quivering. You whimpered such perfect little mewls of pain as her enormous hand-penis stretched you.'

Even now, I licked my lips, remembering how he had kissed me softly, outlining my trembling lips with his tongue.

'I did so want to comfort you, beloved, to hold you through your pain. I wanted to share the O of your lips as you gasped when the dildo slid all the way in for the first time, your startled smile as your bottom suddenly accommodated, the beatific grin as Sondra leaned down and sucked your clit in reward. Your suffering, oh, my Isobel, it was so pure and desperately needing.' I shivered as I remembered how Adrian's voice had choked with emotion. 'I was so proud when you arched your bottom up to her, begging so wantonly, looking into my eyes even as you screamed at Sondra to please, please, fuck your ass and make you come! I could see when the pain turned to pleasure. My darling, even when I twisted your nipples, you opened yourself for more.'

I sunk my fingers into my sopping pussy, relishing the musky sex smell that again wafted through the room. Adrian had put his fingers to my nostrils as he spoke.

'I came when you gushed in her face, Isobel. My pants were soaked with my jism, as they will be tomorrow.' The memory of his softly spoken commands echoed in my ears. 'You will think of Sondra's dildo in your bottom while you finger yourself tomorrow. When you display yourself for the men in our bedroom, you will think of Sondra's tongue on your clit and her fingers in your cunt, and of how she made you wiggle and squirm and plead.'

I slid my hands lower, shivering as I remembered his

final words. 'Some day, my Isobel, perhaps I will take your beautiful bottom with my cock.' He had kissed me once more as I drifted off to sleep. 'Some day, perhaps I will let someone else have you there, and I will watch.'

. I dreamed that day would be today. I whimpered, pinching my clit, my body flushing hot at the memory of Adrian's words, and at the thought of the foreman taking me. Adrian had known I would peek. He always knew exactly what I was doing. I licked my lips again, savouring the pussy-soft skin inside my mouth, the smooth, silken band of muscles so like the one Sondra had awakened last night. Perhaps the foreman would lick and suck and tongue-fuck me to climax first. Or would he pepper me with quick, hot, desperate kisses while he pressed his thick full shaft to my now awake and hungry anus?

Would he diddle my pussy or suck hard on my nipples to keep me open as he sank his cock deep into my arse? Would he gift me with an orgasm so overwhelming my husband again would come just from watching?

Suddenly, I understood what Adrian wanted from me today. The voices around me droned like bees as I pressed my legs together, then opened them again and started circling my pleasure nub with my pussy-soaked fingertip. With my other hand, I dipped my fingers in my cunt. Grunting like an animal in heat, I moved one juice-slicked finger to press up against my tight little anus. I gasped as my finger slid in, my lips grimacing first in pain, then curling in pleasure as my bottom relaxed. I heard the catch in Adrian's voice as he stopped speaking. I rubbed faster, moaning and panting as I stroked my clit and noisily pumped my fingers in and out of my holes.

My fingers weren't as long as Sondra's dildo had been. They weren't as full and thick and hot as the foreman's cock would be. He would fill me, have me squirming like an animal as he skewered me. Maybe some day, Adrian would let the foreman fuck me up the arse while Sondra filled my cunt with her fingers and her supremely talented mouth slowly, exquisitely, mercilessly teased an orgasm through my clit. Adrian would stand back and watch, stroking himself, his beautiful cock spewing white semen all over my belly as he called to me, 'You are beautiful, my Isobel. My wife. The whole world is jealous of what you give me so freely.'

And I would come. My clit and pussy and anus would clench and the climax would wash over me and I wouldn't be able to stop. The sound of flesh on fabric and of men panting and gasping would fill my ears, the way it suddenly did now. Adrian's harsh breathing would flame over my skin. My cunt would convulse around my hands as I screamed out my climax, as I shook and screamed out Adrian's name, as I screamed it over and over and over again.

My ears rang with the sound of my voice, with the grunts and growls of men who were beyond control climaxing around me in the room. The world turned hazy red and my body dissolved into the blessed relief of knowing I had once again pleased my beloved, my Adrian. My hands fell to my sides, the faint smell of semen and the honeyed scent of my own juices filling my nostrils in the suddenly quiet room. I stretched luxuriously and rolled over as though to go back to sleep.

From the corner of my eyes, I peeked at the men again. I couldn't see Adrian, but the others were coughing discreetly and looking away, again adjusting themselves. All except for the foreman. His burning blue eyes were glued to mine. His face was flushed as he ran his hand surreptitiously over the obscenely distended front of his jeans. I winked at him and lifted my pussy finger to my lips, sucking it into my mouth. The foreman closed his eyes on a silent moan, and the quiet spasm shook his body, his hand grasping his crotch as he breathed deeply and the dark wet stain slowly covered the front of his jeans. I blew him a tiny kiss and smiled as I snuggled into the sheets.

In the distance, I knew that Adrian's sudden laugh had nothing to do with business. The foreman and I had played the game to my husband's satisfaction. The distinguished gentleman would get the contract, and the foreman would be commanded to come back and finish the job. We would play again.

Something to Remember You By

Tracey Allyson

S he watched him slide his cock into the woman who squatted on all fours, pushing her arse up towards him. He began to thrust forcefully, his buttocks clenching and unclenching from the effort. The woman moaned and sat up slightly as he leaned over her, roughly grabbing her breasts. He started to speak in short sharp gasps, but this was drowned out by a furious voice that cut through the heavy sexual atmosphere like a freezing cold knife.

'Cut, for fuck's sake cut!' the voice said. 'Christ, Aaron, I thought you were supposed to be a professional. I know this isn't a close-up but even I can see your bloody dick's slipped out and you're faking it.'

Aaron Adams released his grip on the woman, who was now calling someone on her mobile phone. He turned and looked coolly at the owner of the voice. He was angry; usually nobody could tell when he was faking.

'Hell, sugar,' he drawled, drawing deeply on the cigarette he'd just lit. 'Seems to me it's so long since you saw a dick I'm surprised you even noticed.'

Not one crew member laughed; nobody spoke; they all respected her too much for that. In fact, it seemed to Megan, the owner of the voice, as if everybody had stopped breathing.

'Oh, I don't know, Aaron,' she said in a steady tone. 'I'm looking at you, aren't I?'

Laughter erupted through the set. The lighting crew had to put their precious bulbs and gels down to stop themselves from breaking the equipment, and even the normally emotionless, consummate professional camera crew and cable staff were giggling and nudging each other in the ribs.

'We'll break for half an hour while the dick gets hard again,' she said caustically.

She slowly walked to the tiny makeshift room she used as an office, calling out instructions to her beloved crew. She sat down and bit her lip. His words had stung, but there was no way he would ever know. Working in the porn industry had its benefits: sex on tap, sex any time, anywhere and in any format; it just wasn't her that was having the sex. For the first twelve months she'd put it down to the fact that she saw sex every day, then that she was just too tired or too busy. After that she just tried not to think about it. She had a fantasy, though, a very specific one – she just hadn't had the chance to try it out yet.

There was something about this conceited American; something in him that made her think things she'd never thought before – like maybe getting the other side of the camera and trying the merchandise for herself. That's all they were to her, the men she filmed every day: pieces of meat, blips on the schedule that she had to pamper, psychoanalyse when they couldn't get wood, and ply with alcohol when it really was time to tell them that the show was over and gravity was taking its toll. But he was different. Maybe it was because, at 42, he was a little older than she was used to dealing with. He was very tall, but then so was she. He had short dark hair that was slightly peppered with grey and a cock that made her feel as though most of the male actors she'd worked with had only just reached puberty. His body was good for his age; granted there was the tiniest hint of middle-age spread, but somehow that just added to the appeal, like fantasising over your father's best friend when puberty kicks in. Or maybe it was his accent. He spoke in a low, controlled drawl that made her want to touch herself at night. Cliché after cliché went through her mind, but her train of thought was rudely interrupted.

'Who the fuck do you think you are, you uptight bitch?' he asked, his face almost purple. He was naked as he stood in front of her, his cock partially erect. 'You talked to me like I was some kind of half-wit, wet behind the ears jerk-off, in front of everyone.'

'That's because you acted like some kind of half-wit, wet behind the ears jerk-off, Aaron,' she shot back scathingly, trying to keep her eyes off his cock that still glistened with wetness from the cunt of the actress he'd been fucking, albeit fleetingly, on set.

'They may cut corners in Hicksville, USA, but here people like to get what they pay for. You are paid to fuck when I say fuck, how I say fuck and where I say fuck, and out there you weren't fucking at all.' The power and arousal she felt when she said the words made her squirm in her chair.

'Oh, you are something, baby,' he drawled. 'You honestly think you're in control of me, don't you?'

'I own you, Aaron. You have been paid a shit-load of money for this job, you're working with some of the most beautiful women in the business, and you're staying in one of the best hotels in the area while my production company picks up the tab. Therefore, until we finish this shoot, you'd better believe I'm in control of you.'

127

'Really,' he said, pushing the door of the tiny office shut. 'Well right now I'm on a break and I feel like relaxing.'

He leaned back against the door and slid his hand down his stomach until he touched his cock. He moved his hand further down until he reached his balls and began to rub them; he was breathing erratically and letting out low sporadic moans. His cock started to rise as he took it in his hand and gently pumped it, exposing the fleshy tenderness as he pulled the foreskin back and forth. She was stunned by his action, but didn't let it show.

'Oh,' she said, trying to stay calm. 'Another audition . . . well, let me see what you've got, Aaron.'

'Oh, you are unbelievable,' he said in a strangled voice. 'You are wound tighter than three dress sizes too small. Nobody could be as crab-apple-pie as you and be getting any.' As he savagely gripped his cock, a tiny white pearl appeared at the tip, he stopped what he was doing, decisively took the tiny drop of liquid on his finger and put it in his mouth, looking straight into her eyes as he sucked it. He began rubbing his balls again and slid slowly down the door until he sat on the freezing concrete floor.

Megan wanted to scream at him, she wanted to run, but she couldn't. She did own him, she controlled him, and this was her very own private show from the big-shot porn star. She saw his hips start to jerk upwards as he began to pump faster now.

'Oh yeah, oh suck it, Meegan, fucking suck it,' she heard him say as his face contorted with pleasure. He was auditioning for her; he was saying lines that she had written and, if he wanted to keep his job, she thought, he'd better keep going. The power she had over him made her feel exhilarated, and she felt a warm trickle of her own juices soak her underwear. But she kept her face blank; he'd never know what his elaborate little cabaret was doing for her. She continued to stare as he started bucking upwards and moving his hand faster and faster. Suddenly he got to his feet and moved towards her. With only the desk between them she could easily have reached out and touched his cock, but she stood perfectly still. He was jerking his hand furiously, his face only a few inches from hers and, as he came, he looked straight into her eyes. She hadn't seen a man climax at such close proximity for a long time, and she bit her lip again as she felt the flesh between her legs start to throb with a hunger for his cock. The thick white liquid shot across her desk, spattering all over her copy of the script they were working from. He leaned both his hands on her desk and groaned; he hadn't come like that in a long time. Usually it was mechanical, but this time it was undeniably real. Pride, however, stopped him from admitting it.

'How do you like them apples, sweet cheeks?' he said arrogantly.

Megan was unsure what to say. She wanted him to get hard again and fuck her into oblivion, but professionalism took over and she found herself slowly clapping her hands.

'Not bad, Aaron,' she said. 'If only you could give that kind of performance when the cameras are rolling then maybe you wouldn't have had to audition for me again. By the way, I hope you can last longer than that in the next scene.'

She took a handful of tissues out of the box on her desk and, pulling a face as though she were dealing with something offensive, wiped his come off her script. 'By the way,' she said, opening her office door, 'my name is pronounced Meg-an not Mee-gan. If you're going to work over here maybe you should take some elocution lessons. See Maggie in wardrobe; she has some numbers you could try.'

The look of disbelief he gave her made part of her feel

sorry for him, but she was still in control; only her own juices running down her inner thighs could give her away.

'We're back on set in ten minutes, Aaron,' she said efficiently. 'I hope you can get wood again by then.'

'You know Freud said –' he shot back, trying to be clever '– that all hostile behaviour is just a thin layer of barely controllable sexual urges. In your case I think he might have been right.'

'Ah yes,' Megan added, slowly walking away. 'But then Bowlby believed that a successful attachment bond between mother and child forms the basis of healthy mental development. In your case I get the feeling you had a lot of babysitters from an early age.'

He stared at the space where she'd been for a long time before leaving the office.

'Son of a bitch,' she heard him curse and then add, 'That is one mean broad.'

Megan pushed open the cubicle door in the toilets and then locked it behind her. She took a piece of tissue with the intention of drying her sodden bush before she went back on set. As she rubbed the hot flesh between her legs, delicious sensations crept through her body. She slid her other hand beneath her top and fingered a rigid nipple. In her head she pictured him lying on a bed, jerking his cock viciously as she watched, telling him exactly what to do. She could feel the pulsations in her cunt getting stronger and she could smell the piquant odour of his come emanating from her script. The orgasm was quick and made her shudder as she leaned back against the freezing wall of the cubicle. Suddenly, the prospect of telling Aaron Adams how to fuck had become very appealing to her. Back on set, Megan was pure professionalism.

'I'm going to talk you through this whole scene, and sort of improvise, but the instructions will be very specific. Listen to what I tell you and go at the pace of my instructions. Quiet on set, we're going for a take.'

The filming bell rang and Megan stared intently at her actors.

'Now, you don't care about him, Michelle,' she called to the beautiful blonde woman. 'Take off your dress slowly; you're teasing him, you're making him want you, but you're looking at him like he's a piece of shit. Aaron, start touching yourself, whatever comes naturally.' Megan swallowed hard as she watched Aaron begin to massage his groin through his trousers. 'That's it, Aaron, you're aroused, but all you do is look at her; you're enjoying the show.'

Somehow Michelle managed to get herself directly in Megan's eye line, which made Aaron look straight at her. 'Now slowly take off your underwear, Michelle, and throw your panties at him. Aaron . . .' she faltered, 'I . . . I want you to catch them and hold them to your face.' She watched him carrying out her instructions, looking at her the whole time. It didn't matter, because he and Michelle would not be in the same shot at the same time until they actually started fucking.

'Now, Aaron, I want you to undress slowly, keep watching her the whole time. Michelle, as soon as you're naked walk over to him and let him put his face in your pussy. Get ready on camera two, they'll both be in the same shot in three, two, one. Now, Aaron, really go for it, eat her. That's it. Now put your hands on her arse as you do it. That's it. Now bring the middle finger of whichever hand is most comfortable to your mouth and suck it. When you've done that, slide it into her arse.'

Michelle's head rolled back as Aaron slid his finger in.

'Good, that's good, Michelle. Now ease her onto the sofa, Aaron, and follow the script from there. We need a good five minutes. No close-ups, no dialogue, and I'll cue when you come.'

Usually, Megan would have busied herself looking at

the next scenes while this went on, but she couldn't take her eyes off Aaron. He gently laid Michelle on the couch and purposefully opened her legs. He ran his middle finger up and down the crease of her sex, making her moan. Kneeling between her legs, Aaron took his cock in his hands and gently pumped it for a few seconds before easing himself on top of her and sliding it in. Megan was so involved in watching his arse clenching up and down, she got a shock when the script editor told her that they had what they needed in the can.

'Now, Aaron, I want you to start coming in twenty seconds. Michelle, start to build, nothing serious, just a convincing climax in five, four, three, two, one.' Megan watched as Michelle and Aaron faked orgasm. She couldn't believe how aroused she felt; she could make him do anything, come whenever she wanted to, and suddenly an idea began to form in her mind.

'That's a wrap, everybody. Thank you very much for your hard work. Drinks are on me later tonight.' Everyone cheered and hugged Megan; she was a dream to work for, fair but firm and, despite her tender years, she got results. Plus, everyone had noticed that Aaron had lost some of his arrogance while he was filming, and they knew it had something to do with Megan.

'Aaron, Michelle, I'd like to see you separately in my office as soon as you're ready.' He walked towards her, but she held up her hand. 'Get dressed first, please, although I'm so used to seeing you naked I probably won't recognise you with your clothes on.' He gave a raised white flag grin and saluted her before walking off to his dressing room. Michelle hastily put on a robe and followed Megan across the dark set. She knew that this probably meant more work.

'You were great, Michelle, very professional as usual. This is for you,' she said, handing over a thick brown envelope. Michelle opened it to see a thousand pounds in crisp twenty-pound notes.

'I don't know what to say,' Michelle began. 'I mean I . . .'

'You don't have to say anything. You worked damn hard to get this one in the can. You saved me ten times this amount in set rental and I know you could use it for the kids.'

Michelle smiled and hugged Megan.

'Thanks,' she said.

'No problem. Listen, we're shooting a dream fantasy piece to insert in the next film. Are you interested?'

Michelle nodded.

'I'll be in touch then.'

As Michelle walked out of the office she passed Aaron on the way in. 'What did the great tyrant want then, a little gratitude in kind?'

'You know what, Aaron?' Michelle said, sidling up to him seductively.

'What's that honey, you want a little extra curricular?' he said, smoothing her hair.

'No,' Michelle said softly. 'I just wanted to tell you that if your cock was half the size of your ego, then you'd be the highest paid man in porn.' She kissed his cheek softly and then walked away, laughing loudly.

'You'd better come in, Aaron. I don't think your self-esteem can take much more,' Megan said, half smiling. He slumped onto one of the uncomfortable chairs as she shut the door. He looked truly deflated and the lines around his eyes seemed a lot more pronounced without the clever concealing of the make-up department. It wouldn't be long, she thought, until some producer took him to a bar and gave him the gravity talk, then he'd be resigned to playing the overweight pool man or the telephone engineer who watches. It was the nature of the business, and it was understood; everybody had a shelf-life and his was drawing to an end.

'How are you, Aaron?' she asked, feigning compassion.

'How do you think I am, Megan?' he said, staring at her like a schoolboy who knew he was about to have the caning of his life. 'I worked my ass off for you, fucking a woman who couldn't stand me touching her, being filmed by a crew who hate me and drinking coffee that catering probably spat in.' He put his head down. 'Apart from that, I'm just fucking peachy.'

'You reap what you sow, Aaron,' she said. But then, realising that she had to get him on side, she relented slightly. 'Look, maybe the set just wasn't big enough for both of our egos, but I got what I wanted from you; we finished the shoot ten days ahead of schedule, which means a nice bonus for you.' She threw an envelope across the desk. He opened it and looked at her.

'Thanks, I'll send it to my mom, she could use the help.'

'Aaron, your mother owns a twenty per cent share of a casino in Vegas and, as your agent, she managed to screw me for another ten per cent on top of your normal fee. I doubt she'd use it to buy herself some carpet slippers.'

'Christ, does anyone ever crack that shell of yours?' he said. 'Or is it just me?'

'Look, Aaron, this is nothing personal; we worked together, we didn't have a particularly good relationship, but I was hoping that now it's over we could at least be friends.'

'Sure, except I'm scared that you are going to eat me alive like some black widow or something.'

'That's only after sex, Aaron,' she said. 'And as your mother is the only member of your family that will ever screw me, you don't have to worry about that.'

'I give in,' he said, getting up and reaching a hand across the desk. 'It would be dishonest to say I've enjoyed working with you, but it was an experience I'll probably tell my kids about.' He turned to open the door.

'Aaron . . .' she faltered. 'Hold on. I didn't ask you in here for a cosy chat; I've got a proposition for you.'

'Interesting,' he said sexily. 'How about dinner first?'

She ignored him.

'I've got a client who is rather selective. They've asked me to put together an erotic short for them. It needs to be pretty full-on, so it would be a closed set – just you and a camera, maybe twenty minutes or so. Are you interested?'

He raised an eyebrow.

'When you say full-on what do you mean?' he asked. 'I know you may not believe this but I've never taken it up the ass from another guy.'

'Spare me, Aaron; all I meant was that it would just be you on your own and maybe some toys.'

'That sounds too easy. What's the catch?'

'No catch, just five thousand pounds for a few hours' work, but if you're not interested there's a few other people I can call.'

'Hey, I didn't say I wasn't interested,' he said almost desperately. Five thousand pounds would pay for that expensive surgeon he'd read about, and a facelift would mean a couple more years as a leading man.

'Good, so I'd like to book you for tomorrow, nine a.m. I'll have someone reschedule your flight home. I'd like you to wear a suit, so I'll ring a couple of designers to see what they can come up with and you'll need a briefcase. Do you have one?'

'Sure,' he said, lying to her. 'No problem.'

'Good. The client wants you to look really respectable and hardworking, like maybe you're a surgeon and you've just come home from a really heavy day. Oh, and don't shave in the morning, I – they want it to look really authentic, like they're spying on you.'

'That's pretty specific – do I get to know who this is for?'

'I'm afraid not; do you still want the job?'

'Yeah, sure, it's easy money, right?'

'Right,' she said, reaching for his hand. 'I'll see you at the wrap party, Mr Adams.'

As she watched him walk away she smiled to herself. Just him, a camera and her; she was going to enjoy this.

Wrap parties were always fairly wild, and someone decided to give this one an S & M theme. The wardrobe girls had been plied with alcohol until they handed over the keys to the costume department. By the time Megan had finished for the night, all that was left was a black rubber dress with matching underwear.

'Oh my God,' she said as she dusted herself in talc so she could slide into it. As the stiffness of the rubber underwear grazed the soft flesh between her legs she squirmed wantonly. She let her hand wander slowly over the crotch of the panties and gasped as she encountered her own hot flesh through a peephole in the rubber. She took her hair out of its tight knot and caught her breath as she glimpsed herself in the mirror. 'I should be in the movies,' she said aloud, and then laughed to herself.

When she walked into the club they'd hired, nobody took a blind bit of notice of her; she looked like one of the dozen or so actresses and models who were inhabiting the bar. Aaron, not recognising her, sidled up behind her and whispered something obscene.

'Save it for tomorrow, stallion,' she threw at him and walked away as he put his head in his hands unable to believe what he'd just done.

Megan slipped away at 3 a.m. She wanted everything to be perfect on the set. She cleared away the tacky living room setting they'd been filming the day before and began to build a perfectly respectable bedroom. By the time she'd finished it looked like something out of an interior design magazine, and she felt pretty pleased with herself. She set up the camera and finally lay down on the bed. She slept soundly for three hours and was awakened by the delivery of two very beautiful designer suits and a long light-fawn trench coat.

Perfect, she thought. At 8.30 a.m. she poured herself a very strong black coffee, trembling at the prospect of what was to come. She had resisted temptation to script any of it, not that she needed to, as this had been in her head for a long time. Aaron arrived at 9 a.m. to find her at her desk – still in the rubber dress.

'Morning,' he said, making her jump. He hadn't shaved, but was dressed in a pale blue shirt and a pair of faded jeans. Megan thought he looked incredibly sexy and toyed with the idea of letting him wear his own clothes, but then she remembered the fantasy she was creating.

'Morning, Aaron,' she said, her voice husky because of her late night. 'Right on time.'

'Yeah,' he said. 'I left the party just after you. I thought I'd better get some sleep if we're gonna get this right for your client.'

'Very professional,' she said, sounding more sarcastic than she meant to. 'OK, if you could try both of these on.' She handed him the suits. 'And I'd like your hair brushed back instead of falling in your face; it makes you look too young and my client has been particularly specific about the look they want.'

'Sure,' he said. 'I'll go and get changed. The set looks amazing by the way. Who did it?'

'I did,' she said without emotion. 'I told you, Aaron, this is a closed set with nobody but you and the camera.'

'Right.' He went off to his dressing room.

She leaned back in her chair. She could feel herself becoming moist at the prospect of what was to come.

He walked onto the set wearing the darkest of the two suits.

'Is this all right?' he asked.

'Oh yes,' she breathed huskily, then regained her

composure. 'Put on the trench coat please, Aaron.' He slid the expensive jacket over his shoulders and was immediately transformed. 'Do you have the briefcase?'

'Yeah,' he said, reaching behind the bed. 'I've had it for ever,' he lied, skirting over the fact that he'd borrowed it from the prop room. 'It's a bit battered, but I thought that would make it a little more authentic.'

'Excellent,' Megan said. 'OK, I'm going to talk you through this step by step, just like the improvised scenes we did on set last week, but here's some background.' She paused, licking her lips and praying silently that he wouldn't notice her nipples were becoming erect beneath the sweltering rubber. 'You're a surgeon, like we discussed; you've just come home from a really tough day and you're wound really tight.' He bowed his head. 'To continue,' she added professionally, 'you throw your coat off, pour yourself a drink and then sit on the bed with your head in your hands, then you drain the glass and stare ahead for a full minute. After that, just follow my instructions, working at the pace of my voice. Are you OK with that?'

'Yeah, no problem,' he said, with none of the arrogance he usually gave in response to her instructions. 'So now we just wait for the person who's shooting for you, right?'

'No need, Aaron, I'll be filming this myself.' She watched his jaw physically drop, enjoying the amazing feeling of power it gave her. 'Does that bother you?'

'No,' he said quietly. 'In fact I can't think of anyone I'd rather be filmed by.'

She didn't want him like this; sentimental conformity wasn't part of the plan or the fantasy. He had to be unwilling but resigned to the fact that he had no choice. If he wasn't, it wouldn't work. She had to get the tension back between them, so she replied caustically, 'Oh, spare me the niceties, Aaron. You get paid either way.'

'You're the boss,' he spat back at her.

She felt a tiny trickle of her own juices pushing through the peephole in the rubber underwear and luxuriated in the knowledge that she could manipulate him to do anything. She opened a box that was sitting on a table nearby.

'I'm going to need you to make use of these, Aaron. I'll direct you if I think you're not doing it right.' She handed him a massive vibrator that had what looked like a serrated surface, and a jar of massage oil.

'What am I supposed to do with these?' he asked.

'Exactly what you are told. I'm going to start the camera running. Come in when you're ready and just do it like we said. I'll direct you the whole time, OK?'

'Yeah, OK,' he said, walking to the fake door on the set.

He walked into the bedroom, threw his coat on the chair and poured himself a drink before wearily sitting down on the bed. He hung his head as he pushed the button on the answering machine and heard it beep, indicating that there were no messages. Draining the glass, he stared ahead as directed.

'Take your cock out,' Megan said. 'Take it out and look at it.' He unzipped his fly and pulled his cock out of his underwear. It wasn't hard, and Megan zoomed the camera in for a close-up. 'Put your finger on the end of it, like you're trying to get it inside your foreskin and start rubbing it slowly,' she demanded. As he did what she said he winced as if in pain. 'Does it hurt, Aaron?' she asked, feeling smug in the knowledge that he couldn't answer her.

He put his head back and carried on with what he was doing and then looked down to see that he was getting the stirrings of an erection.

'Ease yourself back on the bed, keep touching your cock, but pull your trousers and underwear halfway down your legs.' As she said this she pushed her hand down her rubber underwear, found the peephole and, feeling the wetness of her clit, she started to finger herself slowly.

He lay back on the bed and eased his trousers and underwear to just below his knees, still playing with his cock as he did it.

'Now masturbate slowly, Aaron, with one hand. Use the other hand to play with your balls for a few seconds and then push that hand further back and slide a finger into your arse.' He flinched slightly, and this made Megan finger herself more quickly, the power she had over him making her cunt sodden. 'Do it, Aaron, and do it until I say stop.'

He sat on the bed looking like some kind of contortionist, masturbating slowly and jabbing his finger slowly in and out of his arse. She watched him wince for a few seconds more and then barked another order at him.

'You can take your finger out now, Aaron, very slowly, and take your trousers and underwear off completely, then I want you to look around until you see the vibrator. Take it in your hand and then kneel in the middle of the bed.'

She reached into a box beside her and pulled out a huge dildo. Concealed behind the camera, she opened her legs slightly and slid it inside the peephole in the crotch of her rubber panties, still watching him kneeling on the bed.

'Now, keep the vibrator in one hand and start masturbating again. That's right,' she said, making small circular movements with her hips so that the dildo deliciously irritated her. 'Now take the vibrator in your mouth and go down on it.'

He looked at the camera in disbelief; she was totally humiliating him. 'Do it!' she said angrily. He put the cold plastic in his mouth and sucked on it timidly. 'Put more of it in your mouth, Aaron, pretend it's your boss's dick; you're sucking it so you can get a promotion. Keep masturbating; do it a little harder.' She could hear soft little moans coming from his mouth and he began sucking on the plastic vibrator as though he were starting to enjoy it. She smiled to herself, remembering that twelve hours earlier that same vibrator had been inside her. She wondered if he could taste her on it.

'Take it out of your mouth, Aaron. You can't come yet; we've got a lot more to do. Put it down and put both hands on your cock, then start thrusting your hips forward as you masturbate.' He did exactly as he was told. 'OK, now stop, get the massage oil from the table and slowly pour it over the vibrator, then hold it in front of you and jerk it off for a few seconds.' She could feel the waves of orgasm coming over her, but she wasn't ready yet.

'Now get on all fours and put the vibrator up your arse and switch it on.' He looked shocked, but got on all fours and then tried to turn round and do as she said. He couldn't quite reach, so, letting go of the dildo, but leaving it hanging between her legs, she walked in front of the camera and took it from his hand. He looked at her pleadingly, but she wasn't going to stop now.

'I can see you're going to need some help with this one. I'll help you and then I can edit it out later.'

'Sure.' He looked scared.

'Bend forward slightly and put your arse in the air, but keep masturbating.' He did as he was told and waited. All the time she was doing this, she kept grinding slightly, using her taut vaginal muscles to keep the dildo in place. She used her thumb and her middle finger to hold his anus slightly apart; she could see his muscles twitching slightly. She pushed the hard rounded tip of the object against his arse as he turned slightly to look at her. 'Don't look at me,' she snapped. 'I'm not here, remember. Keep looking forward.'

He turned his head back and groaned slightly in anticipation. She slid it in slowly at first, and then heard him say under his breath, 'Oh yeah, oh, hurt me, Megan. Please hurt me.' She rammed it cruelly into his arse and started pumping backwards and forwards as he cried out in excruciating ecstasy. She used the other hand to pump the dildo that was inside her. Suddenly she stopped what she was doing and leaned close to his ear whispering savagely, 'You don't come until I say so. Remember that, Aaron.' With that she turned the vibrator on so that it buzzed away in his arse.

Once back behind the camera, she started barking instructions at him again, watching the vibrator brutalising his arse and his hand desperately jerking his cock back and forward.

'Please, Megan,' he begged. 'Let me come, I can't stop it, please, Megan.'

Megan was sitting on the chair behind the camera with her legs wide apart, driving the dildo in and out of her cunt.

'Not yet,' she rasped. 'Not until I say you can.' She wanted to throw herself onto the bed and let him ram his cock inside her, with the vibrator still lodged in his arse. It was these visions that finally brought her to orgasm whilst at the same time listening to him beg her to let him come.

As reality crept back in she could see Aaron, who was now lying on his back pushing his arse down against the bed so that the vibrator went further inside him. He was playing with his balls with one hand and masturbating with the other.

'That's fine, Aaron,' she said smugly. 'You can come whenever you're ready.'

She didn't need to watch; she just let the camera keep rolling. She suddenly heard him let out a strangled cry, and she was sure it had been her name.

Afterwards, Aaron looked a little awkward. He'd hastily put his trousers on as though, after all this time, he was embarrassed to be naked in front of her.

'That was great, Aaron,' she said cheerily, grateful that the clothes she had on were rubber and wouldn't let the stains of her own come show through. 'I booked you on the three thirty flight back home. If you get your stuff I'll take you to the airport.'

He nodded and hurried off to get his belongings. When he emerged from the dressing room he handed her the suits and the trench coat.

'No, you can keep those, Aaron – another bonus.' She handed him an envelope bulging with money. She was very smug in the knowledge that even with the bonus and the extra £5000 she was still under budget for the film and the money men would be more than happy.

They were silent during the drive to the airport and, when his flight was finally called, he shifted uneasily from foot to foot.

'Take care, Aaron,' she said, kissing him lightly on the lips. 'I hope we can work together again some time.'

'Sure,' he said sheepishly. They called his flight again. 'Hey, Megan,' he said, 'who was the short for anyway?'

'Didn't you know, Aaron?' she said, walking away with a cheeky look in her eye. 'It's for me.' She didn't look to see his jaw drop; she just carried on walking and said, 'I just wanted something to remember you by.'

Melinda

Mitzi Szereto

*I*t hurt at first. But then it got better. Just like they told her it would.

Melinda had never considered allowing anyone to tie her up. The idea of handing her body over to another person – of relinquishing her control and her womanhood to people she barely knew had no place on her list of Things To Do Before I Die. Of course there were a lot of things Melinda would never have considered doing before the night she went to the annual company Christmas party, unescorted and conspicuously alone.

The event started off like all the Christmas parties that had gone before, with nearly everyone in attendance parading their dates before their colleagues, their overly loud laughter and too-bright smiles making Melinda feel more out of the social fray than usual. Not fond of large gatherings, she immediately regretted her mistake in not having coerced her gay friend Joel into coming along with her. He was always a handy escort when she found herself in a pinch, particularly since he knew just when to fade into the background. But tonight Melinda didn't want to be bogged down with a date, bogus or otherwise. She wanted to be available, just in case. She'd even brought along her credit card to splurge on a room in the swanky hotel where the party was being held. Why, she could see the misty green landscape of Hyde Park from the window already!

As it happened, the only view of Hyde Park Melinda ended up being treated to on this wet December evening was the one from the hotel lobby. Evidently the creative head of corporate advertising had far more interesting things to do with his Saturday night than spend it with the office gadabouts, unlike Melinda, who really didn't have anything better to do on this rainy Saturday night. It was either the company Christmas party or cuddling up with the cat to watch yet another television documentary featuring a rhapsodic David Attenborough narrative on the sex lives of creepy-crawly things that live under rocks. At the moment Melinda was more concerned about her own sex life, which had definitely hit the skids.

This recent downward sexual spiral had gained some unwanted momentum thanks to Melinda's involvement with a man from her gym. In retrospect, she probably should have realised that anyone with that many muscles spent most of his time lifting weights and none on building up a career. Therefore it didn't take long for Melinda to decide she could easily forfeit all that hard defined male flesh in return for a steady bed partner with a steady salary and something to talk about beside abs and pecs. For after only a couple of steamy sessions, Blake and his weightlifting paraphernalia had virtually moved into her tiny flat. Granted, they were pretty good steamy sessions as steamy sessions tend to go, though certainly by no means fulfilling enough to warrant her financial support of the man – not even if his tongue claimed the distinction of being as muscular and rippling as the rest of him! Whether at her most exhausted or sexually apathetic, one dose of Blake's hard-working tongue between her thighs would be enough to make

Melinda forget the pile of paperwork waiting for her at the office. It was only too bad the rest of Blake wasn't quite as industrious as his tongue.

As she stood by the bar sipping spicy Christmas punch from a plastic cup and nodding the occasional hello to a familiar face, Melinda's glittery evening bag burned an embarrassing reminder against her hip. The unused VISA card that had been placed inside it with such careful premeditation before she left home for the party now made her feel like a fool. At the time it had seemed like a terribly sophisticated thing to do. But as her meticulously made-up eyes swept across the crowd of revellers searching for the one face she most wanted to see, Melinda realised that the expensive French perfume lavished behind her ears and on the insides of her thighs had been wasted, along with the outrageous sum of money that had gone towards the purchase of her new black dress, which had looked so-o-o sexy when she'd tried it on in the shop. So profound was her disappointment on what should have been a festive occasion that she considered leaving. However, all this changed when her crestfallen gaze met that of a dark-featured young man who looked as out of place as she felt.

Perhaps it was the expression of contemplative amusement in his smoky Eastern eyes that set him so apart from the others in the noisy hotel banquet room. This and the fact that he appeared to be the only male in attendance not drinking himself into a state of obnoxiousness or risking his teeth on the dried-out chicken wings, made his presence all the more noticeable. Or at least it did to Melinda, who found his aloofness strangely appealing. This was not a man who needed to call attention to himself. And neither, for that matter, was his fair-skinned female companion. For he stood in a gaudily decorated corner elbow-to-elbow and thigh-to-thigh with the most stunning woman Melinda had ever seen: an ephemeral white-blonde with eyes as amber as a cat's and the stealthy mouse-baiting movements to go along with them. How was Melinda to know that she would be that mouse?

Although not the sort to be physically attracted to her own gender, Melinda could not keep from staring at the feline young woman whose skin looked like it had been made from finely crushed pearls, just as she found it equally difficult to keep from staring at the *café au lait* young man whose conflicting features were every bit as striking as those of his companion. Melinda knew she was being fairly obvious about it, but she didn't mind if the couple noticed her interest. In fact, she secretly wanted them to. The contrast the pair made against the raucous backdrop of braying corporate types populating the area gave Melinda the impression they had wandered into the party by mistake or else out of boredom and the desire for a free drink. Either that or the Christmas punch had been more punched-up than usual and she had begun to hallucinate. Nevertheless, there was nothing at all hallucinatory about the sudden rush of moisture soaking the gusset of the black silk panties Melinda wore beneath her dress.

No one had spoken in the taxi. The only sounds were those of the London rain pattering teasingly against the vehicle's rolled-up windows and the ever-present chig-chig-chig of the diesel engine as this silent threesome made their way north towards Mill Hill. By now the drunken hilarity of the holiday celebrants had faded to a distant memory in Melinda's ears. Her breath grew heavy and increasingly ragged as she found herself being pleasantly squeezed between the two party crashers in the taxi's generous back seat, the sexually charged warmth of their bodies hinting at the delightful things to come, as did the flirtatious dance of their fingertips upon her widening thighs. Melinda had not said goodbye to her co-workers or informed them of her impetuous decision to accompany the mysterious couple to wherever they happened to be taking her on this soggy December evening. Unwise perhaps on her part, but tonight Melinda did not want to be her practical and reliable old self. Tonight she wanted to be someone else: the kind of someone who didn't care about things like caution.

For the man and woman pressing themselves so provocatively against Melinda's hips and thighs had shown no sign of knowing their fellow partygoers, which confirmed her suspicion that they had not been invited. Although why anyone would have wanted to crash a boring company Christmas do was a mystery. Much as it was a mystery why from out of a roomful of stunning females Melinda should be the one singled out as she stood about drinking punch in her brand-new black cocktail dress – one that looked indistinguishable from all the other black cocktail dresses being worn. Melinda, who did not classify herself as being in the drop-dead gorgeous league, nevertheless grew hotter and wetter by the minute at the thought of what would be done to her after the taxi dropped them at their destination.

Indeed she would be made to feel anything but average tonight, despite the fact that every part of her average self would be fully exposed to these two very unaverage strangers. Her arms would be drawn back and bound with deftly executed expertise in a complex macramé of silken cord that even she would have agreed was a work of art in itself, had she been able to see behind her. Although perhaps it was just as well Melinda could not, since she would have shrieked with embarrassment at the sight of her unfolded buttocks and the lubricated pink plug of latex being inserted between them.

Masculine fingers formed dark fans across Melinda's fleshy rear cheeks as their smoky-eyed owner's female companion dropped onto her haunches to place the intrusive object inside the wriggling backside before her. In her present state of restraint, Melinda's hips would pretty much be about the only thing she could move. Had she tried to kick out with her feet, it would have been impossible. The braided length of cord looping around her ankles had been woven into the elaborate network of knots trapping her arms behind her, forcing Melinda into a pose of helpless subservience. Considering the circumstances, she found it curious not to be feeling any fear when she could do nothing to act in her own defence.

'Relax, Melinda,' the man advised matter-of-factly as he checked her bonds. 'Allow yourself to get used to the pain. Your reward will be so much greater.'

'Don't fight it,' concurred his female partner, placing a not-too-gentle cat's bite upon Melinda's flinching right buttock as emphasis. 'You'll only make it harder for yourself.'

Despite the reassurances of this appealing couple in whose hands she had perhaps foolishly placed herself, Melinda's instincts took over and she tried to eject the foreign presence from her rectum. Her efforts proved futile, however, for the object refused to budge thanks to a unique design that thwarted even the most determined attempts to expel it. The more force she used, the more the latex filled her, expanding like a dry sponge in liquid until Melinda would finally come to accept the fact that she had lost all ability to control what was being done to her body. There could be no going back for her now.

During all this time, not a word of protest would be put forth by the couple's helpless captive. For Melinda's mouth had already been fitted with a gag of sorts: a blue silk kerchief that would have looked more appropriate fluted to a crisp point in a gentleman's coat pocket than in the lipstick-smeared mouth of a bound and naked female at the complete sexual mercy of two individuals whose names she neither knew nor had bothered to ask. Speaking of which, how did the man know her name? Melinda was certain she had not told him or the woman. Actually, she had made a point not to tell them much of anything.

'Everyone has to have a first time.'

The soft feminine purr of a voice startled Melinda, whose recent acceptance of her circumstances had not as yet extended to her latex intruder. So involved had she become in the act of ridding herself of its offending presence that her muscles were as tightly knotted as her bonds. Suddenly she realised how absurdly self-defeating it was to be struggling like this. Deciding to defer to the couple's advice, Melinda tried to relax. She closed her eyes and began to breathe deeply through her nostrils, willing the tension to leave her body until all that remained was a tension in her chest from her wildly thudding heart and an equally wild thudding in her pussy.

Melinda felt the amber-eyed woman's breath blowing a hot caress against her buttocks and she sighed into her silken gag. Having managed to calm down a bit, she would be surprised to discover that what was being done to her did not feel at all unpleasant. On the contrary, the cleverly designed series of ridges she'd observed on the surface of the plug before it had gone disappearing in a pink blur behind her gave rise to thoughts and desires she would never have admitted to aloud. For in the privacy of her mind Melinda caught herself wishing that the object penetrating her was not made of bloodless latex, but of hard male flesh – the engorged heated flesh she had been made to taste before her lips were fitted with the blue kerchief. She could still taste the dark-featured young man's slippery fluids in her mouth, along with the sweeter tang of his partner, whose moist female folds Melinda's tongue had likewise been called upon to please before its capacity to do so had been temporarily stifled.

While pondering what it might be like to be used this way by the nameless man whose hands held her open to the latex, Melinda's thoughts drifted toward such a seduction being undertaken by someone she actually knew, or at least saw nearly every day. Although she'd never confided her feelings to even her closest friends, Melinda had been suffering from a year-long infatuation with a work-mate – in fact, the very same work-mate who had been absent from the Christmas party and for whom Melinda would have gladly forfeited a week's salary in exchange for a hotel room, Hyde Park view or not! Unfortunately Caleb worked in a different department in what seemed to be a world away from her own, which only made it harder for Melinda to come up with a legitimate-sounding excuse to seek him out during office hours. She was a number cruncher and he a creative genius, two factors that didn't do much to bring them together.

Getting a man into her bed had never been a difficult task for Melinda. However, all that changed thanks to Caleb, whose oblivious demeanour shook her self-confidence. Perhaps she wasn't his type. Maybe he wanted a woman who looked like a celebrity or something. Maybe if genetics had blessed her with a few more credits on the impossibly gorgeous side of the ledger, she might have made an effort to strike up a conversation in the canteen or in the courtyard when Caleb drifted outside for a smoke. The problem was, every time Melinda got ready to initiate a casual confrontation, someone else would beat her to it: that someone generally being another female whose physical attributes and in-your-face sexuality far outweighed Melinda's own. Well, Caleb was probably too young for her anyway. For all she knew, he might even be gay. At least this would be what Melinda kept telling herself whenever Caleb turned in her direction, only to look straight through her as his lips sucked the smoke through the filtered tip of his cigarette. Oh, how Melinda wanted her clit to be that filter tip!

Caleb's impervious features shattered into red-hot fragments of pain as the young woman with the latex plug turned her attentions elsewhere by attaching a pair of small metal clips onto Melinda's upstanding nipples. The effect was like tiny teeth biting into the rubbery points and their startled recipient shuddered violently, prompting a disapproving tsk-tsk from her female tormentor, who readjusted the clips so they nipped more cruelly into the sensitive flesh. Melinda resumed the deep nasal breathing that had worked so well to calm her before and the pain in her nipples began to recede, giving way to a vexing heat. It was a heat that gravitated lower and lower and whose capacity to ignite a conflagration made itself apparent when another pair of metal clips were clamped onto Melinda's hairless vaginal lips.

Like the silent young woman wielding these bizarre tools of pleasure, Melinda had also been shaved to a virginal plain, leaving nothing secret and no sensation muted. Granted, she had received quite a shock when she found herself being confronted by a safety razor the moment she had stepped across the threshold of this innocuous-looking Mill Hill house, only to be twisted and contorted until every hair both topside and rear had been hunted down and excised out of existence. Had it been the man wielding the blade rather than his pearly skinned collaborator, Melinda would have been too mortified to go through with the evening. But as the metal teeth of the clips sank provocatively into her intimate flesh and pain and pleasure blended into one, she knew she was ready for anything.

Melinda giggled into her gag at the thought of her tipsy colleagues at the party, the highlight of their evening the free-flowing liquor and the equally free-flowing office gossip, none of which was likely to include her. Good old reliable Melinda, every corporation's wet dream. You could always count on her to stay late and finish the job. After all, she had nowhere important to run off to. There were no Calebs waiting for her at the pub or at that romantic new Italian restaurant with candles and Chianti on the tables; nor were there any bottles of California Chardonnay chilling in the fridge for later when they went back to her place. Indeed, never would these party-goers have imagined the sexy scenario taking place a few miles to the north – a scenario featuring a pair of expertly twittering tongues acting in symphonic harmony upon the innermost contours of Melinda's clipped-open labia. Of course this wouldn't be the first time she'd been underestimated!

Glancing down at the heads of dark and light paying homage to her shaved sex, Melinda shook with the desire to touch this anonymous man and woman who had entered her life only hours ago. She wanted to feel their beautiful faces with her fingertips as their tongues worked with such artistry on her clitoris and its moist surroundings. But part of the bargain of her pleasure had been the inability to exert any control over what was being done to her. The gym-toned muscles in Melinda's arms and shoulders ached with frustration, much as they had ached earlier when going to her knees before the bared and expectant genitals of her hosts, who orchestrated the movements of their guest's mouth to their exclusive benefit, inspiring from Melinda's tongue a boldness she never knew it possessed. Yes, perhaps she even underestimated herself.

It had been easier with the man, who thrust his penis to and fro in her mouth like one might a vagina. Keeping hold of Melinda's chin-length chestnut hair, he pumped her open mouth to the point at which she thought her jaw would break, exacting punitive glances against her throat before finally emptying himself with a sharp cry on her tongue. For the first time in her life Melinda did not experience the urge to spit out a man's pleasure. Instead she wondered if the aloof Caleb would taste as sweet as this dark stranger who had forced himself upon her surprisingly eager mouth. 'How lovely you are,' he replied afterwards in a husky whisper, leaning down to kiss Melinda's sticky lips before surrendering her to the amber-eyed female waiting with impatience at his side. Melinda had nearly forgotten about the other woman, so mesmerised had she been by her unquestioning submission to the man towering above her humbly placed form. However, she would promptly learn that his delicately featured sidekick was not the sort to let herself be forgotten.

Performing orally on another woman would be far more complicated than the straightforward techniques needed with a man, particularly when the recipient happened to be no shrinking violet when it came to making her desires known. Melinda found her hair being grasped in the same manner as before, albeit with substantially more ruthlessness as the expensively cropped chestnut strands were almost ripped from the root. 'Get to it, Melinda!' the woman ordered with a cavalier toss of her white-blonde head, her characteristic kittenish purr now a caustic bark.

Melinda felt a forbidden tingle between her thighs at hearing her name being uttered in conjunction with such a demand. The tingle gained in intensity, reaching near-orgasmic proportions when the young woman proceeded to rub her shaved and fragrant mound against Melinda's lips until arching her cat's spine in orgasm. Although she had never been involved sexually with her own gender, Melinda was not shy to thrust her tongue inside her partner's cream-filled pussy at the moment of her own climax, which had been achieved without any physical means other than the ghostly sensations of the pair of tongues that had gone before. It reminded her of the stealthy orgasms she experienced while asleep and which, upon awakening, would be followed by the discovery of her hands situated in innocent repose at her sides.

Melinda reflected often on that night of self-discovery in Mill Hill. Although she wouldn't have minded repeating the occasion, she hadn't been in contact with the man and woman responsible for giving her so much pleasure. The temptation to flag down a taxi and pay them a visit was one that became harder and harder to resist, especially since she had jotted down the street number of their house upon arriving back at her flat. But Melinda didn't believe they would be there when she arrived. The house had had a temporary feel to it, as if the occupants were just using the place for a quick layover on their way to other adventures, which probably included other Melindas. From what she could recall from the dizzying erotic haze she'd been in, the house had offered little in the way of furnishings – not that Melinda had been particularly interested in interior design that evening! Well, perhaps such things were best left as treasured memories, since it seemed doubtful that the overwhelming intensity of sensation she had been subjected to at the controlling hands of these two name- less and exotic strangers would ever be repeated. Even so, Melinda did not feel at all regretful. The dark young man and his amber-eyed companion had jolted her out of the humdrum dregs of daily life and taught her about her body's ability to achieve pleasure – a pleasure gained through restraint and pain. She had heard about people who got off on such sexual kinks, but had never bought into the pleasure-pain myth. Until now.

By the time she returned to the office after the Christmas break, Melinda had convinced herself that the couple had never existed. What had happened could only have taken place in her mind – a vivid erotic fantasy no doubt inspired by her year-long infatuation with Caleb. As she settled in for the first work week of the new year, she was surprised to find among all the pre-holiday clutter on her desk a tiny box covered in expensive wrapping paper. A late Christmas gift, was her first thought as she searched for an accompanying card. 'Do you happen to know who left this on my desk?' Melinda called out to her assistant when her efforts to locate a card identifying the gift-bearer proved futile. A highly detail-oriented person, it annoyed Melinda when holiday gifts were not given on time.

'It was there when I came in this morning,' came the assistant's unhelpful answer.

Melinda turned the little package every which way, puzzling over its contents. The box looked like the kind that contained earrings or a pendant. Not in the habit of wearing much in the way of jewellery, Melinda relied on her trusty pearl earrings for most situations, especially since joining the conservative ranks of corporate management. She had never been what anyone would have called a flashy person; therefore she hoped this mysterious gift would be something she could use, because if the giver hadn't bothered to leave a card, it was also unlikely a sales receipt had been enclosed in the event it became necessary to return the item.

Melinda waited for her assistant to leave before taking a letter opener to the attractive wrapping paper. She could not understand why her hands were trembling over something so ridiculously mundane as a pair of earrings; she could barely manage the elementary task of prying off the little lid. All at once Melinda cried out with remembered pain, for lying incongruously upon a dainty square of cotton was a pair of metal clips. They looked identical to the metal clips that had been clamped to her nipples and vulva not even three weeks ago. But surely that was impossible!

Melinda felt herself growing wet from the phantom sensations inspired by the unexpected reappearance of the clips and she squeezed her thighs together to calm the chaos taking place between them. Her face burned with embarrassment as she wondered who in the office might have been privy to the lascivious events of several nights ago. A folded square of paper had been tucked halfway beneath the bed of cotton and she plucked it out, hoping for an answer. To her frustration, it provided no clue as to the identity of her bondage-minded gift giver. All it offered by way of explanation was the word Tonight, along with a Maida Vale address. The note had been penned in a meticulous hand, the execution of the letters so tightly controlled and precise that Melinda could feel the intricate weave of silken cording which for one night had placed her in bondage. It would be all she could do to fight the impulse to relieve herself with her fingers right there at her desk.

With a similar sense of destiny to that which she'd experienced on her way to Mill Hill the rainy evening of the company Christmas party, Melinda took a taxi to the address on the note, the distinctive chig-chig-chig of the diesel engine adding an erotic sense of déjà vu to the occasion. The driver deposited her at the wrought-iron gate of a charming ivy-covered mews house, where from behind lace curtains a gentle light illuminated the mullioned windows. Melinda thought she saw a tall shadow move past the one nearest the door, although she could not tell whether the shadow belonged to a man or a woman.

Ever so slowly Melinda made her way up the cobbled walk, taking a perverse pleasure in prolonging the moment before she would at last come face-to-face with the person or persons who had summoned her. For it had, indeed, been a summons she'd received. The handsomely painted front door opened before she would even be given a chance to ring the bell.

'Hello, Melinda.'

Melinda gasped aloud as the wetness that had been plaguing her ever since unwrapping her Christmas gift that morning soaked the gusset of her blue silk panties. She had specifically chosen to wear them this evening because they were the same shade of blue as the silk kerchief the couple from Mill Hill had used to bind her mouth with.

For standing before Melinda was the impervious young man who for the past year had occupied her thoughts and been the inspiration for her orgasms, the man she assumed never noticed her, who looked right through her as if she were invisible. But he was not doing so now. Instead the lips she had so often observed sucking the smoke through the filter tip of his cigarette formed a sardonic smile.

Caleb stepped forward, a safety razor held ready in his right hand. 'You can't imagine how long I've been waiting for this,' he replied softly.

'And she's definitely worth the wait, darling,' came a familiar female voice. Melinda felt a sudden shift in the air as the feline presence of the young woman who had seduced her bound figure came into focus, followed by her smoky-eyed male conspirator.

'I understand you have already met my good friends Stephanie and Naveen?' Caleb looked deliberately into Melinda's astonished eyes, as if the question needed no answer.

Naveen's *café au lait* fingertips reached forward to stroke Melinda's cheek. 'Wasn't it thoughtful of Caleb to have invited us to the company Christmas party?'

Caleb's smile widened. 'Oh, but the party is only just beginning.'

Hands Up

Maria Lyonesse

The Grapes was crowded – even for a city centre pub on Friday evening. The group in the corner were particularly well oiled. Holly almost thought better of it – even took out her mobile to ring Jen and suggest somewhere else to meet. But she couldn't get a signal. Then the barman caught her eye.

'Sales teams, eh?' He jerked his head towards the corner group. 'Won a big contract. Don't suppose I'll see the back of them before chucking-out time. What'll it be, love?'

As she waited for him to fetch her order Holly glanced back to the rowdy group. All eyes were on one man telling a joke.

'. . . and then he says to Camilla, "Can't one just pretend it's a sauce bottle . . .?" '

There followed vigorous hand actions. His audience erupted into laughter.

Holly paid for her drink and fingered the mobile again. If she stood by the door perhaps she could get a signal?

'You're waiting for someone who's at least five minutes late.'

She looked round, affronted. It was the wannabe comedian from the corner group.

'You're obviously alone. No one plays with their glass like that unless they're a little edgy. Edgy enough to have been stood up by, say, between five and ten minutes.'

She met his eyes. They must have been the first thing people noticed about him. An intense pale blue. Meeting them felt like someone – someone intimate, maybe – had taken a palmful of ice and was sliding it down the hollow of your spine.

She'd pigeon-holed him as a drunken jerk. He wasn't drunk. But he was high on something. Success. The crowd's attention.

'I'm waiting for a girl friend.'

'You meeting her tomorrow as well? Say, for lunch?'

'I'm going clothes shopping. Alone.'

'What a waste. I love clothes shopping. So many opportunities.'

He flicked out a business card in explanation. It said 'Owen Carr – Sales Manager, South East. Retail Interiors'.

'Trade you?' he said and when, reluctantly, she'd handed over hers he added, 'Holly? Never had you down as a pensions analyst. Something more arty. You like art? We could meet up at the café in the art gallery – say one o'clock tomorrow? Go on. I'm on a roll. Indulge me.'

Holly was deliberately late. Owen was five minutes later. Meanwhile she'd ordered a cappuccino.

'You don't need hyping up with coffee,' he said, sliding into the seat opposite. 'You need mellowing. They do a good house red here.'

The wine, on an empty stomach at midday, made her feel heady. Like this conversation wasn't happening. Like it didn't matter what she said.

'Why do I need mellowing?'

'You're nervy. Tense. Your hands give it away. They're everywhere at once. Fiddling with things. They need to slow down. Like it says in the song.'

She felt herself redden and imagined it must be as vivid as the wine in the glass. Owen took the glass from her. He lifted her hands and kissed each fingertip in turn. He was in no hurry. He ran his own fingertips down the inside of her forearm – from wrist to elbow, slowly, then back again. She'd never appreciated what a sensitive place it could be. An intimate touch. A pushy one. It assumed they were already lovers.

They had bagels: piquant smoked salmon, calorie-laden cream cheese and peppery endive. As Owen wiped his mouth he said, 'Fancy looking round the exhibition?'

'What's on?'

'You didn't notice the poster?' He grinned. 'Let's see what you make of it.'

He led her into the main gallery. His was a firm, confident grip. One that was used to getting what it wanted. Holly did feel mellow now. And glad she'd let him talk her into a second glass of house red.

The exhibition was a collection of female nudes through the ages.

'Hypocritical,' he murmured as they tagged onto a Japanese party on a guided tour. 'If I was looking at a photo of her in a magazine in my own bedroom they'd call me a sad perv. Because she's a painting on a wall it's art. What d'you think? You feel oppressed by pictures like that?'

She didn't. She thought it was beautiful. The knowing but lazy sensuality on the woman's face. The weight of her breasts evident as she lay on one side. One thigh was discreetly crossed in front of the other. But was it discretion? Holly imagined how the model must have felt – her nakedness being painted, adored like that. She wasn't being coy. She was squeezing her thighs together to keep up the delicious pressure on her clitoris. To keep herself in a slow-burning mood until the artist, her lover, put down his brush, raised his smock and revealed the aching hard-on: her reward for lying still.

'I love it,' she said and with the 'love' licked the taste of red wine still on her lips. 'Every bedroom should have one. Great for getting you in the mood.'

'. . . an experiment,' the tour guide was saying, 'in shade and light. Observe how the sheen on the bowl of grapes in the foreground complements the texture of the model's skin . . .'

'Grapes,' Owen sneered. 'It should be melons. Gala melons to complement her tits.'

In the crush of tourists' bodies Holly felt a hand on her breast. Owen's. It slipped under her jacket and undid the middle few buttons on her blouse. His fingers probed beneath her stiff lace bra, found her plump nipple and rolled it slowly.

'If you're not shocked,' he whispered, 'give me your hand.'

She did. He guided it under his long coat and pressed it against his groin. It was full.

'Undo my zip,' he continued, his mouth pressed against her ear. 'Hold my cock.'

His fly zipper purred down between her thumb and forefinger. She explored and walked her fingers under the elastic, cupped his tense balls and then moved slowly up along his cock.

She was fondling a man and she hadn't even seen him properly yet. He was long and smooth. His erection was firm and confident – like the clasp of his hand. When she closed her fingers around his glans he shuddered and groaned.

'Not so fast, Holly. Slow – real slow. Barely move your fingertips. Then, believe me, no one will know . . .'

She didn't ask him how he knew that. She teased the

very tip of his cock, just circling her thumb. Welded together they moved on through the hall. In the crowd, no one seemed to think it odd they were crushed together.

Was he ever going to come? In front of a monochrome photograph of a naked woman playing the cello – her eyes closed, her devotion to the instrument so complete that penis envy might be a fact – Holly increased the pressure on his cock.

Owen pressed his face into her hair to stifle his moans. But still he didn't come. Not until they'd reached a huge African carving of a standing nude. She was roughly carved from some dark, hard wood. Her Polaris breasts were accentuated by the exaggerated collar necklace and her finger-pointing nipples tipped with gold paint. Owen's whole body froze. He pressed his face even harder against Holly's neck. He gasped. His semen spurted warm into her hand.

Holly, still a little drunk, bit her lip against giggling at the absurdity of it all.

It's Saturday afternoon, she thought. I'm in the middle of a municipal art gallery. I've just masturbated a man I barely know.

Owen produced a wad of tissues from a deep pocket in his long coat. The crowd had thinned.

'I love jerking off,' he confided. 'Anywhere. I'm always prepared.'

He lifted her hand. It was still warm from his cock. He wiped it like a benediction and kissed her palm.

For a moment Holly thought he was going to say something profound but he asked, 'You want to carry on shopping?'

Holly needed a bikini. Owen tagged along. It felt surreal. Did what had just happened make them lovers? He seemed more like a brother now.

'Not there,' he said as they approached one popular women's fashion chain. 'They've got communal changing rooms. I should know – we sold them. Here's a better idea . . .'

She let him talk her into visiting a more up-market boutique with discreet cubicles. She was with Owen. Anything could happen.

As she was trying on a swirly blue bikini it almost did.

The curtain rasped aside. Owen was in the cubicle with her. He fell on his knees before her and the tanga briefs she'd just been debating – would they, wouldn't they go with a tan – were whisked halfway down her thighs.

He buried his face in her pubic hair and breathed in deep. The inrush of his breath was a ticklish, unfamiliar sensation. He was nuzzling her, worshipping her musk-iness. How many lovers had done this so willingly? Holly parted her legs and prepared to be indulged.

Owen's tongue tensed to a narrow point. He drew it backwards and forwards between her labia. It was the same rhythm he'd used to stroke her arm.

His tongue wriggled, probing, deeper into her. It was a warm, inquisitive snake. Writhing in and out a few times, it pulled back, toyed with her clit then buried itself deep in her again.

This was everything. Holly had never known a man do this with such rapture, such total attention. Owen's tongue played her like a singer's with some particularly challenging Italian aria. She tried not to moan aloud. It was so hard. She was used to letting a man know he was pleasuring her. But moan like that and what would they think – the other customers, the shop assistants? How long had she been here? How long till someone wondered if she needed help? The edge of danger was addictive. The frisson of discovery. She could see why it turned Owen on.

'That's fantastic. Keep going. I'm nearly –'

Owen pulled back. He twitched aside the curtain, checked right and left and scarpered.

Holly was shaking. In rage. In excitement. In shock on the pulsing cusp of orgasm denied. The rug had been pulled from under her, leaving her gasping and winded. She felt very naked. She pulled up the tanga briefs without thinking. Too late. Her musky juice was seeping into them despite the plastic hygiene patch. She'd have to buy the bikini.

There was no sign of Owen in the shop. Bastard. What was he trying to do?

She paid the exorbitant price on the tag and marched out into the main shopping mall. Still no sign of Owen. Halfway to the escalator a hand grabbed her elbow.

'On a scale of one to ten, how mad at me are you?'

'Eleven and a half,' she said, shaking him off.

'Mad enough to come home with me?'

She stopped, caught her breath and looked him full in the face. Those eyes again. Pure ice. They could be dangerous.

'I know what you're thinking,' Owen continued. 'I'm some kind of weirdo. Some sick perv beneath the successful businessman. OK. I'm weird. But I'm not dangerous. And you want me to finish what I started back there. I know it. Come on. Humour me.'

Holly didn't move.

'Follow me, then,' Owen said. 'It's only a walk away.' He nodded at her shopping bags. 'I'll walk slow.'

Owen lived in a studio apartment in a converted warehouse overlooking the canal basin. There might have been a lift. But he didn't go that way. Holly followed him up an iron fire escape. The bags were biting into her fingers. She was out of breath.

By the time he'd unlocked the back door she'd caught him up.

'What the hell's your game?'

'You don't like games, Holly? I love them.'

'Bastard.'

'Yeah.' He shrugged off his long coat and backed away from her towards the bright scatter cushions that lay all over his floor. 'Keep it coming. Be mad at me.'

Holly dropped her bags where she stood. She grasped his shoulders and flung him back onto the cushions. She hadn't realised she was going to do it until she did. He went over more easily than she'd expected.

He'd messed her around. He'd left her dangling, randy and unsatisfied. He'd dragged her halfway across town – her feet aching, her back sweaty, her palms raw. She took a smaller cushion and threw it at him.

'You prick!'

'C'mon, Holly. That's beautiful. More.'

She sank to her knees beside him, grabbed the cushion again and swiped at his body.

'Control freak. Arsehole. Don't ever, ever mess me around like that.'

He gasped and rolled at each soft blow. He was fighting with his flies now, shoving his black jeans down over his hips.

'Not the cushion. Your hand. Hurt me, Holly. Fucking hurt me.'

She looked at his arse. It was beautiful. Small, white cheeks with the barest scattering of hair. His cock was like a teenage boy's – standing up high.

'I said hurt me!'

She did. She brought her hand down on his white cheeks. It stung. She hadn't expected that. Owen writhed and groaned beneath her. The tip of his cock strained damply against the vivid cushions.

Holly spanked him again. It didn't hurt so much the second time. Or the third. Her aching, strap-bitten hands began to glow. And the power. It turned her on.

'Cheapskate!' she hissed. 'You usually get a whore to do this? You'll pay me. Yeah – you'll pay.'

'I'm your whore. Make me feel cheap.'

His boyish white buttocks had turned red. She supposed her hands had, too. She didn't care. She'd done that to him. Left those marks on his body. She could do anything.

'You'll be my whore,' she muttered as she spanked again and again. 'I'll strap my dildo on. Fuck you up the arse. You think I like being humiliated? I'll humiliate you!'

'Say it again – the first bit.'

'I'll take my dildo and fuck you up the arse.'

'Yes!'

His cock jumped. He came in a wide arc all over the scatter cushions – the crimson, the purple, the lime green. At once he seized her hands and began kissing them and gasping, 'Thank you, thank you, thank you.' Holly couldn't work out where she was. In amongst the shaking, the anger, the arousal, she felt an ache of something else.

Tenderness.

Owen flipped her back onto the scatter cushions. She realised the strength he hadn't chosen to use before. He rucked up her skirt, snatched down her panties and plunged his face between her thighs.

This time he wasn't going anywhere. He kissed her clit many times and quickly – his lips pounding up and down on her like a sewing machine on cloth. It was maddening. The most feather-light oral sex any man had ever given her but only enough to take her so far. To leave her hanging in a state of utter horniness but not to take her further. When Holly was groaning and biting her finger and kicking her legs Owen plunged his slippery tongue between her labia.

She cried out. Again, dextrous, writhing like a warm snake he played her perfectly. He filled her quim with frantic movement then pulled back and overwhelmed her.

The craziness of the situation turned her on so much. She was close. So close. As Owen's tongue sang raptures up and down her quim, around her tightening nub she felt a long, slow orgasm being born.

It stayed with her. It turned her whole pussy fiery gold. He teased her with his quick tongue, prolonging the rising spasm. When it let her go she still felt golden.

They caught their breath. Owen raised himself up onto one elbow beside her. She could smell her own musky juices on his breath as he said, 'Want to know the story? I love wanking. I prefer it to sex. I can have sex with anyone.' Here he paused and a jealous frisson went through her. 'It takes someone much more creative to give you a first class wank.

'I was a young teen. Mum and Dad were out – big sister's school prizegiving or something. Aunt Hilary was babysitting me. She wasn't a real aunt but that's what we called her. Uptight. Spinster. Pillar of the church. That sort.

'I was reading a porno mag in bed. It was doing the rounds at school. I was really hot. Jerking off so crazily I didn't hear her come up the stairs, open the door to check on me. Too late. There she was in the doorway staring at me and I was coming like a fire extinguisher all over the place.

'She was across the room in two strides. Big, country woman. She used to chuck horses around in her spare time. She rolled me over face down on the bed and said I had the devil in me. I was dirty – corrupted by Lucifer and she was going to thrash him out. She yanked down my blue stripy pyjama bottoms, held me down and spanked my arse so I couldn't sit down for three days.' He sighed. 'God, it was fantastic.

'That reminds me,' he said, straightening his clothing and reaching for a dial-out pizza menu, 'my sister's brat's getting water chucked over it in church next weekend. I hate doing the black sheep of the family bit on my own. Come with me?'

'Won't your folks make assumptions?'

'They gave up making assumptions about me years ago.'

They took the train – past chocolate box countryside dotted with oast houses.

I'd suffocate if I lived here, Holly thought.

At Edenbridge a crowd of French exchange students swarmed through the carriages.

'Let's stand,' Owen whispered.

'When did you become Mr Chivalrous?'

'Just do it.'

Bodies pressed them from all sides. She thought one was Owen's. She couldn't be sure. He was behind her. Her hair was caught in her shoulder bag strap and she couldn't turn her head to check.

Holly felt a hand creep under her skirt. She'd worn a flimsy wrap-around type: just about respectable enough for a family christening. Easy access, though.

The fingers crept up and stroked the stretch lace of her briefs. One slipped inside and began to play with her clit.

'Owen! You just can't pass up a chance . . .'

'Me? I'm not doing anything . . .'

He sounded convincing. That didn't mean he was telling the truth. A thick index finger probed her cunt.

'You think I'm feeling you up? Why me? There's plenty of horny teenage lads in here. French, too. They're mad for it. Bet one's decided to take a chance. Or why just one?'

Another hand began to feel her left breast. It could be coming from the same direction. Or not. She glanced down to see if the hand was Owen's but it had already sneaked under her T-shirt. She could only see the blurred outline as it burrowed under the bra she'd worn for propriety. It pinched her nipple hard.

'These French lads,' Owen whispered again. 'No telling what can happen when they get let off the leash. They don't often get to feel a juicy pair of tits. Or finger-fuck a willing pussy.'

She closed her eyes, leaned into the shape behind her – Owen's or whoever's – and lost herself in his fantasy. That it might be true – the delicious danger – was turning her on so much. Her legs shook.

'You'll send them out of control. Just standing here and letting any one of them grope your cunt or your tits or your arse. They'll think you're up for anything. When we get off the train they'll take you to some out of the way barn and fuck you one after the other. A whole carriage-full of trigger-happy teenage pricks inside you. You'd let them do it, too. Bet you're gagging for a full-on fuck.'

Holly was fighting to keep her breathing under control. Fighting not to moan. The ache of randiness was almost too much. And it was true. She and Owen had spent the last seven nights together. And tried everything but conventional penetrative sex.

She missed the feel of a cock. The way it thrust. The way it swelled and kicked as it was about to come. She bit her lip and grunted. The finger (Owen's, or not?) inside her was drawing slowly – keeping her there. A lover with a slow hand? She was a convert to his way of feeling.

'Quiet,' Owen hissed. 'You don't want the whole train to know. They'll all want some. It won't just be the French boys. That man asleep over there. He's only pretending to be. Why d'you think his legs are rolling apart? He's plumping up. He'll have you. He won't be as quick as the young lads. He'll shaft you till you're raw.'

Holly's legs were trembling wildly. It was happening.

Her orgasm was priming itself but trapped inside. She clamped down. Couldn't scream. Couldn't let go. It stayed like a coiled knot filling her quim, holding her at the clenched moment of climax for half a minute or more. It let her go slowly. She'd never known repression could feel so good.

She reached behind to cup Owen's bulging crotch. He deserved a gift for this – for the wild things he'd sown in her head. She'd kneel down in this full carriage, unzip his flies and fellate him in view of everyone.

'No,' he said, removing her hand. 'I'm saving this.'

After the train ride a taxi dropped them on the outskirts of a village. Owen led her round behind the church.

'It should be about . . .' he groped in the mossy gaps between 400-year old stone, 'here!'

He retrieved a key, unlocked the vestry door and drew her in.

'Owen! What if the vicar's about?'

'He won't be. The christening's not till three o'clock. We've got ages. He'll be in his study on the other side of the village writing letters and listening to Classic FM.'

'How the hell do . . .? No!'

Owen grinned.

'Yeah. Vicars' sons either grow up buck-toothed pious or utter perverts. Guess which way I went.'

Holly chuckled back.

'Bet you were even a choirboy. Fancy a quick game?'

'Why d'you think I snuck you in here?'

He tossed her a robe and began pulling on one himself.

'You be choirmaster. I've wanted to do this for years!'

She tugged the robe over her head. The old cotton had a curious feeling of stiffness and submissiveness to her fingers. Its scent was wholly alien. It tightened the flesh at the base of her nostrils. It invaded her. She was someone else now. Being someone else could be fun.

171

'I've been waiting for this for a long time, too,' she murmured, slipping into her role. 'You and me – alone together after choir practice. I've known you a long time, Owen – in the church, the village, the choir. But I never feel I've got to know you properly. You understand?'

Owen backed away against an antique bureau.

'Please – my father's expecting me . . .'

'He knows you're with me. Safe.'

She had him pinned up against the bureau. She reached under his choirboy's robes and undid his flies. His prick was hard and hot.

'Not such an innocent little choirboy. I've seen the way you look at me. That cheeky way. You aren't new to this.'

'It's a sin. You mustn't.'

She tightened her hand on his cock. She could feel the blood thumping in its veins.

'A sin? I've heard about your degenerate habits. You're going to find out what happens to little boys who play big games.'

She pulled down his black jeans and jockey shorts.

'Bend over. I'm going to give your sweet little arse just what it deserves.'

She forced his head down and tossed his robes up over his back. The juice that was trailing from the tip of his cock she rolled and rubbed into his anus.

'You're puckering, lad. No need to pretend. You've done this before.'

'I haven't. I swear. Please don't . . .'

There were candles on the bureau. Everything from slim tapers to outrageous weapon-sized church candles. Holly stretched out her hand and smiled. That would teach him . . . No. Be fair. She chose one in between, hitched up her robes, parted her wrapover skirt and clasped the thick end of the candle between her thighs. She rested the unsullied wick end on his bullseye anus and pushed.

Owen gasped. Holly felt the rush of power – just like the first time at his flat when she'd paddled his bare buttocks. Owen was at her mercy. And loving it.

She gripped her thighs tight against the wax and rolled and rocked the candle – nudging her clitoris, pleasuring his arse. Owen moaned.

'Sir – you're so big. I had no idea. Don't stop. No – don't stop. Bugger me.'

Holly reached round and grasped his cock. She loved Owen's cock. It was so wicked. Holly teased its length. It shivered. The candle between her thighs was giving enough stimulation to keep her on a plateau of randiness. This was going to be long and slow. And sweet.

She treated Owen more roughly. He could obviously take it. He moaned and sighed and his cock was almost dancing in her other hand. She must have hit the spot inside. The secret, hidden part of a man that makes his orgasm ten times crazier. That makes him your slave.

Owen roared. His cock jerked out of her palm and ejaculated in a hot pumping shower all over his choirboy robes.

She withdrew the candle.

'Oh sir,' Owen breathed. 'That felt amazing. Can we do it again next week?'

He straightened up and turned to face her.

'Mr Choirmaster – sir – there seems to be something funny about your chest.'

He grasped her breasts roughly through the stiff cotton robes.

'The choirmaster never felt like this. I do believe there's a frisky pair of tits under here.'

Still with his hands on her breasts he backed her up against a rail of church vestments. His turn to be in charge. His turn to do whatever he wanted to her.

Owen thrust her against the heavy vestments. The indulgent brocade yielded. There was a venerable mustiness, a faint, spicy tang of something – incense? Holly drew it deep into her lungs. She prepared to surrender.

He pushed the robes up round her neck – then her T-shirt, then her lacy bra. He scissored her nipples between thumb and forefinger and pushed her breasts together roughly. She glanced down. His choirboy robes had fallen back into place but she thought she saw the swing of his rising cock beneath them. Fondling her was turning him on again.

'Yeah – firm and frisky,' he said as he squeezed. 'You're a bad woman. Dressing up and pretending so you could take advantage of me. I'm going to teach you – if you start something you'd better see it through.'

He bent down and took one dark nipple in his mouth, drawing it out with his tongue. She could tell he was getting aroused even without seeing the tented outline of his cock. The note of his breathing told her. The flush at his neck. They'd been lovers for a week. But she knew him. Knew him with a twisted thoroughness – a ram-raiding of barriers – she wouldn't have believed possible.

'You get off on this?' he demanded as he raised his head. 'Dressing up as a man to fondle young boys?'

'Yes. I love it. I love corrupting them.'

'You bit off too much this time. You always pretend to be a man?'

'Always. No one's found me out before.'

'That means you've never been taken like a woman? Never been fucked? Shame. Because I can't promise to be gentle.'

He raised the choirboy's cassock and exposed himself. His eager prick was standing high. Seven nights of foreplay had been leading up to this. Holly shivered like the nervous virgin she wasn't. Owen didn't even pause to slip off her briefs. He pushed aside the lacy crotch and entered her.

It felt right. Like a sacrament. Penetrated by him here

for the first time standing up in a church room with the crush of sumptuous velvet at her back. He fucked her slowly. She closed her eyes and relished his simple maleness. His cock glided in at the perfect angle. Without any effort on her part her clit was being taken to a slow, rising heaven. It was inevitable. She slumped against the heavy brocade and linen and just enjoyed the long slow haul up the rollercoaster knowing something crazy was in store.

She came around him – her quim clasping his cock again and again. It was as sweet and heady as a first ever fuck. The pleasure that only coming with a full, stretched cunt can give.

Owen didn't pause. He carried on, prolonging her golden waves with his thrusting until he kicked and climaxed again.

'Liar,' he whispered. 'You're no virgin.'

'Liar yourself. You said you didn't do penetrative sex.'

'I made an exception. Just for you.'

Later they smiled and held hands as Owen introduced her to his family and other villagers outside the church.

'. . . and this is Aunt Hilary – one of my father's oldest friends.'

Holly looked the woman up and down. Solid. Sensible tweed skirt. The type to send a teenage boy's sexuality into a tailspin?

'I've never met you,' she said warmly, shaking the older woman's hand, 'but I feel I owe you so much.'

Let her work that one out.

Girls Are No Good . . .
If You Want To Have Some Fun

Ms. Steak

Richard Widmark said as the crazed Skip McCoy in
Samuel Fuller's *Pick up on South Street*, 'Girls are no
good if you wanna have fun.' As a female who counts
on other females for fun and frolics, these days I'm
beginning to agree.

I wander the streets like any G.O.D. (Girlie of the
Dawn). I'm called back to the corners and alleys of the
sticky meat market packing area of New York City's
14th Street and the West Side Highway upon returning
from London. 'Girlie of the Dawn' is a term I discovered
in 1993 when I catapulted my life over to London for
one week of sickly sex that opened the magic door to
more and more skanky hellish hedonism. The female
who sparked it all jettisoned herself to the shores of my
Jane Street apartment, and I to her London abode of
squats (and other significant signs of homelessness) from
Camberwell to Stoke Newington, Peckham to Surrey
Quays. Wherever and whatever. It didn't matter if
indoors, outdoors, smelly public toilets in Soho cafés,
well-greased M22 petrol stations – the sex was beyond

anything I had ever imagined. I was hooked and faked love for one year, eventually coming to terms with the fact that what we were doing was a fuck scenario with more emphasis on the fuck than the love. The female in question didn't matter 99 per cent of the time. What mattered was whether or not she was a great lay, no less knew how to spin the webs verbally, physically and mechanically.

This girlie was so fucked up in her masquerading and marauding through the night that I was more and more inspired, and I lay myself on her skin just to feel the stickiness of her insanity, and her desire to wander more and more into the glitter of the London 1993 light. She liked her sex hard, vicious and beyond dangerous in its exhibitionism.

I think it was because of all the wanderings and fuckings that took place at that magic hour between dark and light, and that space in between debaucheries, when the body begins to illuminate and, all of a sudden, the person you are fucking is pure fire in image and in touch, arresting something of an otherness that's beyond human. Few can find this place. I believe G.O.D.s can. I am one. This magic hour was also found in my favourite film, *Days of Heaven*. The little girl narrator watches a tragedy touch itself as the light changes from deep pink to a bruised purple and once more towards acid orange, transforming her world into the wild thing that grew out of control, nevertheless magical. I was watching it all unfurl like a yellow cat stretching through the break of day. After three years of slippage in the London swamp, I can only now speak of the desert and the pieces that crack off and find their way back into the curl of a sleeping and rested body.

In 1985 the meat market of the lower 14th Street Neanderthal regions was my home. I was riding my baby blue 1950s Schwinn (the Cadillac of bikes) at 3 a.m., cruising toward the hooked meat and staring into the red abyss like a Francis Bacon junkie. During the day I was performing Chekhov and O'Neill and at night I was a fucked-up wolf pawing my way through the washed-up trannies, the psycho rent boys and the graffiti artists fucking in abandoned warehouses after making the art of their life. I was staring, riding and learning in the bloodied 80s stench. As I penned 'Girlie of the Dawn' I realised that I – unlike my gay male counterparts – would never be sated from those wanderings. The boys would be sucked off with issued regularity and consistency. 'Girlie of the Dawn' would simply be a G.O.D. because of her crude invisibility in the night and her untouchable, no less unapproachable, demeanour. She would rise out of the ashes of being overlooked and lavish her wisdom from not having scored onto some poor sucker in a coffee shop who could care less about her hopeless copping-for-a-feel exploits.

No one in the 80s even tried to pick me up during those fattened nights of meat. Of course the butchers were all mouthing off, teasing me with their meat products. But no female. Of course, now I see it as impossible anyway. To begin with, I was melting in a fashion limbo of retarded taste. I would dress in 1940s trousers held up by suspenders à la Bananarama doing a Cagney and Lacey moment via Madonna. Complementing that was my shaved head in true Hare Krishna motif making way for the Sinead gangsta look. I wasn't making a commitment toward anyone, not even my fashion sensibility, and I failed miserably in my Little Lord Fauntleroy get-up. How did I ever think I could cruise, no less be picked up? Just because I was working out in major *Terminator* Linda Hamilton bicep mode and doing my Clit Club routine, this gave no guarantees for a New York babe to swagger my way. I was a mess waiting to happen.

But picking up in London was a snap. I am not sure why, because the attitude was just as vicious as in the

NYC scene. Maybe the hormones were hungrier, grabbier and flying freer. Maybe it was that I was an outsider in a strange land. Maybe I was just coming undone and I was slipping.

I wandered and practised in NYC and in London I performed. I guess I just got lucky there. I was a victim of a miracle. From Hampstead Heath's boy-fucking stomping ground, I carried out my sexploits. I was the fag boy with her token boy prize for the hour. It seemed like there was nothing female in what I was doing. Yet the femaleness was protruding. That is what made it all so appealing and sexy. We weren't butch and we definitely were not femme. We chose to languish in the unattainable and ambiguous in-between state which stayed hard and erect and furious in its demand, never cowering and ducking for cover. I can never describe the feeling, yet it still exists. Maybe this state of 'in-betweenness' which is so not lesbionic, gay nor straight, is found in the DNA. This is the playground I fucked in and continue to search for. There are no definitions, no 'namings' of what this was – no less still could be.

I can proudly say that my jaunts lately into the pastis-invested/French bistro 1999 *fin de siècle* nachtmare of the NY meat market, have seen me being cruised by 25-year-old boy galleristas, no less by the glamorous trannies themselves. Maybe my fashion moment is getting clearer, may be it's because my lesbo retro Flock of Seagull's limbo look is now Peter Fonda does *Easy Rider* does Jane Fonda does *Klute* and maybe because I could give a flying fuck about the pick-up moment. My hair is long which means not one female will look my way. It's uncanny, but hair is the most lesbionic focal point. I should just shave my head and prove the point. The girls would flock. I would then take my bald head in hope of head-fucking them just to prove the point that things don't always have to be so shaved, smooth, defined and well-rounded. Like I said, I amputated definitions a long time ago. Fuck the ones that need those signs and symbols to make a move. They think I'm femme, when in fact I'm a butcher that butches. If they only could see the intricate delicate precision points I press onto meat. I take apart the pieces of you, swirling and cutting moments, engravings on skin, reminders of sorrows, hauntings. Recollections of the scream slapping itself onto the walls of executions, dislocations and misunderstanding. I make it all better. I kiss it all away. I can give you what you ask for. I make all the decisions of the flesh, the way only a G.O.D. can. I don't waste your time. This is not about romance and the stars, this is about electrocutions and shock waves travelling to the left temporal lobe of your brain to transport you from heaven to hell and back again, darlin'!

But for the record, females don't cruise other females in dark abandoned spaces in Nueva York, nor in London. Maybe the 21-year-olds do, but if you are beyond 30, *hasta la vista*, baby. True hope is severed from expectation. NYC girlies are married, breeding like Jodie Foster sans partner, or together like Ellen and Anne, then apart and then back together breeding. The 30-something lesbionic would never consider herself a 'Girlie of the Dawn'. She's too busy at home breastfeeding and thinking of Harry Potter's next book for the kiddies, subscribing to *Elle Decor* and doing the Martha Stewart thang. Don't ask, don't tell, is what I say. Most girlies I know who are partnered and doing the child moment have discontinued their curiosities for sex. They look more toward comfort, contentment and home decorations and furnishings. I've always had a problem with the word 'content'. I always picture cows chewing cud. This is 'content' for me. That's cool, but I'm still a selfish sex maniac and I still can't 'get no satisfaction'. I look 29, but I'm 35. I wander late at night like a hawk and I'm still sorting it out. So kill me, I'm a greedy girl with fucking and elevation on her mind!

There is an ancient cemetery on Stoke Newington Church Street in London. The Victorians sure knew how to keep splendour and decorum intact while jacking up your turn-on-level through death. This cemetery is hot. You just walk in there and you can smell the sex and the death all fertilised together. There is something sexy in its disintegration and its exalted Victorian ornamentation, no less the depravity that exudes around each headstone and each bramble bush. It's a wilderness and it is a popular Saturday-strolling, dog-walking and, of course, cruising spot. Boys are doing boys everywhere. Boys await other boys on every bench and every gravestone. In 1993 I was there with my fuck-love-she-thing and we had some amazing fights there. No, we did not fuck, we fought. But each time I walked away from her in flight, just around the bend a boy would follow me in quest of my boyness not realising the tricking going on. These miscalculations took on the proportions of a Marx Brothers' movie and I would always end up in hysterics by the time I exited the graveyard at sundown. The girl in question would run wildly, trying to catch up with me, while the guy thought there was going to be a *West Side Story* rumble and quickly turned the other way. Was there another female to save the day, take me to a tombstone and do me down? Of course not, no single female wanders London, no less New York, alone. I always felt like the only one, in London and in NYC. Maybe on rollerblades, maybe with a little yippy yappy dog as a protector or her screaming child but not à la carte.

Just a few months ago after five years of not visiting the Clit Club, I decided to go one hour before closing to see if there was some sort of specimen of a Friday night leftover that would fancy my eye. I knew ten times out of ten I would be disgusted, wander around the block, bust my way through the biker beer belly blunderings and feel my way toward Florent for an early breakfast.

This was as close as I came to a score. There was a waitress that already brought everything into 4 a.m. focus. Reminding me of the C-girl, a Sydney heart-breaker sort of boy raconteur, but without the swagger and the energy. C-girl is the one who broke the back of this camel. She is the one who sent me reeling back to New York City out of sickness that I would have to breathe in the same air as her. She was the perfect fuck buddy, the perfect specimen, no less the perfect trickster who knew how to do the worst sort of black magic on someone without her even realising it. Ignorance was bliss to her. Stupidity sometimes does save a life. It saved her, but ended mine. The waitress always looked confused, given that I couldn't take my eyes off her and always gave an expression of utter frustration mixed in with pure repulsion. See, when I looked at her, it all came flooding over me. The sensations must have made my face contort into some sort of gruesome configura-tion. Poor thing. Maybe someday I'll just tell her, 'You know, you remind me of someone.'

Sounds like a pick-up line, but little does she know. A whole world explodes each time I steal a glance.

Arriving from London three months ago, my best mate Deborah arrived with a bottle of champagne in her red banged-up Toyota. We were swigging furiously, full mouths exploding out of Kennedy en route back to NYC, bypassing Jamaica Queens, where my mother was dying of lung cancer. I would be with her for one month before she would die. I didn't know the whole story as I was lapping the yellow night away. I only knew that the next day I would be face to face with my mother who I had a life-long commitment to fighting it out with every day of our mother/daughter lives. I was praying we would not fight. Either way, I knew the time would be the last of times. Strength was beyond both of us as I made my entrance back into the New York City howl.

Since then I have been wandering. After the funeral,

December 31, I wandered into Jan 1. For the last few months I wander. I end up in the meat market and I simply make a passage very early in the 5 a.m. grey just to find the sun and make sure it still comes up. Just to remind myself.

The night my father died in 1996, I went to the woman I was working for at the time and who I had begun fucking. I didn't want to do anything but fuck. Fuck until I bled. Fuck until there was no more of me for her to enter into, with her hands, with her fist, with her elbow. I recall wanting her to ram her arm up to my mouth so that would stop the howl and the caw of refusal. I'm a top. I never let anyone fuck me like that. I walked Hampstead Heath in a June daze of overgrown grass fields where I came upon lovers entwined and hidden in the underneath of summer. I realised death brings me to the place of uncontrollable swampy black desire and bottomless pits of nothingness.

I remember that.

I remembered that when my mother died. I guess I lost the hunger to fuck girls in the recollection. The blood lust was gone, along with every other desire to dream on.

I've been a lesbionic since I saw *The Children's Hour* and fell in love with Shirley Maclaine. I was in the second grade and asked my mother what a 'lebeschian' was. No one could decipher the word, no less what this kid was talking about. My father kept asking me what the word was, trying to look it up in the dictionary. So much for my lesbionic career. I was already failing spelling and elocution with a fucking speech defect.

Growing up in the 70s I was taken with Walt Disney movies like *The Three Lives of Thomasina*, Leslie Ann Warrne's completely erotic *Cinderella* (yes, 'The Prince Is Having a Ball' was my favourite song) and of course Julie Andrews in *Thoroughly Modern Millie*. After that came the dysfunctional, drug-temptation: 'I need Prozac but it's the 70s' After-School Specials on TV such as *Go Ask Alice* and *Lisa Bright and Dark*. Then the boy bonding began with David Carradine's *Kung Fu* and of course *Starsky and Hutch* mostly for fashion. Who didn't want one of those Paul Michael Glaser big burly sheep sweaters? It was always a fashion moment with the guys.

Of course religious movies such as *Ben Hur* and *The Ten Commandments* did something to my sense of relating to the male protagonist. I didn't just 'want' Charlton Heston when Aurelius tests his speed in the galleys, pounding those hammers in the most homoerotic scene of Mr de Mille's movie. Testing and teasing to the 'beat' just to prove how fast he could row and how strong he really was. I was dying! No, I wanted to *be* Ben Hur. I wanted, as a strapping well-hung Ben, to bend that old powerful Roman down and nail him on that good Roman ship and make him my sugar daddy! Oh yeah! After that induction into male on male hunger, I made Barbie dress up as Ben Hur and as Moses and let them do their doll thing as dolls would do.

I always considered myself a boy when 'watching'. I think it was *Planet of the Apes* that nailed me down and changed everything. Heston really was every 70s girlie dreamdate at that point in cinema. I mean *Planet of the Apes* was and still is a totally phat and whacked-out film when it comes down to the animal and human scenario. But see, for me it went deeper. It went into Nova, the nympho cave girlie who I realised was the female that completely got me off. When he gets Nova and they do it in the cage, trust me, I didn't want to be Nova, I wanted to be the guy who gets to take that girl in front of everyone, audience of apes included. So much for the beginnings of needing to be watched and needing cave-girlies to send me to the moon and back.

I've always wondered about the geology of the fuck.

I astral-project these days.

I mean when in NYC I walk into Meow Mix and think

of Tallulah Bankhead's line, 'What does a girl have to do to get laid in a dump like this.' I mean really!

All this frustration leads me towards Amsterdam. It was one of those G.O.D. nights several years ago. Yeah, wandering endlessly again. That sandpaper feeling in your mouth sort of night. A night I would end up paying a prostitute to fuck me. Now, forgetting the rare moments of submissiveness aka, father's death, what's unusual is not the prostitute, more so that I let myself be fucked. I consider myself such a butch and such a dom in bed, on the street and in the toilets of certain London hotels. But the calling from Amsterdam was clear. I was just fucked over by Steve McQueen C-girl, 'Girlie of the Dawn' from Sydney, and I needed somehow to get over this. So I called in sick to my temp agency, took a train and then a very, very slow ferry and slurred my way towards Amsterdam. Everything was in slow motion at that point after being dumped by a youthful, smacked out, girl-boy thang. Yet, boringly enough, I found her irresistible. It was a love thang and a fuck thang that took me beyond anything I could have ever wanted. These days I don't want any more. Maybe it just takes time. I hate it when people say, 'oh, let it go, you'll meet someone else'. I hate that when people say that. They have no idea! For females in this fucked-up swamp, there ain't a hell of a lot to choose from these days. Given the Martha Stewart and breeding and bonding moment. Thirty-something lesbionics don't have a melting pot of options. Things are changing. More females of my persuasion are going towards guys or becoming guys. You get sick of the fucked-up ones who can't keep it together. Can't keep the excitement and the passion and the adventure alive, without either doing a kamikaze routine on themselves or an *In Cold Blood* routine on you. I digress. You meet someone for a reason. You fuck someone for no reason or for every reason in the world. There was no replacement for her. But there was relief for the moment and I was going to it.

I paid. Like I was supposed to. I requested the transaction.

And so I'm doomed. Doomed at being a G.O.D. in a carnal operation of calculated pick-ups in the asshole of the world. La Villete, Smithfield's and any other meat market is the place where prozzies would sell their wares. Cities change, prozzies stay the same, but the landscape buckles, rises, melts. The piers, the stink and the creep. The docks and sea fronts same as the meat markets, eroding and falling into the deep. In both places you will find me. Yeah, I'm romanticising and hoping for a time when I try to smell victory and hunger that will let itself rest for a bit. I think of Rome and the trannies there. The slithering snake life to it and the edgy deathlike coil of completion for a night. I feel like Marcello Mastroanni's character in Fellini's *La Dolce Vita*. He just can't get enough of the edge. He has it all, cool RayBan 60s sunglasses, pimpy, paparazzi shoes, but still wants that bleak blackness to carry on for another day and it's usually with a lady of indeterminate profession. He needs the void. The hole within the hole within the hole. And so this 30-something G.O.D. has become obsessed with paying for sex and falling through the wormhole via New York City.

I just need an encounter, a glance, a gaze, en route. In a passage of slipping, the veiling of the skin comes undone. Females cruising females. I only sense young boys now. They come close. In egoless curiosity. And the essence and vapour of these boys always alert me to the stench of the Sydney girl. The one that was perfect but not. The one that is longed for, encoded with desire. She was a trick that repeats itself over and over. The conquest of fleshy sadness elevated to pure bliss, just for a few hours. I would give everything right now to taste it all again. And then be damaged for another year. It's all about a moment of purity. Pure taking. Something Marc Almond calls 'beautiful evil' or just listen to his album *Open All Night*. Listen to his lyrics and that will explain everything. It's that darkness we're not willing to give up. It's a dark sin that keeps us alive and passionate and allows us not to fall into the cracks of mediocrity and suburbia and oblivion and nothingness.

There is a disorder of the senses. The stranger, the twist and the temptation. In Paris the prozzies are delectable to me, no less they laugh at my curiosity. Big, brawny and unattractive to me, but incredibly hardy and volatile and voluptuous. Never in a million years as a very androgynous female who salivates at boyish females would I expect this sort of behaviour from myself. And I'm not the type that would pay for sex. But money speaks. And it all seems so harmless to a certain woman who laughs and then just points for me to go upstairs and follow her. I don't speak French, so it all ends up quite a clumsy mess. But I need this strangeness, unfamiliarity and awkwardness. I also need the practice. To get close to this transaction that is quite empty and harmless. It's something I do in the dark because I need to. For now. That is what this is. It keeps my juices flowing. And why the fuck not? Why dry up in front of the TV or why cyberfuck in a dry ice fantasy of computerised automatic response? I need the flesh, the markings, the grabbing and the recollection of the stink and the sound, the groan and the sweat and the urge. I just need to see the need and all will be well.

Lesbian females are less than bold and no longer daring and fearless. I know, I'll be hung for this. But it is so true! They all look the same here in London. All the signifiers, hair, jackets T-shirts, backpacks. They represent a cliché and as Divine David said,

gay is superficial, wilfully ignorant, Hitlerian, homogenous, plastic, basically disgusting, and gay people because they put up with so much shit and they enjoy being stupid are the dinosaurs of the future. I mean, do I really have to become a total fucking moron to be worthy of love.

And I can't agree with him more. I'm not quite so sure what I'm saying here, I just consider myself a G.O.D. Fuck the lesbo moment.

The straight prozzies I meet become my heroes. Powerful in their service, attitude and appraisal. No bullshit, no drama, just straight up $100 for around the world, so to speak. I look for the fuck in the least 'lesbo' spaces. This is a new episode for someone who usually fucks girls and continues to keep herself intact. Now I pay to be fucked. And that's the only way I want it. For now.

So, I guess what I'm asking for here in this first article of the dawn, this new year, is the hope of finding a NYC brothel that caters to a female such as myself. I mean, I can't be the only one? I'm looking for *la place de jour*, where females can pay females to do them. And do them so good.

Girlie of the Dawn Den of Debauchery. I can see it now!

I'm envisioning a *Johnny Guitar* scenario. Head brothel-keeper is Joan Crawford's character. Tough, strapped in those tight cowboy trousers and pointy boots with sharp-lapelled starched shirt and we're ready to shake our groove thing, 'baby oh yeah'. A huge loft space on top of the meat market. Rooms for every fantasy and convenience catering to the female who wants it at 6 a.m. before her Goldman Sachs banker job, or the one who needs a 'bargain-basement' special student rate to keep her going for the weekend study binge. Red, like the blood of the meat market, like the scent of my deluge, like the dream of my heart for just a tiny whittled moment carving a picture of satisfaction and gold-sated appetites.

Ah, to dream and to envision such a bordello of the year 2000. If spas are making their rounds, my prediction is the brothel for the 'Girlie of the Dawn' will somehow make its way to your shores.

Now a lot of girlies must be saying, 'It's her problemo she can't even get laid in NYC.'

And I would answer, 'Darlin', ain't no problem, I just be needin' a better selection and I ain't seen it at Meow Mix, the Clit Club, or the barren midnight streets of NYC. Cause the girlies that I would want to do, just ain't walkin' these days, they havin' babies Ms Scarlet.'

So let me just pay, and fuck all the details.

Pay, fuck and go. Just the way I like it. And I'm sure a lot of other ladies would agree with me. More than they would care to admit, I'm sure!

So remember, no rest for the wicked and in the words of Marlene D: 'It took more than one man to make me change my name to Shanghai Lil.' Here's to the brothel, to the women that will make you eventually change your name and identity and for adventures that don't have to die once we hit thirty. Ms. Steak in the house and G.O.D.s in the house. Yo, yo, represent Dudette. No doubt.

Thatching
(and Other Rural Crafts)

Roxy Rhinestone

My editor (him wot, without knowing, pays ze bills for ze netsurfing round rubber and PVC sites) was uneasy about my series of articles on traditional Norfolk crafts.

'Look, Christina, it's kitsch. The readers want quaint charm. Not kitsch. Can you really claim that these craftsmen are keeping our rural heritage alive? They're incomers with mobile phones and degrees in media studies. When did they last tug their forelocks? Never. When did they last turn up to work on their dobbins? Never. Is there one single one of them that doesn't drive a four by four? No. Their customers have to email them to commission a job. Go on, deny it, Christina.'

I lay as far back as I could in the dud typing chair and laid it on the line. 'I'm exposing the post-modern, Clive. That's the key to this article, that these guys are craftsmen in a chic way. It's a social comment, a riposte.'

'And you've got a degree in Shiteology.'

'Clive, it's old hat to seek authenticity. It's just like with tourism now. Gone are the days of the *untourist* seeking the unspoilt. Now you have to be a *post*-tourist who relishes the tacky, deliberately chooses that which is fabricated.'

'Bollocks!'

I ignored him, as he intended me to do. He was rather enjoying playing the lout.

'You have to enjoy the *in*authentic, Clive: the Blackpool not the unspoilt village full of locals who've never seen a black man before. Similarly our post-heritage readers can enjoy craftsmen doing it in jogging bottoms and US army boots, instead of baggy old corduroys and braces. These are a new breed of craftsmen who are fascinating *because* they have Psion organisers in their back pockets and know international airports better than they know the county market square! ... Anyway, thatchers and millwrights need their mobiles for safety if they're working in isolated places. Suppose they fell?'

Clive carried on pacing. He learned the art from watching Clark Kent's editor at the Daily World in early *Superman* movies.

'Do they even know what they're doing, these posh hippies? Are they really craftsmen or just bodgers with the gift of the gab?'

I'd say they're highly skilled with their hands and their tools, I thought, my thighs still damp from my last encounter. 'Yes, they've picked the brains of old men, and then applied modern ecological knowledge too.'

'So the series should work for the Green readers then,' he calculated, backing off.

'Oh yeah. Leave it to me, Clive. This will win us awards.'

He went away and read my latest piece, then came back and complimented me, leaning over my shoulder and into my Applemac like it was a mirror in which he could see his own worth.

'Ace. You've really got inside these guys, Christina.'

I didn't say, well, actually they've all got at least six inches inside *me*, thank you very much.

But in terms of my orgasms it had indeed been a successful series so far. I'd interviewed a marshman with a first in Physics who put down his scythe and harvested me, not the reeds, most scientifically for several very slurpy hours in the sun. And Jamie, an ex-Para who was fixing Scouters windmill, had been all for fucking me while I was lashed to the sailstock. The trouble was that a force five wind had got up and the sails would have whizzed around too hairily even for my taste. So instead we'd done it on the fantail platform overlooking all the tiny cruisers on the Broads far below. I'd also had the pleasure of shagging a man who made mawkins, which is Norfolk dialect for the fancy scarecrows. A former pyrotechnics choreographer for music festivals, he attached the scarecrows to burning rope that went off with a crack every twenty minutes to frighten rooks away from the peafields. Traditional method. As he'd lashed me, at my invitation, to the scarecrow, this was rather interesting.

My favourite so far was the master thatcher, last Tuesday.

I had dressed in expectation that there would be ladders to climb, on the grounds that if he wasn't worthy of seduction I would at least enjoy giving him something to gawp at. A white cream skirt with purple lace knickers, and a violet bra whose existence was far from discreet under a buff blouse with buttons that happily undo quickly. The interview was to take place at a hundred-foot medieval thatched barn, deep in the country near Hickling Broad.

There was no one around down Ticklebelly Lane, the farmer on holiday and the tourists far away on the water. The guy was working alone that day. The master thatcher, Ken, was sinewy and brown and wore a T-shirt saying My place, tonight. We shook hands. So that I could get a sense of the texture of his basic material, he sat me on the reeds in the back of his long wheelbase Land Rover while we did the initial talk. I liked the smell of his sweat, it was sweet and stark and mixed with the moist grassy stench of reeds from salty marshes. The reeds pressed against my thighs, warm from the sun as the soft top of his Land Rover was down.

'I'll just brief you on the basics,' he said, but running his appraising eyes over *my* basics. Yes, a brown and sturdy body, good and tasty. And yes, *briefly* clad. This fish didn't seem to be biting, though. So I shifted around to enable him to see my breasts in profile. Still he continued to lecture – which was very irritating. Was he *really* taking me at word, as a journo not a woman!

'The water reeds we use are both different lengths and different types.'

I wondered about *his* reed – medium length and nicely shaped, I thought, but he was giving me a thorough talk. 'Lengths. There are three main lengths you can buy: short, three to four foot; medium, four foot to five foot six; and long – five foot six to six foot. The three types are tapered, cylindrical and big-topped.' I was hoping that his was the big-topped sort.

'The big-topped is most sought after when it's long and coarse,' he explained.

Ah, I bet, I thought, and asked as I licked my lips, 'In what quantities do they, er . . . come?'

'In fathoms, six bunches make a fathom. And in a bunch are hundreds of reeds, mixed up, lengths and types. It's all regulated by the British Reed Growers' Association. I only get the best reeds, from Salhouse and Ranworth. Reed quality varies with the different years and locations. Some like reeds from estuarine salt marshes but I prefer freshwater marshlands. I buy the best and I buy in bulk because the quality varies from year to year.'

'It sounds like a pricey job for an impermanent result?' Would he never smile? If he was not going to go for me then maybe I should just get on with being a journo and then get out. I had, after all, several other fish to fry.

'Say £6,500 for a three-bedroom house with a thousand square feet of roof. My roofs should last seventy years. But because there's so much interest in using local building materials, the reed price is sky high. It used to be about eight pence a bundle in the 1960s. Now it's about £1.70 a bundle plus VAT, though the foreign stuff is cheaper and a lot of customers want a cut-price job doing. You've got ladders and transport expenses to cost in, too.'

The mention of *bed*rooms had me going again. And how long could *he* last. However, Ken clearly had his mind on giving me information that would gain him useful publicity. He drove me round several neighbouring villages to point out roofs in different states of construction. His Land Rover juddered, as those old ones do, which really turned me on, that and watching the gear stick with its large black knob vibrating between us.

'Some people want theirs tidying up, see. Others just liven up their old thatch with a new ridge. The thorough ones, or the ones with money, want you to strip off and re-thatch.' I listened hard to see if he said *strip* with relish, but still he didn't seem to have his mind on me.

'And see the ridges?'

I nodded.

'The patterns on these decorative block ridges show which master thatcher has done it. We all have our different signatures, just like the fishing families each have their own patterns for knitting into guernseys. The trouble is that with all these conservation buggers around you have to get Listed Buildings permission to change the pattern. What you take down should go up

194

again, they say. It leaves no opportunity for customer or thatcher creativity.'

'And so you lose job satisfaction? And presumably it's against the whole spirit of the craft, which was for thatchers to express their individuality?' I thought a bit of incisive empathy might encourage him to express his individuality right up my fanny but no, still seriousness.

'Exactly.'

'. . . What's your signature, Ken?'

'It's personal.'

'Oh, go on.'

'Well, depending on the circumstances, I might, er, show you later, Christina.'

This sounded promising. Maybe.

We got back to Ticklebelly Lane and I took some basic personal details – like he lived in a rainbow-painted converted WW2 ambulance at the leeward side of the dunes near Eccles, with a satellite TV dish so he could see the more international quality news on CNN. He'd trained at the thatching school Knuston Hall in Northampton, then bought a thatching franchise. His next-door neighbours in an old charabanc were two Hungarian circus jugglers, flanked by a guy who tested new software for a computer magazine. Ken himself had studied Economics at Keele and gone into futures in the 80s.

'Did you leave with the crash?'

'No. I ditched it because I wanted a different relationship with unpredictability. I thrive on uncertainty but I also wanted some continuity with past effort and future solidity. Hence this job, and the roofs built to last. Conversely, I had a loft in Docklands that was just going up and up and up in value. And that bored me. Too steady. I wanted a closer relationship with impermanence. Hence the fragile mobile home on the edge, a location that risks flooding from uncontrollable seas.'

While I was still taking in the complexity of his tastes he decided I had been informed enough and began the demonstration on this barn.

'Follow me,' he commanded, and I watched his bottom admiringly as he went up the ladder. Those were surely rural labourer's authentic moleskins he was wearing. I then enjoyed hitching up my skirt to follow. Then stood at the top of the first ladder resting my breasts and belly against the hot thatch he'd set down so carefully over the last few weeks. It was like sunbathing against a huge nest. He was heading up from the gutter line to the ridge, twelve feet above me.

'See,' he called down, 'a thatcher does most of their work standing up or kneeling on ladder rungs. A lot of pressure, bone on wood.' I was rather desperately fancying the pressure of his pelvic bones on mine. And the rhythm in the sun. Yes, it could be wonderful. Instead he was just on about his clothes.

'So, Christina, you need good soles on your boots, and kneelers. That's why I've got these knee pads stitched into my trousers.'

Could be useful, I thought, trying to keep my eyes from gleaming. Men were often too whingy about their knees for my appetites. After all, what's a bit of carpet burn between friends?

'Usually we work in teams, or with an apprentice. If it's a good sunny day and you're working well, putting two hundred bundles a day on a roof, you want someone to fetch it up and down the ladder for you. Saves time, energy – though it breaks the monotony. Thatching's monotonous, not idyllic. I spend a lot of time fantasising.'

I wondered if I could ask about the subject of this but his sudden grin said enough. It was like a flash of hope after all the business talk. Maybe he could only put his mind to sex when he was in high places. He was sitting astride the ridge of the roof, like a cowboy on a horse. I thought he'd look good in chaps, no trousers underneath and was imagining his prick, a nice bit of golden wrinkly flesh set against the dry brown verticals of the reeds. 'Today, now, I'm picking the rubbin, which means to cut off the loose bits of thatch to make the roof look tidy.'

I watched him cut the lengths with his knife and began to imagine how he might neaten me off. Like cutting the hairs on my head. Like cutting my other hairs, a close trim followed by serious study of the underlying structure.

A mobile went.

'Yours, I think,' he said, patting his.

It would be Anna, my lover, announcing that she was back from Phuket. I ignored it. I wanted my ridge trimmed, now. And the rest.

'Not going to answer?'

'This is more important,' I called, without specifying that it was lust not research to which I referred.

'Doing the ridges is more interesting than labouring on the main plain areas. You can generally thatch about a hundred square feet a day and this barn is a hundred feet long with a pitch of thirty foot, so I've been on it for ages.'

'Boring?'

'Could be if I don't have a good fantasy going . . .'

'You know,' he said companionably, 'thatchers are often asked to bury things in roofs – lucky charms, photos, newspapers of that date, love letters.'

'And do you?'

'Oh yes. I've got something in mind today, actually.'

'Mmm?' There was something in his tone that warmed me.

'Something very important . . . To do with you . . . A rather delicate object.

'Hmm?'

'Yes.'

'Going to tell me, Ken?'

197

'I might.'

'Go on.'

'Purple lace, in fact.'

This was more like it.

'I don't know if I could get them off, standing on this ladder,' I pretended. 'I mean, standing on one leg.'

'I, er, think I can help you,' he said. 'Turn round.'

I turned with my bottom to the thatch, my feet still on the highest rung. And he slid down the roof to straddle me. Pressing his body against mine, smelling of marshes and birds and head, he pushed his hand up my skirt and pulled my pants down, not with speedy expediency but slowly. Inch by inch, watching my eyes as they came down. Methodically.

All the time he pressed his thighs harder and hotter against me. Despite being on top of a ladder, I felt more and more relaxed, as if I was just lying back in a hayrick.

And when the knickers were off then he, smiling, undid the traditional belt of his traditional moleskins and demonstrated the ancient craft of grinding a delighted maiden (well, almost) on a thatched roof throughout a summer afternoon.

When he later helped me down the ladder, somewhat shakily, there amid the reeds in the back of his pick-up he further demonstrated the long-enduring qualities of traditional knee pads. I testify, dear reader, that the old rural skills and garments are often the best.

Three days later he emailed me a message: 'Look at the ridge decoration on Ticklebelly Barn.'

It seemed like a kind of boast.

I drove past. There on the ridge, where each thatcher leaves his special design, was not just any old meaningless criss-cross of split hazel of the ornamented ridge but a very purposive pattern. A long horizontal line of linked yoni and phallus. And the occasional letter C, for Christina. I felt very proud.

Ant, the photographer, took the pictures. I bought seven prints for myself and preened at home, the thatch ridge all over my bedroom wall. I was longing to drive people past the barn and show them, see if they got it. The picture that was used in the paper I captioned, 'A ridge of mysterious and unusual design'.

But then in the pub someone told Ant that Ken put on ridges the details of every bird he was currently poking.

'It's like a cross between love message graffiti made by pilots, and the Judy Chicago exhibition that made famous women the sum of their fannies, isn't it, Christina?'

'It's a bloody liberty,' I retorted.

'Don't suppose that one's about you?'

'Of course not. I don't mix business with pleasure.'

'Much!'

Clive, unaware of all this, said the piece was so passionate that my series on rural craftsmen could continue. I would have carried on anyway. These excuses for encounters with rough hands and razor brains were too good to miss out on. And the piquancy was in taking part in history, considering if women in the past had similarly shagged under thatches and up against scarecrows.

I was looking forward to my session with the harness maker. There was such a lot to be done with leather straps and buckles. And then, having a taste for metal, I could set up a session with a blacksmith; bent backwards naked over an anvil sounded attractive, being gently threatened by heavy iron tongs or even a white-hot rod.

I couldn't image what I'd do with mole catchers. But I'd just heard of a besom maker, and I'd always wanted to be lightly beaten by a birch broom. This one used heather and sold them to racing stables. Heather was, apparently, good for sweeping the spaces between cobbles. And there are quite a lot of cracks in me that would relish the firm approach that only a master craftsman could supply.

Nita

Kathryn Anne Dubois

'*D*o you know why your mother gave you to me?'
the man with the onyx eyes and deep voice asked.
His lightly calloused hands slid down her arms, stroking
as he spoke, to entwine with her fingers and then up
again. Slow rhythmic strokes.

Nita was confused. This man wished to buy her. That
she understood. But not for pleasure like Serena was
bought two years before by a younger man from the
city. Nita would be a wife, her mother explained.

She studied this strange man with his gentle touch,
who had laughed when she asked about his fields. Nita
was strong and had been taught well the duties of wife,
yet he told her that she would not be cooking for him.

A moist breeze drifted through the open windows of
her family's hut, riffling the curtained door between the
two rooms. The thin cotton of her dress clung to her in
the heavy humid air.

His eyes glittered as he slipped one long finger under
the thin strap of her dress. Nita didn't understand many
things, but her sixteen years had taught her some ways
of men. They liked touching women. She had seen this
at the market, male hands slipping under the skirts of

village girls and the flushed pleasure in the men's faces – the playful horror in the girls as they slapped away the seeking hands.

A strange tightness between Nita's legs tugged at her when she would see this.

'Are you afraid?' the man murmured, lifting the strap and letting her dress slip off her shoulders with the movement. The tattered lace edge hung off the small swell of her breast just short of her nipple, which poked high against the worn fabric. No man had seen her, but she was curiously unafraid. The man smiled, and although he was old – older than her uncles – she liked the rough shadow of his beard and his lips, soft-looking against the dark male features.

She knew now he would touch her, and she knew little of this. Only once had she seen.

It was in their hiding cave that she saw her brother with Serena. He was eighteen, and he had boasted that he had long given up the foolish cave games of his childhood. Nita was disappointed, but she went alone. It was then that she saw them.

Her brother's organ was stiff and long, jutting out from his trouser opening as he lay at the mouth of the cave beside Serena, the sun slipping through just enough that Nita could see. Serena's legs were spread, her skirt hiked to her waist. Liam dipped one long finger between her pink woman folds. He stroked slowly, idly, slipping the tip of his wet finger, glistening from her, along her creases as soft moans murmured past her lips. Nita learned later about that wetness. The tightening had brought it to her, the moist heat, but she never explored her own plump lips as her brother did with Serena. It seemed wrong – it was for men.

'What are you thinking, little one?' The man studied her quietly, tipping his chin down to look into her eyes. His eyes were warm and dark, searching hers. 'You don't look away? You are proud, this pleases me.' His gaze melted into her. 'Tell me what you think.'

'You will touch me,' she replied simply, for she knew not what he meant.

A small smile curved his lips. 'Yes.'

Then he bared her breast, feeling its weight. Her small high breast fitted perfectly in his palm. He examined her closely, wetting his finger and stroking the tip, which was the colour of dark berries.

The pleasant feel of it was new to her, and she liked watching her nipple pout and harden under his touch.

'Your breasts are beautiful, delicate and small, but your nipples are large. They are ripe and eager. I find the contrast erotic. Do you understand?'

His thoughts were foreign, but he brought the tightness to her, in her woman folds. Her skin grew hot.

She heard the outer door open, the plywood swinging on its rusty hinges. The man still played with her, pinching her nipple between his fingertips, making no attempt to stop even as she heard her mother's voice calling to them. This squeezing made her full and restless, her sex lips throbbing with each pinch. She gave a little whimper.

Nita was unsure. Her mother told her to listen to the man, take care to give no insult.

Her mother drew aside the curtain and stepped into the room. The man gave no notice but Nita met her mother's eyes, questioning. The nervous glance her mother returned and the curt nod toward the man was a message for Nita to obey.

Nita's face turned hot. Would the man lift her skirt now? Stroke her like Liam did to Serena? The thought made Nita very warm and a light shiver ran down her spine.

The man brushed her cheek with his fingertips and then drew her strap up. 'I am well pleased.' He turned to her mother. With a short bow, her mother covered her face with her apron and rushed out the door.

Later, when Nita left, her mother cried and thanked her. She was a good girl to help her family, her mother told her many times that day. Her uncles did not come. It was hard to leave the small ones, but, like Serena before her, she would be dutiful.

The man, Enriquez, had a shiny jeep and told her she would have fine clothes in the city. He was only forty-five, not so old he assured her.

'You can speak, little one. You need not be afraid.'

The jeep bumped and tilted as it made its way down the mountain, passing villagers on foot and goats grazing.

Nita wasn't afraid. She was lost. She knew not what to expect. She would not speak until she knew.

His house was grand with trees inside but no animals. Floors of polished rock as smooth as water shone beneath her bare feet and wells spilled water into gleaming basins. His lights needed no pumping or batteries and they lit every room. It was like the magazines the missionaries left.

A woman, Maria, older than her mother, washed her in a pool upstairs and spoke to her of things she knew not.

'The Senior is a good man, odd, an artist. You will like it here. Tomorrow you will be his wife and we will become good friends.'

Maria squeezed sweet-smelling soap on Nita's scalp and she scrubbed her head. 'Such lovely hair,' she murmured.

She stood Nita before her and dried her, examining her nipples and hips. 'Turn around, child,' Maria whispered. 'Yes.' She stroked her small buttocks. 'The Senior will enjoy you.'

Nita saw the girl who was herself in the looking glass as Maria saw her. Her nipples were large like the man said, and she thought again how he touched them. She was thin but her muscles were sharp from her work in the valley and because of long walks to the village.

Maria smoothed scented cream over her taut skin and her flesh came alive. This was new, too.

Her gown for sleeping was white and very thin. Nita could see her dark mat of hair and her nipples. Maria smiled.

He came to her soon with the dark liquid her uncles never allowed. And as she drank from the carved glass, a cool breeze sifted through his sleeping room and under the hem of her gown. As the liquid warmed her belly, she grew light-headed and even smiled at the man Enriquez.

'Come here, Nita.' His voice was rough and soft and his eyes like flames. It was then she saw his organ, like Liam's, hard and thick, coming out of his robe. She shouldn't look, but she did.

He took her hand and brought it to the round tip, red and warm. An animal sound came from his lips when she explored the pearly drop seeping out. Liam had that, too, before he caught Nita watching and then got angry.

She wondered. She wanted to lick it and didn't know why. She didn't know much, only that he would want to touch her.

With sure hands he untied the ribbons that caught at the shoulders of her gown and let it drop to her feet.

She liked it when he skimmed his palms over her breasts and down her belly, then turned her to stroke her bottom. He smiled when she made no protest at his urgings. 'Turn this way, now this, let me see. You are beautiful.'

She felt pleased and the tightening was pushing at her, coming in little throbs.

Then his tongue was on her, licking her nipples and down her belly. She watched with curiosity as his tongue travelled down to her thighs and even her feet.

He scooped her up in his arms and laid her on the large, high bed covered with cool cloth, soft for sleeping on. Her nipples tingled with the breeze and she thought of when he wet her nipple with his finger.

Tonight he wet them with his tongue. She liked the cool breeze on the wetness and spread her legs without thinking.

He growled like the creatures of the mountains before his head fell between her thighs. She swallowed her breath when he touched her little nub of tightness and licked. Her squeal of delight brought soft laughter to this strange man named Enriquez.

The pleasant joy touched her everywhere, down to her toes, and she wriggled and danced on the bed when his lips suckled her like a baby at teat.

Her body was in flames and every part of her skin ached for his touch. When he next stood at the foot of the bed, she feared he would leave. She wanted more.

'I'm going to fuck you now, little one.' His voice was gravelly and his breathing hard as he dropped his robe. Nita didn't know his words but his organ looked angry. He held it firmly and climbed once again onto the bed.

'Spread yourself,' he commanded, his tone gruff. Nita obeyed.

He kneeled between her knees and pushed her legs up. Her sex was wide for him. Would he stroke and touch her with his organ?

She watched as he separated her sex lips with one hand and, with the other, guided his organ to her swollen folds.

Then she felt the pressure. His organ was spreading her and her eyes flew to his. She didn't speak, just stared.

'This is fucking,' he said, his voice tortured and then his eyes closed. He moaned the animal noise.

Nita pulled away but he grabbed her hips and pushed himself into her, quick and hard. She bit back the pain, would not speak, but her woman folds burned. He filled her. The power and strength of him, the thickness was splitting her apart. When she struggled against him, he rocked in yet farther, up to her waist.

He grunted and settled against her, his weight strong and large, keeping her still. Just when she thought she couldn't stand any more he began to move. She cried out, but he stifled her with his tongue, plunging into the soft depths of her mouth, his tongue tangling with hers. She bit his tongue. She didn't mean to. He growled in response and plunged into her, over and over. He pushed her knees up and sank deeper still.

She turned her head away from him. When she opened her eyes she saw in the looking glass that he had propped himself on his elbows and was watching as he entered her. Her knees were drawn high and her breasts swelled, the tips pointed as though reaching for his lips. He licked them, the tip of his tongue circling and teasing. She felt the answering tug in the tight nub between her legs and the pulling as he sank into her more easily now.

She spread her thighs wider and the pull across the little nub grew tighter and she moaned. Then he stroked her with his thumb. She shuddered and arched to him.

He ploughed her and bit her nipples, all the while stroking with his thumb and the pleasure grew until her whole body tightened – too tight.

She bit into his shoulder as she burned. She punched at him, hitting. She would explode, die.

And then she did. Her body racked and shuddered under him, the warm heat of pleasure stripping through her quickly and making her shake. She cried at the bliss she felt, the delight over every inch of her body. Then she collapsed.

After a long moment, she opened her eyes to him. He loomed above her, his chest hard and shaped with muscle, the dark mat of hair spongy and soft-looking.

She ran her fingers along the bulge of his arms and he quivered beneath her touch.

'That is fucking,' he whispered and then he arched his neck and closed his eyes. She thought he was thinking, but then he growled deep in his throat and shoved himself deep. He grimaced, the cords of his neck rigid, and then she felt him pumping into her. His organ throbbed.

He lowered his head and buried his lips in her neck, breathing hard.

It was not long before Nita realised this was her job, this fucking.

Enriquez would not allow her to cook or clean. Maria convinced him to let Nita tend the flowers, but she was to wear only a sundress when she did so, with no panties. He liked to slip his hand under her skirt when he wished. Now she knew what those male hands wanted at market.

Sometimes his fingertips ran lightly over her lips, while other times he would slip one long finger into her and then lick off her sweetness.

She grew to like this sex play and his gentle examinations of her body, the petting and sucking, the stroking and teasing her, like she was a ripe fruit – a feast for his pleasure.

In time she learned to suck him and lick with skill. The feel of his seed spilling over her nipples excited her, the liquid hot and smooth. She massaged it into her skin, stimulating her nipples and licking off the stickiness from her fingertips.

'Stroke yourself,' he would say to her after he spent himself like this and she would. He liked to watch her play with her aroused lips, the little bud hard with tension and sensitive as she stroked and pinched herself. Many times he would get hard again while watching her and spill over her sex lips as she convulsed gently under his lecherous gaze. The flood of warm liquid at the moment of her crisis heightened her bliss.

As her breasts grew into her nipples he became distant and sulking. At first his displeasure confused her, but as her hips rounded and she grew bolder in their sex he rejected her. By the time she was eighteen, he hardly touched her, and she was left bereft and wanting.

He lost himself in his art now. She could arouse no passion in him. Maria comforted her, but could not explain.

The men he met with praised his work. They saw the longing and the torture of his drawings. Sensuous lines and shadows drew the eye to the centre of his paintings, always sad figures, usually indecently clad, women whose nipples were red and pouting against their milk-white skin unlike Nita who was brown, her nipples large and dark.

'Go to him,' Maria murmured as the men smoked their Cuban cigars and twirled their brandy in large snifters, discussing the work of Toulouse-Lautrec and Matisse.

Marie tugged Nita's fitted black dress so that her breasts swelled dangerously over the delicate piping of the scooped neck. She then slid her hand through the side slit and drew down the top of Nita's stockings, allowing the elastic lace to peek through. Maria ripped the slit so it travelled halfway up Nita's thigh.

'He will like this,' Maria explained, 'when he sees the eyes of the other men on you.' She slid her fingertips over Nita's nipples and the surprise of it caused Nita's tits to swell and harden. Maria gave them a final pinch and they stood at attention. 'You have no panties?'

'No,' Nita assured her.

'Go.' Maria handed her a tray of drinks, and she entered the heavy-panelled drawing room with trepidation, unsure of Enriquez's response. She was never privy to his work sessions and only showed herself at select parties, draped as he had instructed, to adorn her body and tempt the male guests. But never was her dress as provocative as when she dressed for him only, as she was today. But now his colleagues would see how this dress moulded her body with no underclothes to confine her. Her breasts swayed and moved under the filmy fabric, the feel of it stimulating her nipples as much as the thoughts of the men's eyes on her.

Enriquez gave a start when he saw her. The men's heads turned in her direction. She registered their instant interest by the light in their eyes and the drop of their mouths. A man with dark wavy hair tied at the nape of his neck leaned forward and studied her, the curl of his lips revealing his pleasure.

'What is it, Nita?' Enriquez snapped.

She stopped abruptly, the tray teetering its contents. The young man with the ponytail leaped up and took it from her, placing it gingerly on the coffee table, his eyes now level with her cleavage.

'You may go now,' Enriquez ordered.

'Enriquez.' The deep voice of another man came from the armchair. The amusement in his dark brown eyes melted over her. 'Is this lovely creature your wife? No wonder you've kept her hidden all this time.'

Enriquez waved his hand dismissively.

'Do you paint her?' The question came from a large framed man perched on the edge of the couch beside her. 'If not, perhaps you should,' he suggested, while his eyes raked over her as though she were an object rather than a woman. With a surprised jolt, she felt his cool palm on the silk stocking of her thigh and then he stroked.

Enriquez appeared not to notice or he didn't care. So deprived was she of sexual touch that she welcomed his boldness and longed for him to slip his fingers between her thighs and caress her. The lewd thought brought moisture to her sex and she throbbed deliciously, so quickly aroused. Instead, she half-heartedly pushed down on his wrist. The other men watched with delight.

Enriquez seemed mildly curious, making no move to stop him. The man slid his hand up further, until it was impossible to miss his hand travelling up her skirt, over her hips, and then around to the front of her belly. Another few inches and his arm would hike up her hem, allowing the slit to reveal her naked sex for all to see.

She groaned at the thought of exposing herself to the male audience and then smiled at the thought, suddenly wanting to spread herself wide for them to feast their eyes on.

'Strip her,' Enriquez ordered nonchalantly. 'See if she makes a good subject.' The men surrounded her quickly and in one sweeping motion they slid off her dress and gazed at her as she stood before them in nothing but her black silk stockings and heels.

She caught her reflection in the long gilded mirror. The curve of her buttocks, high and rounded, and her breasts full and heavy with nipples like large copper pennies. She reached up instinctively to squeeze and pinch the ache from them as her arousal grew.

The male eyes danced with lust and their bulges strained against the thin fabric of their trousers. She needed them. She ached to be filled.

One seemed to sense her urgency and slid one finger between her legs and then let it ease into her hot wet depths. He pushed at her clit with his thumb and she exploded. Warm convulsions tore through her, causing her to collapse within the circle of men.

They smiled and laughed as they laid her out on the floor and lifted her knees. To her shame, they spread her wide.

'She's soaked, and I get the first taste,' the man with the gravelly voice chuckled as he dove between her thighs, sucking and licking, thrusting his tongue deep.

Enriquez stood aside and watched, a mixture of

disgust and pride etched in his expression as he allowed each man to take their turn, each one bringing her to greater heights of ecstasy with their tongues and their fingers but, still, it was not enough. She needed to be filled.

'Can we take her, Enriquez?' the handsome man with the wavy dark hair asked. When Enriquez nodded, he pulled on his zipper and yanked out his massive cock. 'Place her against the wall,' he growled, his voice vibrating with lust. 'Spread yourself wide and open yourself with your fingers. Show me lots of wet pink.'

The other two men lifted her and held her against the smooth floral wallpaper. Her husband's eyes glittered. She watched him reach into his trousers and release himself. His eyes closed on a groan and then opened again as he slid his hand around the gnarled veins that ran along his cock and circled its head. Her husband gave her a soft smile just as she felt the pony-tailed man take her hand and bring it to her own sex.

Enriquez's eyes dropped to her fingers as she spread herself for the man crouched in front of her, his large purple-veined cock hard and angry.

He aimed the wet tip of pearly come over her clit and teased her first, slipping and sliding over her sensitised bud. The tantalising heat and pleasure tore through her until she knew soon that she would be begging all the men to fuck her.

'You like that, little one?' It was Enriquez's voice that rose above the others as he stroked his member faster and groaned.

She nodded and whimpered, thrusting her hips harder against the swollen cock, reaching up to offer herself, yearning for him to impale her.

'Pinch her tits,' Enriquez ordered. 'She likes that.'

A large male hand on each side of her covered a breast and pulled and pinched on her large tits, scraping with their thumbnails, the friction agonisingly delicious. They pinched hard, making the pleasure that stripped through her a painful ache.

'Please,' she whimpered. She spread her legs wider, pulling back her sex lips, fully exposing herself. Enriquez's eyes riveted on her pink folds and he licked his lips. She imagined his lips on her, wet and soft, full, the way he used to pleasure her. She longed for him.

The man positioned himself at her entrance and thrust deep. She cried out and he groaned.

'You are so tight,' he moaned. 'I don't think Enriquez has used you in a while.' He grinned lasciviously and hilted deeper.

Enriquez sprang off his seat, his cock bobbing before him. 'Get off her,' he ordered.

The man looked surprised and then imploring. 'Let me finish,' he pleaded.

'Not now,' Enriquez snapped. 'Let me at her.'

He dragged the man away and shooed off the men at her side, dropping to his knees to lick her, long hot swipes between her swollen lips, his tongue darting inside and then flicking along the tip of her clitoris.

'No more,' she begged. 'Please fill me, my husband.'

He growled deep in his throat and took her down onto the rug with him. 'Sit on me,' he demanded.

She straddled his powerful body and eased herself down on his throbbing member, watching it fill her and disappear between her tender folds.

He groaned and arched up, sinking deeper. She fell across his chest, rubbing her nipples across his coarse wiry hairs.

It was then she remembered their audience and wondered about the sight her bottom made, enticingly tilted up to the three erect men surrounding her.

The handsome man's penis was wet and glistening from her. He grinned at her and ran this thumb along his length until it too glistened with moisture and then he placed himself behind her. She saw her husband nod to the man and then felt the man's hands on her warm bottom, stroking her full globes. She squirmed with pleasure at the feel of it, but then gasped when she felt his thumb probing her most secret place. She tightened at the intrusion and he stopped.

Her husband crooned to her. 'Open yourself to my friend.'

She straightened. *Was this done?*

He pinched her nipples hard, sending waves of desire cascading through her body. When the tall man, who had been standing aside, dropped to his knees beside them and watched, she shamelessly grabbed his hand, bringing his fingers to where she and her husband joined.

The stranger stroked her clitoris with deft fingers as her husband fucked her with slow sure thrusts. The heat of pleasure grew quickly and she gave herself over to the torturous stimulation with wild abandon. The probing thumb of the man behind her pushed gently, just passing her tight rim. She felt herself open and welcome the invasion as her pleasure grew.

'Ah,' the man beside her chuckled. 'She is liking that now.' He petted and swirled his fingertips over her hardened nub.

The man behind eased her forward so that she laid once more against Enriquez's chest. She rested her head along the warm corded muscles of her husband as she felt the man in back press his thumb deep into her tiny hole, probing gently. She pushed against him, wanting to be filled.

Her husband reached around and grabbed her buttocks, spreading her wider, and then she felt the thick pressure.

The man was pressing her with his cock. The pleasure pain was shocking. Her husband slid his penis out almost completely as the other man sought entrance.

'Oh,' she moaned. 'It's too big.'

Her husband pinched her nipples again while the men who watched stroked her sex lips and teased and played with her. She opened to the pleasure of so many male hands at once, each of their faces filled with lust for her. The power of their need filled her as much as did their bodies.

The cock started sinking into her thickly, the feel of it hot and tight in her virgin hole. She gasped when she glanced in the mirror to see herself impaled by two men, the one behind slipping slowly between her buttocks, easing in, his member hot and throbbing. He pinched her bottom and then spanked her and laughed.

The other men chuckled as her initial expression of alarm turned quickly to a groan of pleasure. He spanked her again and thrust between her bottom. The hot shocking feel of it sent her desire soaring and caused her to moan aloud.

'Fuck every hole,' her husband growled as he slipped into her again, fully and deeply as the man behind withdrew.

They alternated thrusts, in perfect synchronisation, as though they had done this before.

Nita was tight with arousal, moaning with each thrust, slick and smooth, slipping easily in front and then behind. 'Faster,' she demanded as they kept up the steady rhythm, and as the man behind alternated stroking her hot globes and then spanking her. The tall man turned her face to him and offered his penis. She licked at it greedily. He held the back of her head and guided himself between her lips.

'Ah,' he sighed with relief as she engulfed him down to his root and then slipped her lips along his shaft in withdrawal. He pumped gently, his fingers sifting through her hair.

'Mmm, she is lovely this one. Such beautiful tits, such clever lips. I want to fuck her next but I don't think I can last with her skilful . . . oh . . . oh.' He held her head and pumped his seed down her throat. Nita milked him and squirmed and rocked her hips against the two cocks impaling her.

They both thrust up as one, splitting her apart, the pleasure unbearable. She came in long shuddering groans as they pumped furiously into her, releasing their semen in hot thick spurts. Their hot sticky liquid seeped from all her openings, her mouth, her bottom, her cleft. Then she felt the third man come all over her nipples.

He laughed when she smoothed his seed over her engorged nipples and massaged the silky cream into her breasts.

The men sighed and crawled upright, throwing themselves onto chairs and sofas, hastily drawing their pants up from around their ankles and belting them. Her husband reached for his box of Cuban cigars and offered it around.

With a curt wave of his hand, he instructed her to serve them their coffee. 'We have work here. And you've interrupted us.'

When she started to protest, he levelled a hard glare. She paused a moment before giving him a sly smile and then her gaze swept over the men collapsed around the room.

With a careless toss of her hair, she reached down, picked her dress off the floor, and walked with a spring to her step, straight out the door.

The Trouble with Guys

Verena Yexley

'No, Tony, I'm not cancelling my date with Paul. I told you when we started going out months ago I'm not interested in settling down with any one man. You're a sweet guy and we've had good times, but I have no intention of being exclusive with you or anyone else. Now, go out clubbing and pick up a nice piece of ass to amuse yourself with and I'll see you at work on Monday.'

Beth hung up the phone with a quiet sigh. Why did it always seem to come to this, the whiny insistence that she should be satisfied with just one lover? Men were all the same, they all wanted to save her from herself, from her inclinations to spread herself around, test the waters and sample the wares. What was it about guys that made them want to become monogamous? Didn't all the experts with all their research insist men had roving eyes and were hard wired to wander, generously planting their seed in multiple women to ensure their own genetic survival? She had certainly seen enough of them doing the seed planting bit, but was becoming more and more sceptical about the moving on part of the theory. Sometimes she wondered if she shouldn't carry around a crowbar to pry them loose when they started to stick like glue.

She shook her head and chuckled softly at the amusing image of prying men from her body as she headed purposefully in the direction of her bedroom. She still needed to finish her make-up and slip into her dress, assuming Paul would be precisely on time for their first date after all the weeks of pursuit. She wondered, not for the first time, if he was as good at fucking as his flirting and his ego suggested. Walking into her room she continued smiling at the memory of just how outrageous his flirting had become before she finally agreed to take him up on his repeated requests.

As she sat down in front of her make-up mirror she savoured the small catch of excitement radiating around her solar plexus. Like a sudden in-drawn breath her body stirred with expectation of the upcoming seduction, a new unknown body to explore with new tastes and textures, the excitement circulated around the bottom of her diaphragm. In a little while, when she was actually with him, her pleasure zone would move lower, focus more specifically then spread all over her, under her skin but always connected to her sex and bum.

She wiggled her bottom on the chair, moving to mush her panties into her already wet pussy. There was a brief temptation to touch herself, to spread her legs apart while she sat on the hardback chair and pleasure herself. Instead, she tucked away the image for later when she could do it for Paul. This time she got both the catch in her tummy and the throb of her pussy as the image of later and all it implied began to flit through her mind.

The make-up was on in minutes, her practised hands and the little she used making it a quick and simple exercise. She slipped on her black wool dress, arranging the front opening to line up with the slit in her black satin slip. Picking a stray hair off the shoulder she stood in front of the mirror to check her finished image. The woman returning her stare was not too shabby, she thought with affection; for an old broad she cleaned up quite nicely really.

The short-sleeved dress fell down her body softly, gently outlining her generous portions. At forty-three she was old enough to appreciate the benefits of a good support bra and could afford the cost of the sexiest ones. Her full-sized breasts held high and inviting would look even more delicious when the dress came off. The control top pantyhose rounded her tummy and hips to present to advantage her classic hourglass figure. Short frosted blonde hair gelled back in a youthful cut and make-up that looked like no make-up at all completed the image of an average woman who really hadn't done anything special to look so good. Her green contact lenses might make someone take a second look but even that would not shatter the image of a well-kept mature lady. And if she threw in a smile, something never too far from her lips anyway, she could lead just about any man to question the social brainwashing about younger being better.

Which thought led her naturally to the real secret joy of older peri-menopausal women. Her matured sexual appetite might appear to mimic the raging hormones of adolescence but her imagination and skills were matched by nothing a twenty-year-old could inspire. No matter what they said to the contrary, younger women were always holding on to the naive wish that this time, with this man, it might be different somehow, he might be 'the one', the rescuer of her dreams. Beth had the advantage there too: she didn't need rescuing nor did she harbour any misguided youthful fantasies about giving up her sex for possible future benefits. Her appetite and her imagination were used solely for the purpose of fulfilling her own hedonistic desires. She did what she did with whomever with the singular intent of enjoying the bliss of sexual stimulation and ultimate satisfaction.

The buzz of the doorbell brought her attention back to the matter at hand and with a last quick look at her mirror image she padded off in stockinged feet to answer the summons. When she opened the door for Paul she was momentarily surprised by how small she felt. At six foot four plus whatever height he got from his shoes he dwarfed her own relatively tall body. When they hugged briefly she felt almost smothered and strangely vulnerable. The feelings weren't unpleasant, simply unexpected and easily overshadowed by the powerful surge of desire the sight of his large male body and the brief physical contact stirred in her. For a moment she was tempted to suggest they skip the restaurant and stay at her place instead but knew the expectation and flirting through dinner in a public place would only heighten her desires.

As it turned out dinner was everything she hoped it would be. Paul was an accomplished flirt. They started cautiously at first but as the wine caught up, their sexual innuendo quickly surpassed any similarity to subtlety. Beth took advantage of every opportunity to touch his hands across the small table and once, when she returned from the washroom, she made a point of standing behind him and running her hands over his shoulders and down his pecs, stopping to gently squeeze when her fingers found his hard nipples.

When she sat down he took one of her hands and turned it palm up tracing a circle with the tip of one finger, then licking the tip a moment later he returned it to her palm and wandered it up her inner wrist. At the contact she had to make a conscious effort not to moan out loud, could only shake her head mutely when the waiter returned to enquire about dessert preferences. By then there was no doubt they would head back to her place and the sweet desserts hidden beneath their clothes.

During the short taxi ride he held her hand and

continued to tease the soft skin of her inner wrist with his fingers. Simply tickling her forearm lightly was stoking the fires in her pussy. When he raised her hand to his mouth and began to lick her fingers she had to fasten her free hand to his inner thigh and slide it up to discover the size of his delight. Finding his bulge she let her fingers explore it almost as softly as he was touching her wrist but when he pushed her palm into his face and bit the meaty skin below her thumb she squeezed, smiling at his sudden stifled gasp.

The moment they reached the stairwell for the climb to her second-floor apartment he pushed her against the wall. When he finally stopped using his mouth to tell her how much he wanted her, what he wanted to do to her and captured her lips with his, the sensitive place below her diaphragm had gravitated permanently down to a point between her unsteady legs. She felt their weakness as an adjunct to her desires, the images he spoke flitting across her mind, pulsing to the beat of her heart and the throb in her pussy. While he explored her mouth with his tongue she searched his chest with her hands wanting to feel the hardness of his muscled body beneath his crisp linen shirt.

'We better take this upstairs before one of my neighbours comes,' breathless, she whispered the suggestion into his ear.

'Not until I feel how wet you are.' He slid his hand up and under her dress, pushing it between her thighs until his palm was cupping the damp gusset of her underclothes. Looking into her face he moved his roaming hand to the waistband of her panties, slid it under the elastic and down the front of her belly until it met the smoothness of her mound.

'Oh, very nice. Did you do this just for me? Or do you keep it shaved all the time?' Without waiting for an answer he caught the back of her head and with a tight grip on her short hair, forced her mouth to his. After he released her he wondered out loud just how far the shaving went as he slowly inched his hand down her mound to the very top of her slit, dipping in gently to lay a fingertip on her clit.

With one hand exploring her pussy and the other holding her head Beth felt the continuous surges of her arousal. She liked the idea of force in her sexual exploits and given Paul's physical size it was easy to imagine he would take her whether she wanted him to or not. There was no not about it: she wanted him and she wanted him in the dirtiest, naughtiest ways possible. But she really didn't want to get naked in the stairwell of her apartment building.

Covering his roaming hand with her own she suggested, 'Let's go upstairs. You can pretend I'm an innocent with my lovely smooth pussy. Perhaps we can play doctor and you can teach me all about my secret private places.' Rather than releasing his hold, his hands tightened where they were, his breathing became loud in her ear and for a moment she worried she might have stirred him too much.

He sounded hoarse when he finally spat out, 'This doctor has every intention of giving you just what you need, honey. And the first thing we need to do is find out why you're so wet down here.' The hand he had between her legs suddenly became individual fingers roaming and fiddling within the many folds of her swollen flesh until they were just as suddenly pulled away. 'You see, look how wet my hand is, look what I got from between your legs.' He put his slick fingers in front of her face, the waft of her desire spreading around them. 'Taste it,' he ordered her. 'Lick my fingers off and then we can go upstairs to my "office".'

A small part of her mind cheered wildly at the direction he was taking their play. Even as she gripped the wrist of his wet hand she silently applauded his skill in creating a fantasy for them to play out. With the rest of her mind thoroughly committed to her sexual stimulation and satisfaction she threw an innocent look at his face and hesitantly moved his cream-slicked fingers towards her mouth and began to lick.

'There's a good girl,' he encouraged. 'You taste good, don't you?'

'Yes, sir,' Beth said in a tone intended to convey a hesitant reply.

With a lascivious twinkle in his eyes, he took her hand in his and led her up the flight of stairs.

Not until they were in the apartment and walking down the hall to her living room did Beth understand something was definitely wrong. Instantly she realised lights were on; she knew she had turned them off when they'd left hours earlier.

'What the hell are you doing here, Tony?' She couldn't help the rise of her voice as she entered her bedroom only to find him sitting on her overstuffed bedside chair. The smile on his lips could not hide the nervousness in his eyes as he looked at her angry face.

'Elizabeth, please don't be mad. Let me explain –' the darkly handsome young man began, but she cut him off with a look.

'Get the hell out of here Tony, now!' Standing in the doorway waiting for him to get up and go she wondered suddenly where Paul was and why he was silent.

'No, Elizabeth, just listen. I'll do anything you want if you just let me stay. I need to be with you.'

Still standing at the bedroom door she was beyond simply being pissed off by Tony's unexpected visit; she was beginning to wonder if more was going on than she knew. A suspicion confirmed the next moment by Paul's whisper from behind her. 'Let him stay Beth, we can have some fun.' Warm breath tickled lightly in her ear quickly followed by the soft stroke of his tongue. It wasn't much in the way of an appeal but she knew she didn't really want to miss the opportunity she was almost certain Paul and Tony had somehow planned. She knew just what she could do to them before the night was over if they wanted to insist on swinging as a threesome.

'Anything I say, right, Tony? You too, Paul?' She wasn't sure if he had expected that but Paul nodded his head at her question.

'OK, both of you unzip and pull your cocks out. I want to be able to see just how much fun you're having. And guys, you stay where I tell you to and no touching unless I say. Understand?' She smiled as both men nodded their acquiescence.

Tony stood to unzip his pants and let his erection hang out boldly in front of him. He watched quietly as Beth smiled at the sight of his long slender penis, knowing how she appreciated his size and why she liked it so much. It bobbed in the air as he watched her walk towards him as though it were tracking her approach. He could do nothing but stand there and feel the strain on his stomach as his body anticipated whatever she was about to do.

At the touch of her fingertips lightly caressing his smooth satin skin he felt the blood rush to the head of his dick and his legs suddenly felt lifeless beneath him. When he wobbled slightly, her touch and the anticipation of his reception finally catching up with him, it was her instructions to Paul that kept him on his feet.

'Paul, come and stand behind him, put your arms around his chest so he won't fall down.' She backed up a step as Paul moved over to them, his own erection solidly leading the way. Before he could pass by she stopped him with a hand to his chest, her gaze fixed on his cock. At this, her first sight of his delight, she knew her plans for the guys would work out better than she could have imagined.

'Very nice, Paul. I'm glad to see all that bragging actually comes with a very substantial package to back it up.' She eyed him a moment more before motioning him behind Tony. While Paul's arms wrapped around him, Beth held Tony's cock in her hand and felt the rush of blood and excitement the contact from Paul caused. She knelt in front of the two men wrapped as one and brought Tony's cock to her face. She loved to play with a lover's penis, enjoyed the texture and the movement, loved too the image of her apparent supplication to their maleness as she knelt between their legs. She especially relished licking off the first drop of dew and kissing their swollen cocks as they watched.

All these thoughts danced through her mind as she knelt in front of Tony and teased him with her breath. With one hand she stroked him, enjoying the smoothness of the skin, the texture of the large pulsing veins filling with blood. When the first drop of clear fluid seemed ready to drip from the end she held it to her lips and licked the dew with just the tip of her tongue. She turned the lick into a sucking motion and pulled the head of his cock between her lips as her hands wrapped around it. Tony's circumcised penis made it easy to access his tiny hole and push in her tongue as though trying to penetrate him.

Although she could have been content to continue as they were she had no intention of letting the men have pleasure from her for any duration, at least not until much later. She licked the underside of his cock, rubbed it across her cheek and under her chin. The feel of it on her face was deliciously erotic; the idea of such a very private body part touching so blatantly her very public face, the naughtiness of it, made her vision blur and the knot in her stomach tighten.

Staying where she was she looked into Tony's face as he watched her taste him and with one last lick and a final kiss she moved her head away as she gripped with both hands and squeezed. She was pleased with his gasp of surprise and jerking arousal as he responded to the stimulation. Letting go she instructed, 'OK, Tony, get behind Paul now. But first drop your pants, but keep your jockeys on. Paul, you drop yours as well.' She watched from the floor as both men silently complied. For all she had a terrible thirst she planned to have a taste of Paul before she sent one of them to bring a bottle of wine to the bedroom.

Then, at the sight of the transparent wetness waiting for her on the end of Paul's beautiful cock she decided thirst was not going to be a problem for a time. But before she touched it she wanted to examine the position Tony had taken behind him. Staying on her knees she moved herself to look at the joining of the men as Tony wrapped his arms around Paul's large chest. With just their jockey shorts on Tony's dick was pressed upward along the crack of Paul's cheeks, snuggled into the cotton briefs. She slipped her hand between the men, pushing Tony into the crack more deeply. 'Keep it there, Tony, push it up while I taste the flavour of his cock.'

Sticking out from the slit in his shorts Paul's dick bobbed up and down, dripping a clear filament from the tip. Hypnotically reaching towards it Beth caught the fluid on her finger, hungry to taste his discharge. She moved to kneel in front of it, devouring it first with her eyes. Thick and long, she wallowed in the pure aesthetic beauty of its shape, the tiny purple veins throbbing, the head twitching. The primitive look of the uncircumcised flesh excited her; it seemed to enhance its length and size. Softly, she blew warm caresses on it, wanting to see it twitch and jerk before covering it with her mouth.

With deliberate slowness she tickled the tips of her fingers along its length and across Paul's weighty balls. When her fingers reached the bottom of his scrotum she moved her hand up his behind, until she felt Tony's sacks. With a quick squeeze she stretched further between Paul's legs until her arm was up his crack alongside Tony's warm, dripping cock. She smiled when she felt the firmness of Tony's flesh, thrilled by the image of the two men folded together.

'Tony, reach down and hold Paul, I want you to feed him to me.' She watched both men for their reactions. Tony's hand slid down Paul's torso, reaching for the other man's cock. He held the base firmly in both hands as she opened her mouth to receive it. 'Tell me what to do, Tony,' she instructed him quietly.

'I'm going to feed Paul's cock to you, Elizabeth, and I want you to kiss it and suck on it,' came his immediate reply.

Ripples of desire surged through her stomach to her womb wetting her panties. Breathing in the smell of Paul's musky penis and Tony's hands, she laid her lips around the covered head. For a moment she wandered her tongue across the tip, sucking the liquid still oozing from the tiny shadowed hole. Inhaling deeply as she worked she took more of the thick cock into her mouth, pulling it to the back of her throat. When her lips came up against Tony's hands she slowly backed down the shaft, covering her teeth with her lips and biting down.

'Pull his foreskin back.' She watched as Tony complied, noticed the shallow grunts sneaking from Paul's open mouth. 'Now run your hands up and down, like you're jerking him off.' Her pussy dripped at her own words, clenched as she saw Tony stroke Paul's cock more vigorously.

'You like that, don't you, Paul?' She saw his body shudder as Tony kept up his hand movements. Before Paul could shape his reply she captured the head of his jerking dick in her mouth and traced the ridge exposed by Tony's hold on the skin. 'Tell us, Paul, tell us what you like.' This time she waited to hear him say the words.

Through short gasps of breath Paul obeyed. 'I . . . like what Tony's . . . doing.' He was almost groaning, would have fallen but for Tony's body holding him in place.

'What's Tony doing that you like, Paul? What about his cock – do you like how it feels stuck in your crack?' Beth was enjoying her wickedness and getting thoroughly turned on to boot!

'Jeez, Beth.' Paul looked down at her through glassy eyes, clearly struggling with stimulation, possibly struggling with how he was being aroused. His eyes followed the other man's hands as he finally told them, 'I like Tony rubbing his hands on my dick and I like his cock sticking between my ass cheeks.' Suddenly, Paul barked out a short squeal as Tony squeezed harder on him, pushing his cock more firmly into Paul's butt.

Beth was surprised to discover how erotic she found watching the two men touch. They looked beautiful moulded together: Tony's hands, slightly darker than Paul's skin, looked competent as they slid up and down the other man's cock. She suddenly wanted to see more of their bodies.

'Tony, stop playing with Paul and unbutton his shirt, but stay behind him.' The movement of Tony's hands stopped immediately, left the weeping cock and moved to Paul's shirt front. While she watched him follow her instructions, she bent forward and kissed Paul's abandoned cock, delighted by its constant unsteady quiver. It seemed to follow her mouth, trembling with need when she moved away again.

When Tony had Paul's shirt off, leaving the man standing only in his jockey shorts, his cock lancing about in the air, Beth continued. 'Now, Tony, run your hands up to his nipples and touch them the way you touch mine. I'm going to lick some more of this lovely discharge off his cock and suck his balls for a while.' She waited to see Tony's hands searching Paul's torso for his nipples, flooded herself again with the image they made. She felt Paul shudder head to foot as Tony's thumb and finger began to squeeze and pull on his firm little buds.

She bent her head to her own delight hanging between his legs.

While she sucked his heavy sacks into her warm mouth she ran her hands up his bum, feeling Tony's patient erection, feeling the sodden spot on his shorts from his oozing dew. She poked her finger into the space between Paul's cheeks, pushed her hand in to replace Tony's penis. When Paul's legs spread without a word from her, Beth clenched her own muscles with anticipation, thrilled by his compliance. She slid her hand under the leg of his jockey shorts and up his crack, searching with her fingers for what she wanted. When she felt the hard dip of his puckered anus she rested the tip of a finger on it and listened as he laboured for breath.

Slowly, lightly, she stroked the opening of his cavity, coaxing it to relax. It was slick from his sweat, slick at the entrance as she pushed her finger a little more deeply. Against her cheek his cock was batting at her, leaving a trail of transparent cobwebs. When it jerked against her face again she captured it in her mouth and assailed the tiny hole. With her tongue attempting to enter him her finger pushed more firmly into his opening, crooking in and stretching out the entrance. She felt him swaying above her, let his cock fall from her mouth, and looked up to see Tony rubbing the palms of his hands over Paul's erect nipples. Now it was time for her to get a drink.

'You boys stay just like that. I'm going to change and get us a bottle of wine. Tony, I think you should just use one hand on his nipples; he seems to need someone holding onto that throbbing baton he's wielding.' The noise trailing from Paul's mouth made her smile. 'And, Paul, don't even think about coming. Tony, you can take him to the edge but don't let him go over.' With her final order she went to her closet to change.

Looking across the room at the two men, Paul standing

with his nipples and penis hardening at Tony's skilled manipulations, their eyes closed, Beth marvelled at her good fortune. She would have to thank Tony for his persistence; her irritation over his whiny phone call earlier in the evening had vanished, even his intrusion into her apartment was of no account in the face of what she was now seeing. Perhaps there was something to be said for sticking it out with men over time, only she was beginning to suspect it had to be more than one man.

When she returned to her room with the wine and glasses she stood for a moment simply drinking in the sight of the entwined couple. 'Tony, stop fondling Paul. Paul, turn around and take Tony's shirt off.' Many long moments passed before Paul was able to comply, he seemed ready to fall. Whether out of compassion for the man or because he liked touching him, Tony kept his hands on Paul's waist and steadied him. When the shirt was off Beth walked to the two men and stared at the twin cocks pointing at each other, dripping filaments of desire from their very different-looking dicks. She reached out and took one in each hand, pulling the men closer until she could rub them together. Her pussy was in spasm over the eroticism of the action, over the grunts and groans of pleasure escaping both men's mouths.

She cupped the head of each cock in a hand, filling her palms with their wetness. When she was coated she held her hands to their mouths. 'Lick yourself off me,' she instructed. Their tongues instantly began to clean the stickiness from her palm and fingers, shivers of sizzling desire cascading from her hands directly to her soaked pussy. 'Tony, on your knees.' He knelt immediately, knowing what she would say next. 'Lick that wet drip off Paul.' When his tongue snaked out to run over the tiny hole oozing with juice she reached down and held the shaft.

'You like that, don't you, Paul?' she asked redundantly.

'Yes, Beth,' he whispered, sounding choked.

'Do you know what I have on, Paul?' she asked next, knowing he hadn't seen what she had changed into.

'No, Beth.'

'Tony, stop licking his cock. Lift my shirt up and tell Paul what you see.' It seemed to take an effort for him to leave Paul's body, his gaze lingering hungrily.

He lifted her shirt, his eyes on a level with her groin. 'She's wearing tights and panties that have no crotch. I can see the slit of her pussy lips and –' Tony turned to lift the back of her shirt, '– I can see the crack between her cheeks all the way to the top,' he finished, letting her shirt-tail fall.

Her mind was burning up with infinite ideas as ever more erotic visions assailed her. She wanted to orchestrate the naughtiest scenario she could conjure. Her cunt was dripping, reflexively pulsing in and out; her lips protruding from her crotchless pants were so swollen they felt as though they were weighted.

'Tony, now tell Paul what I like most about your cock,' she continued, wondering if perhaps that information had already been shared.

'She likes the size of my cock,' was his knowledgeable reply.

'Now tell him why I like the size of your cock.'

'Because it fits perfectly into her ass hole.' From his knees Tony looked up at her then over at Paul's cock. It was twitching wildly as they talked, the foreskin folding over the head like a hoodlum, fluid filling the tiny cavity.

'Paul, go to my bed and bend over, put your hands on the mattress and spread your legs.' She wondered if he would continue to submit. When he turned away and headed towards her bed she had to put her hand out for support at the sudden rush of excitement that swamped her senses. She waited for him to assume the position she demanded before she turned to Tony.

'Crawl over to the bed, go to the end and stay on the floor when you get there.' The power she felt at ordering these two capable men about was something she thought she could easily find habit-forming.

When the men were in place she poured herself a glass of wine. Her eyes surveyed the scene waiting at her bed, Paul bent over with his legs spread wide, his blood-filled penis hanging down, never still, never quite dry. And Tony, compliant as ever on all fours like a puppy dog at the end of her bed, patiently waiting for her orders. With another sip of wine Beth sauntered over to her waiting playmates.

'Either of you lads want a drink?' she asked innocently.

'Yes, please,' 'Yes, Elizabeth,' were their tandem replies.

Motioning for Tony to stand she offered him the wine in her glass, waited for him to drink, then refilled it and told Paul he could straighten up for a drink as well. Standing with the two men, their cocks sticking out from their underwear, she felt more fluid seeping between her open crotch and wondered who to choose to lick it off.

'Get on your knees, Paul. Tony, come stand beside me.' She waited until both men were in position.

'Paul, I'm dripping with wet, I want you to lick my pussy but I don't want you to touch my clit. Can you do that?'

'Yes, Beth, I can lick your pussy without licking your clit.' He inched over to her legs, pushed her shirt aside and licked her exposed mound. Beth spread her legs apart, her breathing rapid as she waited to feel the stroke of his tongue on her sodden sex. She put her hand on his head as he parted her with his fingers and licked the stickiness coating the folds of her pussy.

Mind-melting bolts of electricity surged through her at the contact; her grip on his head became a handful of hair as she felt herself swoon. When the sensations threatened her control she motioned to Tony and pulled Paul's head from between her legs. 'Suck Tony's cock, Paul, I want to watch you give him head.' Gawd, but she loved these guys!

She wondered at the skill with which the men ate each other, noticing how Paul had deliberation and purpose in his movements as his mouth took in Tony's suspended cock. Tony laid his hands on the other man's head, holding him gently as he moved up and down the erect shaft. When Paul's hands reached around to hold Tony's buttocks she realised she would orgasm by simply watching the two men make love at her direction.

'Paul, move your mouth away for a second.' She saw him hesitate. 'You can go back to it, I just want to pull Tony's shorts down,' she assured him. When his mouth let go of Tony she swiftly pulled off the jockeys, noticing pink marks on his butt where Paul's hands had been. 'Suck on him again, Paul, but don't let him come.' It was the most beautiful sight she could imagine as he reached for the other man's penis; she had no idea two men together could look so aesthetically pleasing.

Throwing pillows in a pile on her bed she made herself comfortable, taking up the bottle of wine to wet her dry mouth. She spread her legs apart feeling cool air trace a pattern around her bared pussy. She felt decadent, resplendent in her comfortable bed, the wine bottle on the bedside table and the two lovely men touching each other.

'Gawd, you guys are beautiful!' she breathed suddenly, unable to keep the wistfulness from her voice.

As she watched, Paul's hands crept back to Tony's firm, slim buttocks. His fingers dug in and out to a rhythm only he could hear. His mouth moved tenderly over Tony's slender bullet-hard cock. His nails dug in each time his mouth filled with the other man's erection. She delighted in the masterful way his mouth moved, purposeful calculation evident in every action.

'Paul, come up on the bed and kneel backward in front of me.' She waited.

Long silent moments passed, the light suckling sounds the only disturbance to the stillness. Gradually Paul dragged his lips from Tony's cock, kissed it gently as he cupped it in his hands and withdrew. When he was standing, Beth had Tony remove Paul's shorts, taking time to admire his complete nakedness. Once he crawled into position on the bed, his bare ass pointing at her, she ran her palms across his tightly rippled buttocks, slowly pulling the sides apart to expose the angry brown bud of his anus. Her heart fluttered at the sight, relishing the moment of discovery.

With gently prodding fingertips she methodically probed deeper into his already slick, tight opening. He was very slowly rocking his hips back, squeezing and relaxing his rectum in an effort to ease her penetration. When she reached the tight ridges of his inner sphincter muscles she crooked her finger teasing the muscles with her searching touch. It took only moments for Paul's movements to become obvious, exaggerating the spread of his legs, rocking back and forth on his hands and knees. Beth's finger sank deeper inside him, pulling back to the sensitive ridges and probing urgently.

'Tony, get up here and kneel in front of Paul. Feed your cock to him.' She was dripping, tiny multiple orgasms rippling through her body, her vision fading to haziness and primitive sexual images.

It took only seconds for the threesome to coordinate their movements. When Tony pushed his cock into Paul's waiting mouth Beth pushed her finger hard into Paul's virgin rectum. In an instant the three bodies blended their rhythms in a synchronicity of motion. At one end, Paul's mouth ravaged Tony's cock, a hungry animal sating his appetite. Beth's finger sank knuckle deep into Paul's ass, another finger working its way in, stretching him unkindly. All three bodies slid back and forth in unison, locked tightly in a tableau of erotica.

For a time Beth lost her soul to the pure hedonism of their actions, falling through visions of graphic bestial acts they had not yet explored. The feel of her finger inside Paul, pushing a second one in to widen his taut opening, watching through bleary eyes the rapture on Tony's face as Paul sucked on his quivering cock, sent spasms of desire through her like thunderbolts. She wanted to feel full, needed to have what she was giving Paul.

Withdrawing her fingers, she threw pillows to the floor and followed quickly on all fours, pointing her crotchless behind in the air. 'Tony, fuck me the way I like the most. Paul, you mount Tony.' No argument from the men: everyone was waiting for this moment.

It took no time for Tony to take her from behind, grabbing her hips and dipping his swollen purpled cock to her tight puckered rectum. He slid in slowly, both of them savouring the constriction of the space he invaded. Beth opened her mouth, letting sounds and words flow, completely consumed by the moment. She felt the pressure as Paul's body slid behind Tony's waiting bum, lost the rhythm of Tony's penetration while he stilled to feel Paul assault his ass. The noise escaping his mouth was loud and guttural, a string of filthy words and desires heightening their shared arousal to near explosions.

Beth panted and screamed as Tony's attack on her intensified, his thrusting cock slamming into her, pushing to the back of her hole, filling her like nothing could, pulling almost out only to pound back in again. She managed to turn her head slightly and caught sight of Paul squatting behind Tony's moving butt, shoving his dick into the other man and keeping the rhythm Tony used to assail her behind. She shuddered at the sight, thrown beyond her control into the swirl of carnal lusts as her body was racked by waves and waves of gut-twisting orgasms, her mouth open silently screaming for more.

As her body went limp beneath him Tony let her down gently, maintaining the movements of Paul's penetration. His erection dripping, his balls swinging forward each time Paul battered into his ass, the sound of Paul's testes making a staccato noise to the movements, were like a choreographed dance.

Sliding out from under the men Beth crawled to her bedside table to find her double-headed dildo. When she rolled over to push one end into her mushy pussy, the men's hooded eyes watched her movements, maintaining the rhythm of their coupling. One end of the long flexible phallus slipped into her, the other end hanging out obscenely from between her legs. She crawled behind Paul, grabbing his bucking hips to steady herself, moving up his buttocks to mount him. His movements slowed slightly as she forced the head of the dildo into his wrinkled rectum, sinking it in until her hips joined his cheeks.

She fucked Paul in the ass as she fucked herself with the other end of the jellied penis; their motions became frenetic, the constant pounding of their penetration building to a final screaming climax that ripped through all three almost in unison. Gathering what little strength she had left Beth threw herself in front of Tony, telling him, 'Do it on me, cover me in it,' and opened her mouth to taste the come directed at her face. Moments later, feeling more thick cream running over her mouth she opened her eyes to see Paul and Tony stroking the final wad of juice from each other. When they squeezed out the last drops, when their erections were easing, the men collapsed beside her, the sound of their gasps for breath filling the pungent air.

It was no big surprise to Beth when she awoke later to find herself alone. The note propped on the pillows said it all: 'Dear Elizabeth, Thanks for a really great time. You were right earlier tonight when you told me to find a nice piece of ass for my amusement. I did and he's great!! Thanks again.' It was signed, 'With appreciation, Tony.'

Pulling the blanket over herself, she snuggled down to go back to sleep, chuckling. Guys! They were just so predictable. She smiled as she drifted off, wondering if the boys would be busy all week.

A Great Job

Juliet Lloyd Williams

'You're joking,' Simon muttered. He pushed one hand through his dark brown hair. 'I won't do it.' He turned to the man next to him. 'I don't know about you, Nigel, but there's no way I'm working for a bunch of yakking females for the week.'

Nigel studied the dusty ground. One steel-capped boot scraped at the stones. 'I need the job and if this is all they've got, then that's it.' He bent and picked up his worn bag. 'But if you can't stand the heat . . .' The rest of his sentence went unsaid but he knew it would make its mark.

'You calling me a chicken?' Simon snapped, taking one step towards Nigel, who shrugged. 'I'm not a coward. I just don't fancy working for some chicks who're playing at builders. Bunch of butch lesbos, I'm telling you now.' As he spoke, he grabbed his bag. 'I won't have anyone saying I'm a coward.'

With his back to Simon, Nigel smiled. He knew exactly how to handle Simon. He just hoped his temporary employers would be able to do the same.

The building they'd been sent to stood at the corner of the street, a shadow of its former self. Scaffolding surrounded the front of the building and on the third level Nigel could see someone working.

'I'm surprised they're not scared of heights,' Simon grumbled as he climbed out of the car. 'Women should stay at home or work in offices. It's because of this lot that we can't find full-time work.'

'Don't let them hear you talking like that or we'll have no work this week either.'

The woman on the scaffolding peered over the edge. 'You the new guys?'

'That's us,' Nigel got in quickly before Simon could open his mouth.

'Door round the back,' she told them.

The door was propped open with an empty milk crate. They stepped inside. It was the usual sight: bare walls, rubbish gathered in corners, wires hanging from the ceilings, the lingering smell of dust.

'Through here,' a voice yelled.

Through the door into the second room they were beckoned. Bent at the waist, plastering the bottom of the wall, a woman worked. 'Nearly finished,' she said.

'Nice arse,' Simon muttered under his breath to Nigel who cringed. His friend was right, the lady did have a nice arse, and the tight, cut-off denim shorts she wore highlighted that. In fact, the shorts were rather too short. Not that Nigel was complaining, but he didn't want to be caught ogling his new boss's backside before they'd even started the job. He glared at Simon whose eyes were on stalks. Nigel nudged him with his elbow and glowered. Finally Simon dragged his attention from the lady's behind to look at Nigel.

'What?' he mouthed.

'Don't . . .' Nigel gestured to the woman who was still bending over, finishing the job. Simon shrugged and returned to staring at the bottom and long shapely legs.

She'd done it deliberately as soon as she'd heard them enter the building. The scuffing of their boots on the floor had made her aware of their presence and she had risen from her usual squatting position to thrust her bum in the air, a position she knew they would appreciate. She stood and turned around to have her first look at the new guys. They were both tall and well-built, muscled from all the manual work and attired in the usual scruffy jeans and plaid shirts. Both had brown hair but one was dark brown verging on black and the other quite fair. In fact, the fairer one looked rather nervous.

'Hi, I'm Jill,' she said as she walked towards them and held out one hand. Nigel's fingers curled around hers and he introduced himself, then Simon, who thrust his hands into his back pockets. Jill hid a smile and stretched her arms over her head, arching her back. An action which thrust her braless breasts against the thin fabric of her T-shirt. Nigel, she noticed, tried not to look at the puckered nipples but Simon stared avidly. A good start.

'Right,' she said. 'Leah's on the scaffolding doing the pointing and Andi's gone for supplies; she should be back any time. All the rooms have been rewired and we've plastered most of the walls, so we need skirting boards.'

'That's me,' Simon said quickly.

'You all right pointing, Nigel?'

'Sure.'

'Right then, see you later.'

Simon, in all fairness to him, was a good worker, in spite of his tendency to ogle her. Not that she was complaining: she liked men watching her. As she told Andi later, she was going to enjoy this week.

'So what are they like?' Andi asked as she moved the wood she'd just bought.

'The usual,' Jill answered. 'Nigel's a bit quiet, quite shy with women I should imagine, but the other one is just full of himself. Eyes on stalks. He'll be the fun one.'

Andi shivered. 'I can't wait.'

'Best get some work done then. Work then play,' Jill told her.

Andi smiled. 'It's playtime I love.'

Simon moaned some hours later when Jill told him they only stopped for a quick sandwich and definitely not long enough for him to nip to the local for a quick pint. His moaning stopped when she told him they'd finish early that afternoon.

Jill glanced at her watch: time to finish, well, work at least. Simon's work had slowed considerably this afternoon; they'd have to do something about that. He was a good worker when he put his mind to it, but he was so easily distracted. Earlier she'd wandered through and asked him how he was getting on, and he'd stopped working just to talk to her. And he paused every time she bent over, or stretched, which she'd noted carefully.

'Go and find Andi, will you, please?' she asked.

By the scowl on his face she could tell he didn't like it. He'd soon change his mind. Noiselessly, she followed him. As she'd guessed, he was peering round the door. From the gasps coming from the room, Jill assumed Andi was up to her usual trick. She could see her now, perched on the old chair with one hand tucked inside her shorts. The other hand would be inside her top, squeezing her breast. It was quite a sight, and one Simon would enjoy.

There was a scuffle of boots which made Jill scuttle into the little side room. Nigel wandered in and was about to speak when Simon glared at him. From her hiding place Jill saw Simon gesture Nigel forward. Frowning, Nigel did as his friend requested. His face when he peeked around the corner was an absolute picture; Jill had to bite her hand to stop herself from laughing out loud.

'What's going on?' Leah asked as she entered the room.

The two men jumped, guilt etched on their faces.

She walked across the room and saw what they had been watching, as if she didn't know. 'Have you been watching her?'

Eyes downcast, Nigel nodded.

'If she plays with herself where anyone can see her, that's her problem,' Simon said.

Leah smiled. 'Oh no, that's your problem. Get in there.'

Simon rushed into the room but Nigel was reluctant.

'Go on.' Leah pushed him forward.

Jill came out of her hiding place and smiled at Leah. 'It's going to be a good afternoon.'

They entered the room in time to see Andi climax. The men were transfixed. Andi had pulled her top down and her sun-tanned breasts spilled over the material. One hand was firmly clamped around one breast with the nipple peeking through her fingers. Her shorts were undone and her other hand could be seen moving under the fabric. She had her legs spread wide, then suddenly she stiffened and moaned. Jill had seen it before but it still made her shiver with longing.

Andi opened her eyes and smiled, totally unsurprised at her sudden audience. Slowly, she brought her hand from her pussy to her mouth. She licked delicately at her fingers. 'Tastes good. Want to try some?'

When neither man moved, Jill walked to her friend and slid her hand over Andi's stomach, past her damp pubic hair into her hot, wet sex. Andi moaned and moved against her friend's fingers. Jill coated her fingers in Andi's moisture and then reluctantly withdrew her hand. She held it in front of her nose and smelled the fragrance.

'Bloody lesbo,' she heard Simon mutter.

Smiling, she walked up to him. In spite of the distaste in his words, she noticed the bulge in his jeans. She held her hand in front of his mouth. 'Lick it,' she ordered.

'I bloody won't.'

No sooner had he said the words than he yelped in pain. Leah stepped into his view and waved the belt she had wrapped around her hand. 'Want to try again?' she asked.

'Lick it,' Jill said.

'No way!'

Leah stepped back and struck him again. Simon turned and made to take the belt from her, but was too slow and Leah darted out of his reach.

Jill stepped towards him. He watched her warily. Slowly her hand reached out to cup the bulge at his groin. The wariness faded from his eyes. Her fingers fiddled with the zip and lowered it. It rasped around the quiet room. All she could hear were the others breathing. Gripping jeans and underwear, she dragged them past his erection, then she sank to her knees in front of him.

Her fingers teased his cock, then she brought her mouth close enough for him to feel her breath on his sensitive flesh. Immediately his hand came to the back of her head and tried to push her forward. She moved back and looked up at him. 'Put your hands behind your back.'

When he didn't comply, she made no move to touch him again. Reluctantly her message filtered through and he did as she'd said. She smiled and touched her lips to his shaft. He moaned and she kissed the length of him. Out of the corner of her eye, she saw Leah move towards him. She knew she would begin touching him and before he knew it his hands would be tied.

When he yelled, Jill smiled and moved away. He mouthed and swore as he struggled with the ties that bound his hands.

'Listen, Simon,' Jill said. 'You won't get free; Leah's ex was in the navy and he taught her how to tie the best knots, so you may as well give up. It's useless.'

Her words sank in and he stopped struggling.

'We're not going to hurt you. In fact, you'll find it

pleasurable, very pleasurable.' Her fingers cupped his erection which to her joy was still hard. 'You're going to enjoy this,' she told him.

He grimaced as Andi walked towards him as he knew what would come next. Although he grumbled when she held her hand to his mouth, he did as was previously ordered and licked her juices from her fingers.

'That's better,' Andi said. 'Nigel, go and get the pile of dust sheets from the next room.'

A dazed Nigel struggled back with the sheets she'd asked for. Jill helped him arrange them on the floor.

'Right, who's first?' Jill looked thoughtful. 'Leah, how was Nigel's work?'

'Excellent. He worked well all day. And he tried really hard not to ogle my breasts when I took my top off.'

'Simon, however, was constantly ogling and he stopped working quite a lot.'

'I did not,' he denied.

'You did. In fact, you spent a lot of today looking at my arse. Would you like a closer look?'

He looked so eager Jill almost laughed. Did he think they were going to reward him for his behaviour? She nodded to Leah who slowly dragged her T-shirt over her head then ran her hands over her breasts. Her pink nipples were already puckered with excitement.

Jill felt a shiver of longing run up her spine. Her heart pounded and between her legs she could feel her pussy wet and thrumming. This was what she loved. Leah flicked the button on her shorts undone and then sank onto the dust sheets.

'Come here,' she ordered Simon.

He swaggered across the room and sank to his knees, struggling with the ties. 'Let me free.'

'Later, when you've shown us you can behave. Right, take my shorts off.'

'And how am I supposed to do that?' he grumbled.

'Use your imagination.'

It took a while but finally he used his mouth to undo the zip and wriggle the material past her hips.

'At last,' Simon groaned. 'Now untie me so I can fuck you.'

There was a slap as the belt hit Simon. 'Don't be so presumptuous,' Jill told him. 'We're not here to pleasure you, in fact it's the other way round. How good are you at oral sex?'

Simon looked aghast.

'Not very good then.' Jill smiled. 'Maybe a few lessons will improve your skills.'

Leah slid the shorts off and lay back.

'Go on then.' Jill nudged Simon. 'You can't do any good for her there.'

He shifted closer between Leah's parted thighs. After a muttered expletive, he lowered his head and licked Leah's sex.

Jill laughed and slapped him across the back with the belt. 'Start subtly,' she told him. 'Do as I say. You have to start slowly. Blow gently on her pubes.'

Leah shivered as Simon blew her damp curls.

'See how she likes it.' Jill leaned close so that she could whisper to Simon. 'Now lick the creases of her thighs, then blow gently on the damp skin. Touch her sex. Lick the join. Sticky, isn't she? Work your tongue between her lips. Really taste her. Nigel, come and help him.'

Nigel joined Simon and looked at Jill for instruction.

'Part her sex lips, gently.'

He did as he was told. Both men gasped. Jill laughed. 'Found her little friend, have you? Take it out of her, nice and slowly, so she appreciates every move.'

Nigel's fingers found the end and he pulled gently. The dildo slid out of her. Leah moaned at its loss; Jill could well imagine how she felt, suddenly empty and horny without it.

'We all wear a little something while we work, just to encourage us and remind us what happens when we finish,' Jill told them. 'Lick her lips with long sweeping strokes.'

Leah moaned as Simon's tongue slid over her hot, swollen labia. It was so good after so much arousal. She writhed under him, trying to get his tongue to touch her where she needed it most. She felt fingers on her shoulders. It was Jill. 'Keep still,' she was told. It was a struggle when all she wanted to do was come but she kept her hips still and let Simon tongue her.

'Lick right up to her clitoris, lick around it quickly then glide back down.'

Leah's breath snagged in her throat as Simon touched her clit, but it wasn't enough to trigger her orgasm and she groaned in dismay.

'Nigel, slide your finger into her sex, now add another and wiggle them around.'

For Leah Jill's words describing what would happen before it did was so erotic. She could picture the men's hands and mouths before they touched her. Suddenly, she realised there was another set of hands on her; Simon must have been freed.

'Now kiss her.' Leah moaned at the thought of his tongue sliding into her open sex. 'Kiss her as you would her mouth.' Simon's tongue thrust into her pussy then slowly explored the wet flesh. She moaned long and loud which made Jill laugh. 'See how much she likes that. This is what you want.'

Jill sank to her knees by Leah's head and held her arms high above her head. She noticed Nigel's avid look and smiled. 'She likes to be tied up.' The red flush that stole over Nigel's face gave Jill food for thought; maybe Nigel had fantasised about being tied up too. They'd soon find out. Leah shifted and Jill dragged her attention back to Leah's pleasure.

'Lick that patch between her sex and her arse. She's very sensitive there.' Leah shivered as the man's tongue

245

trailed over the ticklish flesh. She barely heard Jill's next words.

'Wet a finger in her sex. That's it. Now slide the tip into her arse. Go on, she loves it. Nigel, make your fingers into a V and part her lips just above the clit. Push two fingers into her sex. Now lick her clit and watch her come.'

As soon as the men completed the actions, Leah's body heaved and she came, moaning and writhing under the hands and mouths. Her hands were immovable above her head, her sex was filled, there was something in her arse and her clit was being licked; it was irresistible and Jill knew it.

Leah's moans trickled to a stop and Jill watched as the men loosened their grip on the woman. There was a scuffle as Andi came back into the room and dropped the toolbox at Jill's side.

'Thought you might be needing this.'

Jill smiled and opened the box. The two men craned their necks to see what was inside. Waving one finger at them, Jill admonished, 'Not yet. Maybe later.' There was a rustle of paper and both men stared.

'Anyone hungry?'

Nigel shuffled forward and went to take the chocolate bar from her hand.

'Come here.' Nigel followed her to the chair and watched as she slid her shorts to her ankles. She kicked them to one side. Like Leah she wore no panties. Her T-shirt was quickly removed and she sat naked on the chair, shivering at the coolness of the wood against her heated sex. She leaned back and parted her legs, revelling in the men's sharp intake of breath. One hand trailed down her naked side, encouraging the feelings that this afternoon had already brought. Slowly, she reached her mound and, aware of all the eyes watching her, she slid her fingers into her sex and removed the dildo that had filled her all day.

'Taste it,' she ordered Simon. Simon was less reluctant this time and grabbed the black object from her hand. Obediently, he brought it to his lips and sucked her juices from it. He was learning quickly, Jill thought as she unwrapped the chocolate and held it out.

Nigel reached for it but Jill snatched her hand back. 'If you want it, you're going to have to eat it and me.' His eyes widened as she slid the chocolate into her gaping core with the end protruding lewdly. 'On your knees.'

Nigel slid to the ground between her parted thighs and gazed at her open pussy.

'Put what you learned to good practice. I want to come by the time you finish the chocolate.'

His tongue caressed the crease of her thighs and she smiled. He was a very quick learner. His hot breath fanned the damp flesh making her shiver. But then he'd had a good teacher. By the time he nibbled at the chocolate she was already desperate to come. One touch of his tongue against her clit and she would orgasm. But Nigel seemed in no hurry as he licked and caressed between nibbles on the confectionery. The chocolate was melting inside her and dripping slowly out of her, mingled with her juices. Something which Nigel seemed to be enjoying immensely.

'Hurry up!' she muttered as he pulled the bar slowly out of her so he could eat some more.

There was a slap of leather against flesh and Jill screamed, startled by the unexpected sting on her breasts.

'Patience,' Leah snapped and wound the belt around her hand for emphasis.

Looking down her body, Jill could see the red line across her breasts, highlighting the sting that accompanied it. Her puckered nipples burned like fury but it only made her desperation more acute. She opened her mouth, saw Leah step closer and wisely shut it again.

Nigel's fingers tightened around her thighs, pushed

them further apart, making her more accessible. The bridge of his nose rubbed gently on her clit and she moaned and moved, trying to get closer to him. Automatically her fingers wound themselves in his hair and she squirmed under his kiss. The chocolate was finished but his tongue swirled in her sex, removing the last traces of sweetness. As he licked, he rubbed his nose harder against her nub. Jill moaned, then thrust hard against his face, forcing her orgasm. Her body stiffened as she came, her fingers curling around Nigel's head, moaning her pleasure. A moan that raised the fine hairs on the back of everyone's neck.

'Bloody hell,' Simon muttered. 'He's good.'

'Damn good,' Jill told him as she kissed Nigel's lips gently. He tasted of chocolate and of her. His face was flushed and one hand plucked at the tight denim that covered his crotch.

'Need to come?' Jill asked as she smoothed her lips back and forth over his.

He nodded, reluctant to admit his need.

She stood and held out one hand to him. He took it and followed her across the room to the dust sheets. She let her fingers trickle up the front of his shirt until she came to the top button, which she slid through its hole. One by one she undid the buttons and let the shirt hang loose around him. Her fingers itched to touch the warm flesh beneath the material. She laid her palm flat against his chest. He was hot and hard, all muscle beneath her hand. Sweaty after a hard day's work. Her pulse leaped and her pussy tingled in spite of her earlier orgasm. She wanted him deep and hard inside her. Wanted him now. And she could take him, she had no doubt about it. Looking at the front of his jeans, he was as desperate as her, but it wouldn't be fair. He needed more pleasure than that. The pleasure of three women enjoying his body at the same time, while his friend looked on.

She slipped his shirt from his shoulders, then dragged

her attention from his muscled torso to his jeans. The zip snagged on his erection, making it difficult to undo. When it was undone, she dropped to her knees and brought her face to his groin.

'Oh God,' he moaned as she mouthed against the denimed erection.

Her scalp prickled as he slid his fingers into her hair and dragged her closer. She obliged and let her mouth trace the length of him through the material. He thrust against her.

Reluctantly, she drew back and his fingers untangled themselves from her hair. Her fingers caught the waistband of the jeans and so very slowly she revealed his boxer shorts and hairy muscled thighs.

'Lie down,' she urged.

He needed no second bidding and lay down on the dust sheets. She quickly untied his shoes and stripped him, leaving him clad only in his boxers. Andi flopped onto the sheet next to him. She trailed her fingers up his chest and smiled as a shudder shook him. Using her fingertips only, she explored the contours of his chest, an action which made him moan deep in the back of his throat.

'Good, isn't it?' she asked.

Nigel could barely manage to nod his head.

'What about me?' a voice demanded – Simon.

'Your turn will come,' Leah told him.

'Well, get a bloody move on then,' he muttered as he rubbed the front of his jeans. 'I'm fit to burst.'

Leah brought the chair forward and made him sit down. 'Put your hands behind your back.' This time he didn't argue and obeyed immediately. Leah tied his hands to the chair. 'Now you won't be tempted to play with yourself.' She glanced around. 'But I think you should have something else to stimulate you. Just watching Nigel isn't good enough. Andi, your panties please.'

Andi grinned and lifted her hips high in the air to

strip her shorts and panties off. Nigel watched her avidly as she revealed her sex. Leah took the underwear and held them in front of Simon's face.

'They're very wet, she must have been so turned on all day. And they're very pungent. Are you turned on by a woman's smell?' she asked.

At Simon's groan, she smiled. 'You are, aren't you? Oh good.' With a few deft movements, Andi's panties were wrapped around Simon's head. He took a deep breath and shuddered.

'I know,' Leah soothed. 'Imagine how you're going to feel watching Nigel and the girls and smelling Andi.' She glanced at his bulging trousers. 'Let's get these jeans off you.' She undid his jeans and freed his erection. 'There's nothing to rub against, so you shouldn't come. I'll be very unhappy if you do,' she warned.

With one last look at the tethered man, she walked to the dust sheet where Jill and Andi were caressing Nigel.

'What do you want us to do?' Jill asked Nigel.

'I don't know,' he muttered. 'Anything. Everything.'

Jill nodded to Leah who made Nigel put his arms above his head. Quickly she used a piece of rope from the toolbox and tied his arms above his head. The groan Nigel gave sent shivers down Jill's spine. He did fantasise about being tied. Briefly, she wondered what else the man dreamed of.

She pulled a large feather out of the toolbox and held it in front of Nigel's eyes. 'Imagine what this will feel like as it touches your body.' She flicked the feather over his nipple and watched as he quivered. 'If it feels like that there, how will it feel gliding over your cock and your balls.'

Nigel's eyes screwed up tightly and he muttered under his breath.

'I know how it feels when it touches my sex. It's so light, almost not there but it tickles and makes me squirm. I wonder if it'll make you squirm.' She accompanied her words with a short sweep of the feather across his chest and down his belly. It dipped in his belly button making him jerk his hips. 'And when it touches my clit...' She flicked the feather lightly over the tip of his cock which wept.

'Oh, God, please,' Nigel moaned.

'Please what?' Andi demanded as she began licking his nipple. 'Please, release you.'

'No,' Nigel almost shouted. 'No, please...'

'Say it,' Leah encouraged. She sat at Nigel's head and nibbled at his ear.

'Fuck me!' he snapped.

'Not yet,' Jill murmured as she traced the length of his twitching cock with the feather. 'Part your legs.'

With a reluctant sigh, Nigel did as he was told and parted his thighs, giving Jill better access to his balls. The feather slid over each one. Nigel moaned and thrust into the air. Then she teased the creases of his thighs before returning to his cock.

'Suck his cock, Andi.'

Andi sighed happily and relinquished her tonguing of his chest. She straddled his body with her sex towards his face then took the tip of his dick into her mouth and sucked gently.

'All of it,' Nigel moaned. 'Suck all of it.'

Andi lowered her head and took him fully into her mouth. Giving a heartfelt groan, he thrust his hips up again and again. With one hand, Jill cupped his tightening balls and drew the feather up his inner thigh. Nigel reacted as if shot and jumped, moaning wildly. Her hand shook as she moved the feather to her final goal, and slowly let it glide across his anus. Nigel exploded with a muffled groan of pleasure and came.

Dimly, above Nigel's moans Jill heard Simon mutter a loud curse. She turned towards him.

'I'm next,' he demanded.

A smile formed on Jill's lips. 'What do you want?' she asked huskily. 'Tell me what you'd really like.'

His forehead creased for a second then he said, 'I want to see two women fucking.' He nodded at Andi and Leah. 'Those two. And then I want to fuck your arse.'

Andi reached out and stroked Leah's face.

'Yeah,' Simon moaned. 'Go on.'

Nigel moaned softly as the two women kissed. He shifted slightly to give them room and to be able to watch them.

'Get over here,' Simon ordered Jill. 'Untie me now.'

'In a minute,' she said.

Simon's eyes didn't move from the two women who were busy exploring each other's bodies. Leah's hand slid over Andi's smooth damp skin from her shoulder to her hand. Andi shivered at the touch and moaned. She reached out and cupped Leah's breast. Simon took a deep breath. Jill smiled. Wasn't this what most men fantasised about? Two women making love. It certainly made her horny just watching them. The sight of breasts touching breasts as they kissed softly, gently, yet with all the passion of a male–female kiss. It was such a soft sweet loving that no one could fail to be aroused at the sight of it. And looking at Nigel and Simon, neither were they unaffected. Both sported rather startling erections. Jill's mouth watered. Surrounded by sex, both masculine and feminine, was an unbelievable aphrodisiac.

Leah gasped and dragged Jill's attention back to the women. Andi lay back on the sheets near Nigel and pulled Leah down with her. Leah slipped between Andi's parted thighs and thrust gently, rubbing their two mounds together.

The air was redolent with the scent of sex and sweat and the dry dusty concrete smell of building work. And Jill loved it all. Watching Andi and Leah, she shivered as the women slowly manoeuvred around until their sexes were above the other's face. Simon closed his eyes against the sight. He rocked back and forth against his bonds, not pulling to get free but enjoying the constriction. Nigel's eyes flicked from the women to Jill. He looked questioningly at Jill when Leah plucked a pair of small balls from Andi's sex.

'Love balls,' Jill told him.

He nodded rather vaguely, but then was entranced as Andi parted Leah's fragrant folds and dipped her head. The movements were slow and secure; they both knew what the other liked and were only too willing to comply.

Nigel tapped Jill with his foot. 'Untie me. Fuck me,' he moaned.

'How?'

'What?'

'How do you want me? On top? Underneath? On my hands and knees?' she asked as she freed him and passed him a condom from the box.

Her words made him flinch as the mental pictures formed in his mind. He wavered as if seeing Jill in every possible sexual position, then he said, 'On your hands and knees.'

Shaky hands arranged her in the position he wanted, facing, she noticed, the two writhing bodies of Andi and Leah. Not that she was complaining; she loved watching them together. They made such a picture, such a lewd picture as they greedily took and selflessly gave.

Nigel grasped her hips and positioned his erection at her sex. With one deep thrust, he was inside her. He felt so good, so hot and hard. His fingers dug into her flesh as he withdrew and thrust again. The position opened her up to him and he moved deeply in her. She jerked back against him, wanting him now with a fervour that couldn't be denied. In front of her Andi and Leah squirmed, moaning and slurping. There was sex everywhere. In front. Behind. She could smell it, taste it, hear it and now with Nigel thrusting into her, feel it. One hand left her hip and cupped her mound. She gasped as his fingers slid between the wet folds and circled her nub. Her hips shot back against his, making him moan and renew his efforts. With his cock in her pussy and his finger on her clit, she couldn't fail to come. Her sex contracted around his and she screamed with pleasure. She barely heard the muffled sounds of ecstasy coming from Andi and Leah. She felt Nigel come as he pulsed inside her. She flopped on her stomach still feeling the ripples of orgasm flicker through her. Nigel collapsed beside her, one hand on her bare bottom.

'Oh God,' he moaned somewhat shakily. 'Amazing.'

'Do something bloody amazing for me,' a voice yelled – Simon.

Jill rose on rubber legs and walked across to the chair. Her fingers shook as she tried to untie the knots. At last Simon was free.

'Well?' he demanded.

'Well, what?' she said.

'Are you going to fuck me?'

'No, I am not,' she answered coolly and before he could look at the other two women, she said, 'and neither are they.'

His mouth dropped as he stared at the bodies on the sheet.

'Nigel worked very hard today,' Jill told him sweetly, 'so he was rewarded. When you learn to work that way, you'll be rewarded too, but until then . . .' She shrugged. 'I'll allow you to pleasure yourself now, but I'm forbidding you to fuck your wife tonight. You are married, aren't you?' Simon nodded. 'You can pleasure her with your mouth or your hands but that cock stays out of her, do you hear?'

With a reluctant air of acquiescence, Simon nodded. 'No sex.'

'I mean it, Simon. We'll punish you tomorrow if we even *think* you fucked her. Understand?'

He raised his head and met her eyes. 'I understand.'

'Good. Now you can come.'

Simon's hand clutched his sex and he began to rub himself. His eyes were tightly closed. Probably picturing everything he had seen today, Jill thought. Or imagining how he would be rewarded tomorrow, if his work was up to scratch.

She smiled smugly. God, this was a great job. She loved working with her hands, in more ways than one. She also liked teaching as well. Teaching men how to behave and how to fuck was just exquisite. A real pleasure. And of course pleasurable for their wives and girlfriends too. And what with their being so short-staffed all the time, they saw a lot of different men. All in need of training.

Visit the Black Lace website at
www.blacklace-books.co.uk

BLACK LACE

Black Lace Booklist

Information is correct at time of printing. To avoid disappointment check availability before ordering. Go to www.blacklace-books.co.uk. All books are priced £6.99 unless another price is given.

BLACK LACE BOOKS WITH A CONTEMPORARY SETTING

☐ SHAMELESS Stella Black	ISBN O 352 33485 1	£5.99
☐ INTENSE BLUE Lyn Wood	ISBN O 352 33496 7	£5.99
☐ A SPORTING CHANCE Susie Raymond	ISBN O 352 33501 7	£5.99
☐ TAKING LIBERTIES Susie Raymond	ISBN O 352 33357 X	£5.99
☐ A SCANDALOUS AFFAIR Holly Graham	ISBN O 352 33523 8	£5.99
☐ THE NAKED FLAME Crystalle Valentino	ISBN O 352 33528 9	£5.99
☐ ON THE EDGE Laura Hamilton	ISBN O 352 33534 3	£5.99
☐ LURED BY LUST Tania Picarda	ISBN O 352 33533 5	£5.99
☐ THE HOTTEST PLACE Tabitha Flyte	ISBN O 352 33536 X	£5.99
☐ THE NINETY DAYS OF GENEVIEVE Lucinda Carrington	ISBN O 352 33070 8	£5.99
☐ DREAMING SPIRES Juliet Hastings	ISBN O 352 33584 X	
☐ THE TRANSFORMATION Natasha Rostova	ISBN O 352 33311 1	
☐ SIN.NET Helena Ravenscroft	ISBN O 352 33598 X	
☐ TWO WEEKS IN TANGIER Annabel Lee	ISBN O 352 33599 8	
☐ HIGHLAND FLING Jane Justine	ISBN O 352 33616 1	
☐ PLAYING HARD Tina Troy	ISBN O 352 33617 X	
☐ SYMPHONY X Jasmine Stone	ISBN O 352 33629 3	
☐ SUMMER FEVER Anna Ricci	ISBN O 352 33625 0	
☐ CONTINUUM Portia Da Costa	ISBN O 352 33120 8	
☐ OPENING ACTS Suki Cunningham	ISBN O 352 33630 7	
☐ FULL STEAM AHEAD Tabitha Flyte	ISBN O 352 33637 4	
☐ A SECRET PLACE Ella Broussard	ISBN O 352 33307 3	
☐ GAME FOR ANYTHING Lyn Wood	ISBN O 352 33639 0	
☐ CHEAP TRICK Astrid Fox	ISBN O 352 33640 4	
☐ THE GIFT OF SHAME Sara Hope-Walker	ISBN O 352 32935 1	
☐ COMING UP ROSES Crystalle Valentino	ISBN O 352 33658 7	
☐ GOING TOO FAR Laura Hamilton	ISBN O 352 33657 9	

- [ ] HOP GOSSIP Savannah Smythe — ISBNO 352 33880 6
- [ ] GOING DEEP Kimberly Dean — ISBNO 352 33876 8
- [ ] PACKING HEAT Karina Moore — ISBNO 352 33356 1

BLACK LACE BOOKS WITH AN HISTORICAL SETTING

- [ ] PRIMAL SKIN Leona Benkt Rhys — ISBN O 352 33500 9 £5.99
- [ ] DEVIL'S FIRE Melissa MacNeal — ISBN O 352 33527 O £5.99
- [ ] DARKER THAN LOVE Kristina Lloyd — ISBN O 352 33279 4
- [ ] THE CAPTIVATION Natasha Rostova — ISBN O 352 33234 4
- [ ] MINX Megan Blythe — ISBN O 352 33638 2
- [ ] DEMON'S DARE Melissa MacNeal — ISBN O 352 33683 8
- [ ] DIVINE TORMENT Janine Ashbless — ISBN O 352 33719 2
- [ ] SATAN'S ANGEL Melissa MacNeal — ISBN O 352 33726 5
- [ ] THE INTIMATE EYE Georgia Angelis — ISBN O 352 33004 X
- [ ] OPAL DARKNESS Cleo Cordell — ISBN O 352 33033 3
- [ ] SILKEN CHAINS Jodi Nicol — ISBN O 352 33143 7
- [ ] ACE OF HEARTS Lisette Allen — ISBN O 352 33059 7
- [ ] THE LION LOVER Mercedes Kelly — ISBN O 352 33162 3
- [ ] THE AMULET Lisette Allen — ISBN O 352 33019 8
- [ ] WHITE ROSE ENSNARED Juliet Hastings — ISBN O 352 33052 X
- [ ] UNHALLOWED RITES Martine Marquand — ISBN O 352 33222 O
- [ ] LA BASQUAISE Angel Strand — ISBN O 352 29988 2
- [ ] THE HAND OF AMUN Juliet Hastings — ISBN O 352 33144 5
- [ ] THE SENSES BEJEWELLED Cleo Cordell — ISBN O 352 29904 1

BLACK LACE ANTHOLOGIES

- [ ] WICKED WORDS Various — ISBN O 352 33363 4
- [ ] MORE WICKED WORDS Various — ISBN O 352 33487 8
- [ ] WICKED WORDS 3 Various — ISBN O 352 33522 X
- [ ] WICKED WORDS 4 Various — ISBN O 352 33603 X
- [ ] WICKED WORDS 9 Various — ISBN O 352 33860 1
- [ ] WICKED WORDS 10 Various — ISBN O 352 33893 8
- [ ] THE BEST OF BLACK LACE 2 Various — ISBN O 352 33718 4

Please send me the books I have ticked above.

Name ....

Address ....

....

....

....

Post Code ....

Send to: Virgin Books Cash Sales, Thames Wharf Studios, Rainville Road, London W6 9HA.

US customers: for prices and details of how to order books for delivery by mail, call 1-800-343-4499.

Please enclose a cheque or postal order, made payable to Virgin Books Ltd, to the value of the books you have ordered plus postage and packing costs as follows:

UK and BFPO – £1.00 for the first book, 50p for each subsequent book.

Overseas (including Republic of Ireland) – £2.00 for the first book, £1.00 for each subsequent book.

If you would prefer to pay by VISA, ACCESS/MASTERCARD, DINERS CLUB, AMEX or SWITCH, please write your card number and expiry date here:

....

Signature ....

Please allow up to 28 days for delivery.